THE FAIRY TREE

A SHADOW HARBOR MYSTERY

BY

KAREN COTTON

BOOK WRITING
P I O N E E R

Table Of Contents

Acknowledgement

I would like to thank my sister, Jeanne, and my brother-in-law, Johnny. My sister so patiently and consistently encouraged me along the way to continue with my dream of writing and publishing this book. She never stopped believing that I could do it and that I should. Thank you, Sissy. And Johnny, thank you for always being there for me. I think you both have a little magic in you!

Karen Cotton

Kcotton51@yahoo.com.

Dedication

vi

I dedicate this book to my amazing husband, Roy Cotton. You never gave up believing in me and you were always willing to listen to my new plot ideas. Thank you for catching my mistakes and for all of your help all through my project.

THE FAIRY TREE

A SHADOW HARBOR MYSTERY

Chapter 1

Daniel Donovan had painstakingly built the tree house years ago, crafting every beam and board with care, even though he couldn't shake the unease that came with the thought of his little girl being suspended more than thirty feet high in the air. It made his heart pound with a mixture of fear and unease. But his headstrong daughter begged and pleaded nonstop until he had given in, not that he really stood much of a chance when his little angel climbed onto his lap, wrapped her arms around his neck and planted teary kisses on his cheek.

Although Rylie possessed the face of an angel, with soft curls framing eyes that sparkled with mischief, it was evident in the determined set of her jaw, the defiant tilt of her chin, and the way she approached the world with an unshakable confidence that belied her tender age. She already showed signs of developing a fiery, independent spirit that was so much like her mother's. When she smiled, a small dimple winked near the corner of her mouth, and a devilish glint lit her emerald green eyes, Donovan's eyes, or so Grandpa Donovan claimed. The strawberry blonde hair that fell to her shoulders was the exact shade her mother had when she was a little girl.

It was hard to believe that they had lost Alana so many years ago. Rylie had been spared much of the pain of losing her mother since she had been too young at the time her mother passed away to fully understand what had happened. But for Daniel, the ache of her absence was a constant companion.

He missed his wife terribly, which some thought was why Daniel had such a challenging time denying his young daughter anything, including building her a tree house.

Once Daniel accepted that he had lost the battle and sat down to design Rylie's treehouse, he was determined to make it extraordinary. He poured his heart and imagination into every detail, creating a magical retreat where her little girl could dream her wildest, most outrageous dreams. With its whimsical design, complete with a cozy loft and a rope swing that dangled invitingly from a sturdy branch, it became a haven of wonder—a place where her daughter's imagination could soar as high as the treetops. What he didn't know was that someone else also desired Rylie's tree house to be extraordinary and did so by encircling it with very old Fairy magic.

Rylie's tree house was perched in the heart of an ancient Sycamore tree, nestled among its wide, sturdy branches. The tree's gnarled bark told stories of countless seasons. It was a perfect view of nature and craftsmanship, a magical hideaway elevated high above the world where dreams felt closer to reality.

The gingerbread trim, delicately arched windows and a thatched roof made the treehouse look as though a Fairy had whisked a cottage from the cliffs of Ireland and nestled it among the majestic branches of the Sycamore.

A star carved into the door, fitted with a small pane of glass, allowed Rylie to view who was seeking entry. The design caught the sunlight, forming playful star-shaped shadows inside the treehouse, adding a touch of whimsy to her magical retreat. Daniel placed a slim iron bar across the interior of the door, making it a simple measure to secure from howling winds on a stormy day or a means to keep unwanted marauders from barging in uninvited.

The ladder extending from the base of the Sycamore had thirty-six steps to reach the tiny porch, far more than a typical tree house ladder - but Daniel had designed the steps to accommodate Rylie's short legs.

The arched doorway faced west and looked over the back porch of Rylie's house. To the east, Daniel had installed an arched window, framing it with intricately carved wooden shutters. Each shutter was adorned with vibrant wildflowers etched into the wood, painted in hues of yellow, blue, and pink that brought a touch of nature's beauty to the little sanctuary.

Often, when Rylie and her cousin, Colin, spent the night in the tree house, Rylie kept the shutters open so she could catch the first rays of sunlight spilling into the room.

This quiet Friday morning of June found Rylie sitting curled up in her favorite chair, which really was an enormous, overstuffed red satin pillow she had confiscated from her Aunt Ana's garage. Aunt Ana and Uncle Patrick, Colin's parents, had chuckled over her insistence on keeping the pillow, but they didn't deny her once she had her heart set on it.

While she waited for her cousin, Rylie glanced around the treehouse and her lips curved into a satisfied grin as she remembered how she persuaded her father to paint the walls a bright yellow. Over the years, the color had faded to a mellow shade, one that reminded Rylie of the lemonade her housekeeper, Hannah, made on sweltering summer afternoons.

Pinned on the walls were some of her drawings, which captured her vast imagination in the colorful figures of the Fairies she so often daydreamed about.

Two of her drawings had little blue ribbons attached to the lower right-hand corners, a sweet reminder of Rylie's growing artistic talent and the pride it was already bringing her. Each ribbon added a touch of triumph to the vibrant sketches, symbols of her creativity and the joy she found in bringing her imagination to life. The ribbons were the prizes she had won at the Shadow Harbor town fair last year for taking first place in the art show. She had been the youngest artist to ever walk away with not one but two first-place prizes, and what made it even more amazing was that the show had been her very first competition.

The tree house was the perfect place for Rylie and Colin to plan their grand adventures.

Colin's father and Rylie's father were brothers. Colin had been born only a couple of days before Rylie popped into the world and from the moment they could crawl, they were drawn to each other, and over the years, they had become not only co-conspirators but best friends. Family friends often joked that the cousins were like two halves of the same coin — where one went, the other was sure to follow. Whether they were plotting treasure hunts, staging daring rescues, or simply sharing whispered secrets, they were a team as natural and enduring as the sun and the sky.

Rylie glanced over to where the old sea chest sat flush against the back wall. She remembered the excitement she felt when she and Colin discovered it while exploring her father's attic.

She saw herself seated on the dusty floor in the dimly lit corner of the old attic, surrounded by shadows that danced in the faint light filtering through a small, grimy window. She was facing the exotic old chest, its ornate carvings barely visible beneath thick layers of dust. Despite the years of neglect, the beauty of the chest shone through—its intricate patterns and inlaid brass accents hinting at tales of distant lands and forgotten treasures. With Colin kneeling by her side, they wiped away cobwebs and years of dust from the top of the chest. They made numerous attempts to open the chest, but to Rylie's growing agitation, the sea chest remained stubbornly sealed. No matter how hard they pried or how much force they applied, its chunky brass lock and stout hinges refused to budge as though fiercely guarding its secrets.

Tilting the chest, they searched for the hidden lock and heard items rolling around inside. Curiosity mixed with a dose of pure mischief had the pair decide to confiscate the chest and move it to the privacy of the tree house before continuing their efforts to open it.

It had been a formidable task hauling the cumbersome sea chest from the attic. First, they had to maneuver the bulky chest down the narrow back staircase that led from the attic directly into the kitchen without bumping into the walls, or dropping the sea chest altogether, or knocking out one or both of the cousins in the process. Then silently sneak out through the kitchen's back door, go all the way across the backyard and up the wooden ladder into the tree house, all without alerting the housekeeper, Hannah, of what they were doing.

When finally, they made it. The chest was placed near the far wall, and a thoroughly exhausted Rylie plopped down on her pillow.

She wiped a thin line of sweat from her forehead, leaving behind a dusty streak and then rubbed her grimy hands on her jeans. She was more than willing to let Colin contemplate the mystery of the locked chest. With a slight frown, Rylie knew she no longer possessed even an ounce of the patience needed to discover the secret of the lock. It really was best for them both if she just stayed out of Colin's way and let him try to open it. Heaving a sigh, she turned her attention to the discarded drawing she had been working on earlier in the day.

The sea chest was solidly built, its frame exuding a timeless durability. It resembled a treasure chest from a long-forgotten era—sturdy and spacious enough for both cousins to sit on comfortably, as though it had been made for such a purpose. The ancient wood, although still beautiful, had its share of scars from years of use.

Across the top and attached to the front of the chest were two thick leather straps secured on both ends by gold buckles. The buckles were quite unusual, unlike anything Colin had ever seen before. They seemed to be large, scaly dragon feet with four curved, jet-black talons jutting out on each foot.

Attached to the lid and positioned in the middle of the chest was an enormous dragon.

The dragon crouched on two powerful, muscular legs. Its long, slender neck and robust body were covered with small scales of deep sapphire blue interwoven among larger golden scales that glowed in the sunlight. Two glittering crystal ovals of emerald green formed eyes that glowed fiercely in the dragon's pale green face. Through jagged teeth, fiery blood-red flames spewed forth from the dragon's mouth.

Wide, leathery wings fanned out from the body as if the beast were ready to take flight at a moment's notice.

A silver-tipped barbed tail encircled the top of the chest and curled down around the body of the dragon, coming to rest on the front of the sea chest.

As Colin stared at the beast with fascination, he was certain he saw the emerald eyes blink and the tips of the serpent's forked tongue twitch.

Tiny hairs at his nape sprang up, and a chill skittered down his spine. Colin had the strangest feeling that the dragon's eyes tracked him as he examined the chest.

An unbidden thought flashed through Colin's mind: the dragon had been placed upon the chest as a guardian of what once lay within.

"Wh-where did that come from?" he mumbled. He shook his head as if trying to shake the peculiar thought from his mind and returned his focus to the sea chest.

After completing his examination, he was unable to detect any type of lock attached to the chest, yet he knew it was locked. Hadn't both he and Rylie tried repeatedly to open it?

Colin loved the challenge and thrill of solving a difficult puzzle and he was determined he would find the secret to this one.

After little more than an hour had slipped by, Colin solved the puzzle. Whoever had crafted the hidden lock was incredibly clever. A smug smile slid across Colin's face when he heard the distinctive sound of the locking mechanism clicking into place.

"Yes!" he exclaimed, shooting a fist into the air. He looked over at Rylie, excitement and satisfaction lighting his eyes.

"I figured it out, Ry. This is so cool! You have to see how the lock works and check out the stuff inside."

Colin demonstrated how, by turning the head and then the tail of the dragon in a series of twists, a low growl sounded, and the lock snapped open. At least it sounded like a growl to him, Colin thought.

They discovered that the sea chest once belonged to their great-great-grandfather, Rylie Aidan Donovan. The Grandfather that Rylie had been named after.

The chest stayed hidden in the attic, covered with layers of dust for many, many years — abandoned and forgotten.

Upon opening the chest, Colin made several discoveries. Inside the thick lid, their grandfather's name had been carved. The embedded letters were surrounded by Fairies caught in flight. Laughing leprechauns, some holding tiny pipes with even tinier puffs of smoke curling up toward the sky, rested among a sea of flowers.

As Rylie gazed at the beautiful scene, she trailed her finger along the indented groove of the carved letters, feeling the satiny smoothness of the wood.

For just an instant, she felt an invisible tug, as if she were being drawn toward the scene and specifically the Fairies. But the excitement in Colin's voice snapped her back. "Look at all these things, Ry."

The treasures that had been rolling around inside were very old. There was a scroll, faded and yellowed, tied with a bit of string; a compass that fit in the palm of a man's hand; a round magnifying glass with a long brass and leather handle; and a spyglass — the type used aboard ship in times past.

A very wicked-looking dagger encased in a leather scabbard suddenly captured Colin's full attention. Carefully, he removed the dagger from the chest and gently pulled it free from the scabbard.

The handle of the dagger had been fashioned from a rich, dark wood that felt sleek and smooth to the touch. Carved into the handle was a beautiful Fairy wearing a tiny crown encrusted with a rainbow of glittering gemstones.

Rylie looked up at Colin. "The dagger is beautiful. Grandpa Rylie must have believed in Fairy magic," Rylie said with wonder.

"I don't know," Colin said. But it looks like he has Fairies on almost all of his stuff. That's weird."

Colin removed the other items from the chest and closed the lid. He placed the scroll on top of the chest, gently untied the fragile string, and carefully unrolled it, taking care in smoothing out the folds.

The scroll turned out to be a hand-drawn map of a small village. There were markings that resembled tiny cottages surrounded by a forest of trees. Further along the map, more cottages were scattered along the edge of a cliff, their placement suggesting they overlooked the vast, restless sea below. The faint, delicate lines of the drawing hinted at an artist's careful hand, capturing the charm of the place in intricate detail.

"I see an 'X' marked on the map, but I can't make out the words next to it," Colin said.

"Try using the magnifying glass," Rylie suggested, rolling her eyes.

"I was just going to do that," Colin replied, reaching for the glass. Using the front of his shirt, he attempted to wipe off the layer of dust that had settled on it. But he found the years of grime were glued to the glass and not easily wiped away, so Colin puckered up and spat on it, then once again used his shirt to wipe the glass clean.

"Ewe, you are so disgusting!"

"Thanks," he said with a lopsided grin as he held the magnifying glass over the lettering.

The words Fairy Glen appeared next to the "X". He noticed a tiny cottage delicately etched on the far side of what appeared to be a wide, open meadow. The cottage seemed isolated, as if guarding a secret, its placement inviting curiosity and a sense of mystery.

"Fairy Glen," that's the same name as Aunt Molly's shop. I wonder if she knew about this scroll?" Colin said.

"Probably," Rylie snarked, "since her shop has the same name. Do you want to go over there and ask her?"

"Yeah, if you want to," Colin mumbled as his eyes continued to roam over the map.

"Why do you suppose Grandpa Donovan put that 'X' on the map, Colin?"

"How do you know he's the one that made that mark?"

"I don't know for sure. But it's his chest, so the map is probably his, too. Besides, it does look really old. When my dad gets home, let's show it to him; maybe he knows something about it. Then afterward, we can go talk to Aunt Molly."

Chapter 2

Later that afternoon, the sound of the approaching truck brought Rylie and Colin racing from the backyard toward the front driveway. The cousins skidded to a stop, cornering Daniel just as he stepped out of his dusty pickup truck. His jeans were streaked with grime, and the faint scent of sawdust clung to his flannel shirt, proof of a hard day's labor. Yet, the weariness etched into his features melted away instantly and was replaced by a wide, genuine smile at the sight of his kids, their energy a balm to his tired soul.

"What are you two up to?" Daniel asked with a chuckle.

"Come on, Dad, we need to show you something," Rylie shouted, grabbing Daniel's hand and tugging him toward the backyard.

"Okay, okay. Just slow down a little... Where are we headed, anyway?"

"There's something we want to show you in the tree house," Colin answered.

"But you have to promise to keep it our secret," Rylie pleaded. "We found an old sea chest in the attic and hauled it up." She glanced at her father to gauge his reaction.

"Wow, you found that old chest? Grandpa showed it to me once when I was a kid, but I really wasn't into old sea trunks back then. Don't ever remember seeing it again. How in the world did you two manage to lug that old chest all the way up there? It must have weighed a ton. What did Hannah say about you doing that?"

"Well, it wasn't exactly easy," Rylie hedged. "It took us forever and I thought Colin was going to drop it on me when we were going down the stairs from the attic. But then, we climbed up the ladder; he was pulling, and I was pushing, and we finally managed to get it into the tree house. I was so scared that Hannah was going to hear us with all the noise we were making or look out the kitchen window and see us, but she didn't because she was on the phone in the living room talking to Devlin." Rylie smirked, making kissing noises.

Barely covering his laugh with a cough, Daniel said, "How did you manage to get the thing open?" he asked, looking from Rylie to Colin. "I thought there was something really tricky about the lock on it?"

"Colin figured it out. It only took him about an hour or so; I never would have gotten it," Rylie confessed. "Colin's much better at puzzles than I am."

"Really," her father teased. "It's hard to get you to sit still for very long unless you're working on one of your drawings."

As they reached the ladder, Colin waited a moment for Rylie to start up then he followed her. The cousins entered the tree house and waited for Daniel to join them.

"Okay, so what's up?" Daniel asked, looking from one to the other.

"Show Uncle Daniel the map, Rylie."

Rylie brought her father over to the chest and unrolled the scroll, then pointed to the 'X' marked on it.

"Do you know anything about this 'X' and the words <u>Fairy Glen</u> printed next to it?"

Daniel picked up the scroll with care, the aged parchment crackling softly under his fingers. He reached for the magnifying glass that Colin had left lying on top of the chest. Holding the lens over the intricate markings, he studied the faded lines and symbols with growing interest. "This," he began, his voice tinged with awe, "this is a very old drawing of a village in Ireland. I vaguely remember my grandfather, Ryan Donovan, talking about a map that Great, Great, Granddad Rylie Aiden kept stored in this old chest. It was supposed to have been a drawing of the area where he lived as a young man back in Ireland.

"The story goes that Grandpa Rylie dug up the Sycamore tree – the very one holding your tree house somewhere in a Fairy Glenn located in the back woods on his property in Ireland.

"He brought the tree all the way from Ireland aboard ship and planted its roots here in our yard well over 200 years ago. That is really all I know about the legend.

"You might want to talk to your Aunt Molly. I think she knows a little more about the legend than I do. There was something about Fairies and magic in the story, too, but I have to tell you, I never really paid that much attention to the tales Grandpa Ryan told when I was a kid, not the way your Aunt Molly did. It is just make-believe anyway — a family myth. Kind of a Donovan family Fairy tale, I guess you could say."

Rylie turned her head, smirked at Colin, and looked up at her father. "I knew we needed to talk to Aunt Molly. She must know something about the map since her shop has the same name. I thought we would talk to you first and then go visit Aunt Molly's shop this afternoon."

Daniel reached over and brushed a smear of dust from Rylie's cheek, a faint smile tugging at the corners of his mouth."Unfortunately, your plan will have to wait a couple of days because your Aunt Molly is away on a buying trip, and she won't return until Friday. Her assistant, Jenny, is watching the shop for her."

Frustration rolled over Rylie's face, like storm clouds gathering on the horizon, her brows knitting tightly and her lips pressing into a thin line. When Rylie decided to do something, she wanted to do it now — patience was not her strong suit. The idea of waiting even a couple of days to speak to her aunt seemed unbearable, her fingers curling slightly in protest. Colin, however, just figured they would find out what they needed to know eventually.

"It's only a couple of days Ry, not that long of a time to wait," Colin cajoled.

"I know," she whined. "It's just so frustrating."

"You want to go in the house and snitch some of Hannah's brownies. You can smell them all the way out here, and I'm sure they'll make you feel a whole lot better," Colin suggested.

"I'm thinking the brownies are probably to make you feel better," Rylie answered tartly, but the grin she gave her cousin took the sting out of her words.

A smile tugged at Daniel's lips. "If you two get caught, don't count on me being able to save you. But I might be able to run a little interference for you."

A few minutes later, the three of them climbed the steps leading to the back screened-in porch. Colin reached the back door first and flung it open. The old springs groaned in protest.

"I thought you were going to oil those springs for Hannah," Colin whispered.

"I sure need to get to it one of these days before Hannah has my hide. It has been on her list of 'things that need fixin', for ages now. The problem is no matter how many items I fix, her list never seems to get any shorter. It's like the thing grows overnight." Daniel grumbled.

"Don't let that screen door slam shut," Hannah called out in warning. "Wipe your feet on the back mat! Oh, and Daniel - I heard your grumblings."

Daniel and Colin exchanged amused grins, the kind that shared a silent understanding. With an exaggerated effort, Daniel made sure the door closed quietly.

All three Donovans knew better than to rile Hannah. She might technically be Donovan's housekeeper, but her role in the family ran much deeper than that. Hannah had been an integral part of the family long before Rylie was born. In fact, she had been in the household when Daniel was a baby, back when she worked for his parents.

Daniel's parents had decided to move to Ireland not long after Daniel married. Since Daniel would take over the family home, his parents invited Hannah to come with them. But the Donovan house had been Hannah's home for most of her life, so she decided to stay with the young couple instead of moving to Ireland. She ran a smooth household, and it was rare that anything got past her.

The enticing scent of chocolate and toasted pecans filled the air in the kitchen, causing Colin's mouth to water.

Stacked on a large oval platter, sitting in the middle of an enormous kitchen table, was the source of the tempting smell. The table was as old as the house. Both were antiques since Rylie Aidan Donovan built the Donovan house and the table in the early 1800's.

The thick pine had generations of scars and scrapes from years past, yet no one would dream of having the table refinished. It was the heart of Donovan's house. Memories of family celebrations and generations of conversations filled with laughter and tears were locked in the table. It had always been the gathering place for all Donovan family events.

Hannah stood drying her hands on a towel, her back turned to the kitchen table, gazing out the window above the sink. She persuaded Daniel to install the large picture window a couple of years ago, and she was delighted she had. She loved the view of her flower gardens, especially in spring and early summer. Her gaze passed over the breathtaking beauty of the roses. She had every imaginable shade, including some unique combinations no one had ever seen before. She had a rainbow of flowers, including delicate violets with their deep, velvety purples; yellow and white daffodils; sweet-faced pansies and clusters of pink peonies. Hannah's gaze drifted to the dragonflies flitting gracefully among the soft pink roses, their gossamer wings catching the afternoon light. A ghost of a smile tugged at her lips as she watched their playful chase, a quiet moment of beauty she rarely allowed herself to savor. She knew that once night fell, the fireflies would take their place, illuminating the garden with their tiny, flickering lights, continuing the dance the dragonflies had left behind. It was a rhythm of nature she had come to cherish, a fleeting reminder of life's simple joys.

Working in her gardens was soothing and gave Hannah a sense of personal pride and accomplishment. Some afternoons, she enjoyed the simple pleasure of sipping tea on one of the stone benches nestled among the vibrant blooms, letting the gentle hum of nature surround her.

The house and property may belong to Daniel, but the gardens were hers. She thought with a quiet smile, a true labor of love. Her sight roamed over the vibrant array of flowers, the rows of herbs, and the thriving bushes heavy with blossoms. She couldn't help but chuckle softly, and she considered how much lovelier her gardens were than those of her neighbors — and the peculiar reason why.

Yes, she would greedily accept all the credit for the splendor, relishing the compliments she received from her family and friends, but secretly, she knew the Fairies and their Fairy magic was what made her gardens spectacular.

She had kept the secret for so many years now. Sharing it with only one other, someone who truly believes in and loves the Fairies as much as she did. Someone who did not think she was a crazy, old Irishwoman.

I am going to have to talk to her soon. I just know there is definitely something strange going on, she thought. I don't know what, but something is about to happen. I can feel it deep in my bones, as sure as my name is Hannah O'Hara. Oh, mark my words; the Fairies are planning some sort of shenanigans!

Keeping an eye on Hannah, Colin placed himself directly between Rylie and Hannah, trying to block Hannah's view.

Seeing the cousins' strategy, Daniel decided to add a little diversion himself, so he moved to stand next to Hannah. Placing his right arm around her shoulders, he said, "You really have outdone yourself this year, Hannah. Your gardens are more beautiful than ever."

"Why, Daniel, it pleases me that you noticed," Hannah said, beaming with pride as she continued looking out the window.

"What is the name of that tall yellow flower, the one with a sort of crown on its head?" Daniel asked, feigning ignorance, as he slowly moved his left hand behind his back and signaled Colin to make his move.

"That one is a daffodil. It happens to be one of my favorites."

Seeing the signal, Colin then gave Rylie the thumbs up, and Rylie slowly reached toward the plate to snag a couple of brownies.

Although Hannah was still turned away from the table, her voice rang out loud and clear. "No, no, you don't, Missy." With both hands resting on her plump hips and a twinkle in her eyes, she turned and scolded, "I'm wise to your antics. Both of you need to go and wash your hands and faces and then you may have a brownie. Where in the world did you get into all that dust? You look like you were dusting the floor of your tree house with your clothes."

Without pausing to wait for a response, Hannah turned sharply, her narrowed gaze locking onto Daniel with the precision of a hawk. "If you know what's good for you, Daniel Donovan, you'll be washing up as well."

"You know, I was just thinking that is exactly what I should be doing, just as soon as the kids vacate the bathroom," Daniel said with a cheeky grin. He pulled out a chair at the table and sat down.

The cousins raced out of the kitchen, their laughter trailing behind them as they made a beeline for the bathroom downstairs before Hannah could quiz them further about the dust on their clothing.

Just as they entered the bathroom, they heard Hannah holler, "After you dry your hands, don't be petting Josephine and Colin; use the towel, not your jeans."

At the mention of her name, the chubby calico cat sauntered from her corner of the kitchen. She had taken a couple of steps away from her soft, overstuffed basket, where she had been resting most of the afternoon, and slowly stretched, gracefully arching her back. She lowered herself to her haunches and cast a curious look from Hannah to Daniel as if to see why she had spoken her name. Then, her penetrating stare got fixed upon Daniel's face.

Daniel always felt a bit unsettled under Josie's intense stare, her eyes seeming to see more than he was comfortable revealing. Trying to ease the moment, he broke off a piece of the blonde brownie he snagged when Hannah's attention was focused on the kids and offered the tidbit to her.

Josie made quite the production out of taking the offering. Her little nose quivered, and it seemed to him that Josie really did understand everything being said around her. The way her sight traveled from one person to the next, as each one spoke, gave the appearance that she actually followed the conversation.

Oh yeah, he thought *Josie was not your average feline.* Now that he thought about it, he realized that Josie had always been in his life. As far back as he could remember, Josie had just always been there. The strange thing was that she never seemed to change or grow any older. *Hmm,* he wondered, as he headed to the bathroom to clean up, *just how old was Josie?*

Rylie and Colin reappeared in the kitchen just as Colin finished wiping his damp hands on his jeans.

Two ice-cold glasses of milk awaited them, and they both helped themselves to a chocolate brownie when Hannah joined them at the table.

"After you two finish eating, I would like you to take this plate of brownies to the Widow Pritchett," Hannah said, placing a small dish on the table next to Rylie.

"I ran into her at the market this morning. She seemed rather out of sorts, and I think the brownies will cheer her up."

"Oh, come on, Hannah, absolutely nothing will cheer up Mrs. Pritchett," complained Rylie. "You know everyone says that she is always ornery."

"I heard that even her dog is bad-tempered," Colin chimed in.

"Why would someone name their dog Mr. Prickles anyway unless he was born grumpy?" Rylie added, "Just like Mrs. Pritchett."

Colin jumped back in. "I remember last Halloween when she..."

"That's enough, you two," Hannah interrupted. "Mrs. Pritchett may have a reputation for being disagreeable, but it does not hurt us to be a little neighborly."

Making his way back to the kitchen, Daniel could not help but overhear the conversation. "I must agree with Hannah. I think Mrs. Pritchett is just a lonely old woman. She can't bear the thought of anyone feeling sorry for her, and because of that, she tends to get back up and act ornery."

Seeing the look that passed between the cousins, he added, "You don't have to stay long. And say hi to her for me. You know," Daniel continued, "if you two got to know her a little, you might actually like her."

"Yeah, like that's going to happen," Rylie snorted.

"Go on now, Rylie," her father said. "And be nice."

"Okay. Okay, we're going. Come on, Colin, let's go."

"Hey, why do I have to go?"

"Because Colin, if I have to go, you have to go. Now, come on. Besides, I helped you watch the twins last week, remember? And they were a pain in the . . . neck," she quickly said, glancing at her father. "So, you owe me."

Rylie really didn't mind helping Colin watch her little cousins, Ryan and Rogan, but she loved having Colin in her debt. Life was good.

"Yeah, I remember. You'll probably be reminding me for the rest of the summer," Colin complained.

Rylie picked up the small plate of brownies and headed out the back, impatiently holding the screen door open for Colin.

As Colin reluctantly rose, he quickly snagged a couple of brownies from the platter and sprinted toward the open back door. He flew through the door and was across the yard, headed for his bike before either his Uncle Daniel or Hannah could call him back.

Fifteen minutes later, Mrs. Pritchett answered her front door with a scowl darkening her long, narrow face. Her thunderous look would have most kids turning around and fleeing back down the porch steps and retreating on their bikes.

Chapter 3

The widow Pritchett was a stern-looking woman, her presence commanding unspoken respect if not outright fear. She stood ramrod straight, her posture a testament to years of rigid discipline. She was bone thin, her sharp features accentuated by the severe lines of her face. She wore her thick white hair pulled tightly back from her face and arranged in a perfect bun high on the back of her head. Not a single strand of hair dared to be out of place.

Her piercing blue eyes, icy and unrelenting, darted from one child to the other as if trying to penetrate their brains and see the havoc they planned to unleash upon her and her poor, unsuspecting dog.

"Well, speak up," she snapped. "What exactly is it you two Donovan youngsters want?"

As soon as she finished speaking, a low, guttural rumble sounded from the vicinity just above her ankles, a sound that was both ominous and otherworldly. The frightening sound caused the hairs on the cousins' arms to stand at attention, and the unease churned in their stomachs, transforming the sweet comfort of the brownies they'd eaten into a queasy swirl of regret and dread.

Peeping around the black skirt that hung well below his mistress' calves were two beady, muddy brown eyes and a long, pointy snout. Tufts of black and brown hair sprouted out of its head in all directions, forming the oddest checkerboard pattern as though it had been pieced together by a distracted quilt maker. The patches were uneven and wild, giving the creature an almost funny appearance—if not for the way its sharp, alert gaze hinted at a sly intelligence lurking beneath the scruffy exterior. It looked like a creature born of chaos, one that defied any attempt to tame or predict it.

"Now, now, Mr. Prickles," Mrs. Pritchett cooed, "There's no need for you to get yourself all worked up."

Finally finding her voice, Rylie stammered, "Ah, hi, Mrs. Pritchett." She ignored the icy tingles of fear creeping up her spine, willing herself to stand firm despite the creeping sense of dread. She looked down at Mr. Prickles, saw his upper lip pulled back in a snarl, revealing sharp, crooked teeth, and then back up at Mrs. Pritchett's stony face.

"I'm Rylie Donovan and this is my cousin, Colin. Hannah sent these brownies over for you. She thought you might like them. Oh, and my dad said to say hi for him." Rylie's words seemed to just tumble out of her mouth.

"You're Daniel Donovan's child, aren't you?" Mrs. Pritchett demanded. Her face softened ever so slightly, and the hint of a smile seemed more like a crack suddenly appearing on her face.

"Oh, I remember your father. He was quite the little devil when he was your age. He was always getting into some kind of scrape." Mrs. Pritchett sighed. "But Mr. Pritchett was fond of him.

"You do have your father's eyes, Rylie. Well, you may as well come in. No sense standing out on my porch, giving the neighbors something to gossip about over coffee tomorrow morning."

Colin shot Rylie a look that said there was no way he was going in there, his wide eyes and clenched jaw betraying his unease. The fear etched on his face was unmistakable, but it had evolved — no longer was it solely from the snarling cretin lurking behind Mrs. Pritchett's skirt.

Colin backed up and sputtered his refusal. But Rylie cut him off mid-sentence when she shot him the "double dare you" look and followed Mrs. Pritchett into her front hall. *Dang!* Now, he had no choice but to follow her.

Rylie was surprised at how warm and inviting the entryway felt – a total contrast to the woman they were trailing. The doorway they passed through from the front hall formed a tall, graceful arch.

The first thing Rylie spotted upon entering the sitting room was the enormous fireplace. The icy white marble, with the pale pink marble mantel, was the most beautiful fireplace she had ever seen. An antique glass fire screen sat in front of a perfectly stacked tower of logs.

The romantic scene etched on the glass was of a young couple sitting on a park bench holding hands. The couple appeared to be gazing out over the pond, watching two swans swim side by side. The screen design seemed totally out of character for Mrs. Pritchett, Rylie thought.

The scent of oranges and a spice Rylie knew was familiar lingered in the air. Searching for the source, Rylie's eyes wandered around the large room, and she spotted a pretty, sea-green crystal dish filled with potpourri.

"Please have a seat on the sofa. I'll take the brownies into the kitchen. Would you two like a glass of lemonade?" Mrs. Pritchett asked.

Rylie was surprised to see that Mrs. Pritchett's stern face had softened a bit more. She thought she even seemed a little nicer.

"Okay, thanks, Mrs. Pritchett. That would be great," Rylie said.

As soon as Mrs. Pritchett left the room with Mr. Prickles dogging her heels, Colin nudged Rylie in the arm.

"Are you crazy? What are you doing?" he growled, sounding surprisingly like Mr. Prickles.

"I thought we were only going to stay long enough to drop off the brownies and get the heck out of here!"

"Well, it wouldn't hurt you, Colin Donovan, to be nice for a couple of minutes." Rylie snapped back.

Colin rolled his eyes and slumped further down on the sofa, looking very annoyed.

"Well, it's not like you wanted to come either," he grumbled.

"If I knew you were going to make a darn tea party out of it, I definitely would have stayed home."

Since their roles were seldom reversed, Rylie bit her tongue, determined not to argue with her cousin. Instead, she did what females have always done: she just ignored him.

Rylie really was not as calm as she pretended to be. But there was no way she'd let Colin know that. She forced herself to sit still while they waited for Mrs. Pritchett to return to the front room.

Her gaze returned to the fireplace, and Rylie noticed the picture standing on the mantel in a gleaming silver frame that sparkled in the sunlight. The black-and-white photograph looked ancient, its edges slightly faded, whispering of decades long past. It depicted a man in an old-time military uniform, his posture proud and confident, with his arm draped protectively around a young woman at his side. The woman's face was tilted upward, her delicate features soft with admiration as she gazed into the soldier's handsome face, her dreamy smile radiating an unspoken promise of love and devotion. She nudged Colin, pointed to the picture and whispered, "That can't be Mrs. Pritchett and her husband, can it, Colin? She looks so young and happy, like they were really in love."

Before Colin could respond, Mrs. Pritchett returned carrying a large silver tray holding three glasses of lemonade and a plate of cookies. Mr. Prickles danced circles around her.

It seemed Mr. Prickles could not quite decide whether to be miffed about the invasion of the children into his domain or ecstatic about the possibility of getting one of the cookies on the tray.

He looked over at the cousins and let loose a low, rumbling growl. Then, he turned his head to look up at the plate of cookies, releasing several yips that sounded like part whine and part squeal, a racket Mrs. Pritchett totally ignored.

After gracefully setting the ornate silver tray on the coffee table, Mrs. Pritchett handed them each a tall glass of lemonade and a pink napkin.

"I just made the lemonade and cookies fresh this morning. Mr. Pritchett always said I made the best lemonade in town. God bless his soul. Please, help yourselves to a cookie."

Colin sat up straight when Mrs. Pritchett had entered the room. The scowl he had plastered on his face for Rylie's benefit instantly changed to a grin and he was the first to take a cookie, a big, fat sugar cookie covered with chunky, pink sugar crystals. Just as he started to lift the sugary treat to his mouth, Mr. Prickles jumped up and snatched the cookie in his small, sharp teeth, nearly nicking

Colin's fingers in the process. Then he skidded across the hardwood floor as he rocketed out of the room.

"Mr. Prickles!" Mrs. Pritchett scolded, "Shame on you!" But surprisingly, there wasn't any heat to the scolding. "He is usually so well-mannered. I do not know what has come over him." Mrs. Pritchett lowered her voice and whispered, "It's possible he is a little out of sorts. Jealousy, I think. It is not often that I receive company. And never young people," she quietly admitted. "Please, Colin, take another cookie."

After selecting another cookie and carefully keeping his eye on the doorway, Colin took a huge bite. "Where is Mr. Pritchett?" Colin mumbled around a mouthful of cookies.

"Colin," Rylie whispered, sharply elbowing him, "she's the Widow Pritchett, remember?"

"Oh, right. Sorry." Colin mumbled. "I forgot."

"Mr. Pritchett has been gone for quite a number of years, Colin. It is only Mr. Prickles and I occupying this big house these days. Mr. Pritchett built this house not long after we were married. That was over fifty years ago."

"Is that a picture of him on the mantel?" Rylie asked softly, pointing to the one of the young couple.

Mrs. Pritchett seemed startled. The question pulled her from her memories. She looked over at the picture and slowly nodded her head.

"That was taken not long after we were married," she said, clearing her throat. "Mr. Pritchett had been in the Army when we first married. I adored him in his uniform," she confided, her eyes glistened with moisture.

Mrs. Pritchett sniffed once and gruffly said, "Now, you two hurry and finish your cookies. It is going to be suppertime soon and you should start on your way home. I won't have it said that I kept you from your supper."

"Thanks for the cookies and lemonade, Mrs. Pritchett," Rylie said. "Mr. Pritchett was right. You do make the best lemonade . . . just don't tell Hannah I said so, okay?"

Her only reply was a slight smile and a brisk nod of her head. Then she took a calming breath, exhaled, and found herself asking, "If you two would like to stop by sometime to visit, I would not object."

"Rylie, please be sure to thank Hannah for her brownies and tell her I appreciate her thoughtfulness. You rarely see much of it these days."

"Sure thing," Rylie replied.

"Mrs. Pritchett," Colin began hesitantly, "if you want, I could come by and mow your lawn on Saturday. It looks like it kind of needs it."

"Humph," Mrs. Pritchett muttered. "You think that I can't handle my own yard work, young man? I most certainly can." She just stared at Colin for a moment causing him to break out in a sweat. Then she said, "But I believe it's best for you to stay busy so you stay out of trouble in the summer. I will pay you what I think is a fair wage. And I won't tolerate a sloppy job. I'd rather not have it done at all than to suffer a sloppy job."

A little frown crinkled Colin's forehead. "My Dad says I do a good job on our lawn, and I really don't charge that much, so I guess I'll see you on Saturday."

He had a sinking feeling in his gut, realizing he probably should have kept his big mouth shut and not made the offer. The words had slipped out before he could stop them, and now he could only hope the consequences wouldn't be too dire.

When the cousins started toward the front door, it was the exact moment Mr. Prickles had been patiently waiting for. Toenails clicking on the hardwood floor was the first sound they heard as Mr. Prickles bounded around the corner, letting loose a throaty growl, followed by a series of shrill barks. He chased the cousins down the hall and out the front door. The cousins flew across the porch and cleared the three steps in one jump. They were a blur as their bikes rocketed down the block, not even taking the time to look behind them to see if they were still being pursued.

Mr. Prickles, however, had stopped suddenly, just short of toppling off the top step. He continued his high-pitched yips that remarkably sounded like he was chuckling to himself about how fast the kids could scoot. He turned around and slowly strutted back into the house with the doggie door flap, almost swatting his fanny as he hopped back through the entry.

A short time later, Rylie and Colin rounded the hedge that enclosed her front yard and entered the gate. Colin continued toward the back gate that led to his own backyard.

"I can't come over tomorrow because Mom has stuff I have to do," he called over his shoulder.

"I think I have to watch the twins again, so I'll meet you in the tree house Friday morning."

"Okay."

Rylie watched her cousin for a couple of seconds from her back porch and then shouted, "Hey, Colin."

"What?" Colin asked as he stopped his bike and turned to face Rylie.

"Thanks for being nice to Mrs. Pritchett."

"No problem. I guess she wasn't all that bad after all, but her dog sure does suck. I hope she keeps him in the house on Saturday. I totally forgot to ask her. See you on Friday, Ry."

Chapter 4

Rylie had been sitting in her tree house since early morning. The soft rustling of the leaves and the distant chirping of birds did little to calm her growing frustration and she kept wondering where the heck Colin was. They'd agreed to meet early Friday morning and impatience was edging out her good mood. He should be here by now, she grumbled.

Rylie knew she was being totally unreasonable —after all, a few minutes' delay wasn't the end of the world— but she was anxious to get over to her Aunt Molly's shop and get some answers to her questions.

She shifted her position on her pillow for what felt like the hundredth time, the fabric now wrinkled and warm from her restless fidgeting. With a deep breath, she tried—unsuccessfully—to summon even the tiniest spark of patience. When she heard a scratching sound at the door and a soft mewling, she hurried to the door, yanked it open, and was greeted by a pair of round, curious eyes staring up at her.

Josephine sat on the tiny porch, her golden eyes expectantly looking up at Rylie.

"What are you doing up here, Josie?" Rylie scolded, crossing her arms. "You shouldn't climb up here. How do you expect to get back down? What if I wasn't in here, then what would you do?" Rylie scowled, frustration flickering across her face. She hadn't been expecting Josie—she was expecting Colin.

Rolling her eyes, Josie sauntered into the tree house and headed directly for Rylie's pillow. She stood in the center and pushed and kneaded the cushion with her paws, fluffing it just so and then lowered her body and curled up. Rylie was sure she saw Josie smirk just before she delicately licked her paw.

Laughing, Rylie bent over, scooped Josie up, and then plopped back down with Josie nestled on her lap.

Rylie retrieved the drawing from the floor that she'd been working on and tilted it toward Josie.

"Pretty good, huh? I don't know why, but I've been dreaming of her lately. She's very beautiful, isn't she?"

"Are you talking to yourself again?" Colin asked as he entered the tree house.

"Well, it's about time you got here. I thought you were going to sleep all morning. I was just about to tell Josie about my dream."

Reaching down, Colin ran his fingers through Josie's thick fur; then reached around to let her lick his hand and felt the sandpapery roughness of her tongue lightly scratch his skin.

"Geez, Ry, some of us have chores to do first thing in the morning."

"I do, too, but I got mine done early, sleepyhead," she shot back.

"Okay, okay," he conceded, holding his hands up with his palms facing Rylie. He knew he wasn't going to win the argument, so he changed the subject instead.

"Okay, tell me about this dream of yours."

"It's different than other dreams I've had. In this dream, the people stay pretty much the same every night, but the dream seems to continue, like turning pages in a book, each night taking up where the dream of the night before left off. I've had bits and pieces of this odd dream for the past couple of weeks.

"It always starts on a dark and stormy night. It is pitch black out, and jagged streaks of lightning flash in the sky. There's a man, but I can't see his face because of the darkness and the heavy rain, but he's carrying tools, a shovel, and some kind of pick, I think. He crosses a large field of flowers and heads into a bunch of woods. He doesn't seem bothered by the rain that's pouring over his head and running down his face while he walks through the trees.

"Then I watch as he digs up this huge tree and hovering over his shoulder is the most beautiful Fairy I have ever seen. She's flitting back and forth, peering over his shoulder, like she's really worried about the tree.

"I heard her say, 'So, you decided to bring us with you after all. I knew you'd make the right decision. But it had to be your decision. You just couldn't leave us behind.' She twirls round and round, laughing and shouting . . . 'I knew it! I knew it!'

"The little Fairy was totally oblivious to the falling rain and kissed the man on his cheek.

"Then I heard the man shout, 'Glory, by all the Saints, get back inside where it's warm and dry. You have a family to see, too. I'll see to your home.'

"Then everything changes, Colin. This part is foggy. As hard as I try, I can only remember bits and pieces, but it seems the man is on board a ship and he's looking at the tree he had wrapped in burlap. You know, those sacks we've seen Jake use at his nursery? Then I woke up.

"I've tried to capture how the Fairy looked in my drawing and his ship. So, what do you think?" Rylie asked.

"Your drawing is incredible, Ry. It has to be the best one you have ever done. The ship is awesome. Was the Fairy really that pretty? She seems to sparkle, but you can also see the concern on her face like she is protecting the tree or something. Really weird."

"She's the most beautiful Fairy I have ever seen," Rylie said, "and I've seen quite a few of them in my dreams. But I wonder why I keep having this same dream over and over."

"You have to admit, it's pretty freaky, Ry. I don't know anybody that dreams the same dream over and over."

Rylie shrugged her shoulders. "I don't know. I think it's cool. Anyway, I think Aunt Molly's shop is open now. Even if it's not, she's usually in the back working on something. Are you ready to go? Let's bring the drawing and the map to show her," Rylie said.

"Okay. Maybe Aunt Molly will have some donuts, and I'm starving."

"You're always starving."

Colin scooped up Josie as he climbed down the ladder and set her on the ground.

"Do you want to ride our bikes? That way, you can carry Josie in your basket. She likes going to Aunt Molly's shop. I can carry your drawing and the map inside my shirt."

Rylie agreed and Colin placed Josie in her wicker basket on the front of Rylie's handlebars. The basket had been installed so that she could take her with her.

They headed out the front gate and rode past Mr. Quigley's house next door. Mr. Quigley lounged in his old rocker with his long legs stretched out in front of him on his front porch. You'd find him lounging there most mornings and every evening, with Duke lying right by his side. He never missed much of the goings-on in his neighborhood.

Mr. Quigley lived in the old two-story brick house for the past sixty-five years. The red brick had long since mellowed to a soft pink, and the house had a worn, weathered look about it, kind of like Mr. Quigley.

Rylie had spent many afternoons at Mr. Quigley's playing with Duke while her father made repairs to the old house. Duke was an old black Labrador. He sported a touch of gray hair around his mouth and quite a bit more on his chest. He possessed the gentlest personality. Rylie was very fond of Mr. Quigley and of Duke.

"Good morning, Mr.Quigley," Rylie hollered. "How's Duke doing today?"

"Right as rain," Mr. Quigley yelled back. "We both are doing pretty darn well this morning." He smiled his toothless grin and gave her a little two-finger salute.

"You know, my dad said Mr. Quigley was old when he was a kid," Colin whispered to Rylie, even though there was no possible way Mr. Quigley could overhear him.

"Yeah, my dad told me that too. Mr. Quigley and Duke are always together. I heard that Mr. Quigley had Duke's mother as a puppy and her mother before that, kind of like a family tree in dogs."

They passed several more of their neighbors as they continued riding down Maple Avenue, exchanging cheerful waves and quick smiles. The rhythmic hum of their bike tires against the asphalt mixed with the chirping of birds in the nearby oaks. When they turned right onto Willow Glen Road, the air seemed to shift, carrying with it the faint scent of salt from the bay.

Traffic was light this morning, with only a bright red convertible sports car and a white minivan cruising past, most likely on their way to the marina.

For a tourist town, they had their share of newcomers who chose to settle down in their little coastal village. But most residents were families that had made Shadow Harbor their home for many generations.

Shadow Harbor even had its share of celebrities who frequently enjoyed the peace and tranquility of the Sandy Cove Bed and Breakfast, owned by Pete and Sarah James.

Everyone in town believed it was because the Sandy Cove B&B had a very private, breathtaking view of the ocean with its foamy white caps crashing on a beach of sugary white sand.

The scenic view and peaceful setting did draw people from all parts of the country to their tiny sliver of the Atlantic, but Pete James often boasted that it was Sarah's cooking that really kept the visitors returning.

Being such a small New England town, the residents were proud of their large harbor, which dated back to the early 1600s.

A quaint shopping district was the focal point of the marina. In addition to the antique stores and the huge array of shops, candy-colored carts dotted the boardwalk, offering a variety of wares that townsfolk, as well as tourists, found enchanting.

Vendors tempted shoppers with custom-made, hand-crafted silver jewelry, delicate hand-blown glass figurines and authentic wooden sailboats. A rainbow of colorful silk kites in unusual shapes and sizes hovered over the top of one of the carts, and old-fashioned hand-carved wooden toys sat on wooden shelves. Homemade saltwater taffy that melted in your mouth was just a sampling of the wares they offered.

The marina was where Aunt Molly's shop was located. The Fairy Glen was sandwiched between a bakery and a bookstore. Molly's storefront featured a huge picture window hand-painted with laughing Fairies and mischievous leprechauns perched in and around a beautiful Sycamore tree.

Enticing aromas of freshly baked donuts and buttery, flaky pastries swirled around Rylie, wrapping her in a warm, sugary embrace as she pulled open the front door of The Fairy Glen. The soft tinkling of crystal bell chimes drifted through the air, signaling Molly and Jenny that a customer had arrived. Inside, the cozy shop glowed with golden morning light streaming through the lace-curtained windows, illuminating rows of treats displayed like treasures behind sparkling glass cases.

Chapter 5

Leaning against the service counter, chatting with a customer, was where Rylie and Colin spotted their aunt. The customer had just turned to leave when they heard the ringing of the shop telephone.

As Aunt Molly reached to answer the phone, she waved a greeting to the cousins, followed by a nod of her head that had them heading toward the workshop in the back - with Josie trailing behind them.

Two of Rylie's neighbors were in the shop, too, and by their frowns, Rylie assumed they were engrossed in a serious conversation. Molly's assistant Jenny was also busy showing some ladies a cute garden elf. As Rylie passed by the disgruntled neighbors, she overheard Janet Regan say to her sister, Silvia, "I was just talking to Kathy this morning. She was so upset. I swear there were tears in her voice when she told me Samson was missing. You remember her little poodle Samson, don't you, Silvia? Samson has been gone for a couple of days now and Kathy does not have a clue where he wandered off to. Kathy surely seemed shaken. She brought the dog up from a puppy. Kathy said Sampson usually finds his way home after a couple of hours of exploring the neighborhood, but he didn't this time. She said that had never happened before, and he always returned from wherever he would be if she called him. Kathy almost had her throat sore from all the calling she had done. I could hear it in her voice."

Rylie and Colin both slowed down a bit to pick up more on the conversation. They exchanged concerned looks as they made their way to the workshop. *Can it be what I think it is?* Rylie's mind was so fixated on the conversation that she almost bumped into the door jam.

Kathy lived in the house directly across the street from Mr. Quigley. They often saw Samson wandering from neighbor to neighbor, begging for treats, but usually, by suppertime, he would head home like clockwork. Samson was little for a poodle but had an appetite of a dog twice his size, and he never missed a meal. He was a favorite feature of the neighborhood, as almost all the kids had played Fetch with him at one time or the other. *Samson is missing? That doesn't sound okay!* Colin tried to almost telepathically send Rylie a message, who had seated herself at a table and seemed to have forgotten the conversation they had eavesdropped.

All thoughts of Samson immediately disappeared from Colin's mind, too, when he took a seat at the worktable to wait for his aunt. He glanced at Rylie and smirked. "I told you – Aunt Molly would have donuts."

Colin looked over the variety of donuts available on the plate with the same concentration he would use if he were selecting a mint-conditioned baseball card. In his mind, he was wrestling with the same confusing question he had with the cards – *Which one should I pick first?* He was having some trouble deciding between a white frosted donut dotted with colored sprinkles and a gooey chocolate frosted one covered with chopped nuts. "I guess the white-frosted one can wait. I always eat it first. Sorry, frosty, this time you go second," he mumbled to himself, a toothy wide smile on his face and his eyes locking in on the chocolate frosted donut. Without another thought, he stuffed a huge bite of the confection into his mouth, almost too big to chew, but he didn't seem to be in any kind of trouble managing it.

"The Fairy Glen," Molly said, answering the phone.

"Hi, Molly. It's Hannah. I've been meaning to call you for the last couple of days, but Daniel told me you were away on a buying trip."

"I was. I just got back last night. I heard about a new artist in New Haven who creates the most adorable garden elves. Had to visit him. And he sure lives up to all the chatter about him. They are so cute and colorful, and they have the most darling faces. You must stop in and see my new stock too. You'll just fall in love with the little guys."

"Molly, there's something I must talk to you about," Hannah said from the other end, almost ignoring the excitement in Molly's voice. Molly could hear the turmoil in Hannah's voice as she waited for her to continue.

"I sense an air of . . . oh, I don't know, Molly, something magical in the gardens. The air is crackling with energy. It is almost sizzling and popping all the time. It might not be visible yet, but I can feel it every time I step outside. And Glory has been acting very strangely.

"When I ask her what's going on, she just twirls around me, giggling like she does, then poof – she disappears! It is so frustrating being kept in the dark. I have no idea when she is going to start acting her age," Hannah declared. By then, Molly was engrossed in Hannah's troubled conversation and had forgotten about her elves altogether – a frown wrinkling her forehead. "I haven't seen her act this mysterious in a very, long . . ." Hannah's tirade paused mid-thought and then she said slowly, "Come to think of it, Molly, not since you were a child."

Hannah paused, letting Molly take in all the troubling news. Taking a deep breath, Hannah picked up steam once again. "As for Sunbeam and Moonbeam, well, they just chase Josie around the garden teasing her, so it's impossible for me to get anything out of either of them. They too seem more restless and excited than ever, but I can't be too sure of them; they are always running wild.

"And you know how Violet is? She looks at me, beaming like she is bursting to share a secret. Her eyes get huge, and she starts winding her hair around her finger. Then, just when I think she is about to cave in, she clamps both of her tiny hands over her mouth, shakes her pretty little head and chases off after some butterfly that caught her attention.

"Usually, I can coax Violet into telling me anything I want to know, if I can hold her attention long enough that is. I even tried bribery, and you know that usually works very well with her. All it takes is one of my chocolate chip cookies and she spills the beans. But even the cookie failed this time! Not a word! It is so frustrating. I don't know if I should be excited or worried." Hannah fretted. "One thing I do know is that I am getting too old for all these shenanigans."

The wrinkles from Molly's forehead vanished as she pictured little Violet muffling her mouth, stealing a cookie, and dashing for a butterfly. Her lips curved into a pleasant smile, and her eyes twinkled.

"Hannah," she said softly, "I haven't been in the gardens lately, so I am not sure what the Fairies are up to, but knowing Glory, it does sound like she is up to something. If the Fairy clan is in that much of a frenzy, I imagine it will be nothing short of amazing.

Come to think of it, she's been mellow for far too long, so she probably is planning some kind of mischief."

There was a pause on the line that allowed both women to contemplate Molly's words. Then Hannah heard Molly gasp as if an entirely new, more troubling idea came to her mind.

"Hannah, I wonder if all the excitement concerns ***Rylie***. Don't forget, she will be turning ***twelve*** soon, and you know exactly what that could mean. If there is a chance all this rumpus is about that, we better prepare and be ready. I think I'd better have a talk with her and see if she knows anything or see if anything unusual has happened to her lately," Molly offered.

"Well, just don't be filling that child's head with any nonsense! She spells trouble as it is already!" Hannah warned. "I still haven't recovered from your twelfth birthday and that was a long time ago. I don't think my old bones can handle the havoc that child and her equally mischievous cousin will stir up!"

"Not that long ago…" Molly chuckled. "The cousins are in my workshop now, so I'll call you back after I've had a chance to talk to them. See what, if anything, has happened that should be worried about. I'm sure everything will be fine, Hannah; I just know it will. Just please don't worry."

Molly hung up the phone and stood for a minute thinking, her mind skipping back to recalling her own twelfth birthday. The memories made her chuckle as she recalled the eventful day. Molly wondered just what it was Glory had in mind for Rylie and knowing her niece, there was no way it would be an ordinary birthday.

But it was her next thought that sent sparks zapping her mind like the tiny shocks you feel when you test a battery with the tip of your tongue. It caused her brow to crinkle and delighted laughter to escape. "Heaven help us!" she murmured. "Rylie is not the only Donovan about to turn twelve. Oh, I can hardly wait. It's time the Donovan family had a little excitement to shake us all up."

Rylie glanced up when her aunt strolled into the workshop and couldn't help but notice the gleam in her eyes. Molly wore her glossy black hair in a shaggy cut to just below her chin. She unconsciously shook her head to shake her bangs out of her eyes as she approached the table. With a saucy smile and a slightly arched eyebrow, she greeted the cousins. "Good morning. So, what sort of mischief brings you two to my shop?"

"We've been waiting to see you for a couple of days, but you were out of town shopping," Colin sneered. The look of pure distaste on his face clearly said he thought having to go on a shopping trip was horrible.

"And," Colin added, "You know how Rylie hates to wait for anything. She made me get up before dawn just to come see you."

"I did not," Rylie argued, "but I should have – since he slept all morning. Anyway, Aunt Molly, how was your trip?

"The trip was fun, Minx," she began, handing the two kids a wipe each to clean themselves up. "It turned out just as I expected. I had a feeling the new artist I discovered down the coast was going to have just what I wanted. He has quite a talent. I'll show you what I brought back with me after you tell me what's on your minds."

"Oh, you will love this," Rylie began, plopping the donut on the plate and turning to face her aunt. "Everything's sort of strange. We found this ancient map in an old sea chest. You know that chest that Grandpa Rylie brought with him from Ireland? At least, I think it was him. But even before we found the chest I have been having these dreams. In my dreams, there is this beautiful Fairy and her tree. It just feels like everything is all connected somehow. I don't know how exactly but. . ." she trailed off as if to find the right words, but she couldn't.

Zap! Zap! The tiny sparks Molly felt earlier were escalating. "Why don't you just start at the beginning and tell me everything? Don't leave out even one tiny detail," Aunt Molly directed as she grabbed a chair and pulled it right in between the two, her eyes fixed on Rylie.

Catching her aunt's excitement, Rylie grinned and began her tale. She explained how they discovered the sea chest in her attic and how clever they had been in hauling it up to the tree house undetected.

"Ah, so you were actually able to find the old chest. That's very interesting. Did you happen to mention finding the chest to Hannah?" Molly quickly asked. She was brimming from curiosity inside but was also smart enough to know she should be cautious. Keeping things from Hannah was never a smart thing to do.

"Actually, we kind of skipped that part," Rylie carefully said the words, not knowing how her aunt might react. "We snuck it out of the house and stashed it in the tree house," Rylie confessed.

"So, you not only located the chest, but you were successful in unlocking it? How in the world did you manage to do that?" Aunt Molly asked, intrigued. "I always heard it was impossible to get that old chest open. It seems, as I recall, the last time it was discovered, some of the Donovans had tried, but the only one that was successful was Grandpa Marcus. If I remember right, Grandpa showed your dad when he was a kid, but he really had no interest in it. Then, after a time, the chest just seemed to disappear."

"I don't know," Rylie said with a sigh of relief. She was happy Aunt Molly was excited and intrigued more than she was upset. Glancing over at Colin, she quickly added, "We just discovered it in my attic." She paused, then pointed at Colin. "Well, it was actually Colin who found it."

"The chest seemed to blend into the attic walls, and it was totally covered with tons of dust and spider webs," Colin embellished, taking up the story as if the two were in some kind of play.

The excitement teeming from them told Aunt Molly that Hannah's concerns might be well-founded, but she wanted to know more.

"It was tough getting it up into the tree house, but we managed. Snuck it right past old Hannah without her even noticing!" Colin boasted and then raised a closed fist to fist-bump Rylie. Rylie gleefully obliged.

He then went on to explain in detail just what it took for him to figure out the tricky lock.

"Actually, it was very complicated, but I kept working on it until I got the right combination of twists and turns. I can't really explain it, Aunt Molly, but it was as if I just knew each twist or turn I had to make. It just popped into my head, and I knew exactly what I had to do. You should see it, it's cool. I didn't tell Rylie, but I swear the dragon on the front of the chest looked right at me and . . . blinked."

"Why didn't you tell me?" Rylie exclaimed.

"Because I figured you'd just tell me I imagined it. But I know what I saw," he said defensively.

"Yeah, right," Rylie grinned. She shot a look at her aunt, put her right index finger to her head, and twirled it around. It wasn't really that she didn't believe Colin as much as she was miffed he didn't confide in her.

An uncharacteristic flash of temper crossed Colin's features, and he growled, "See, that's exactly why I didn't tell you."

"Hey, come on, you two. You didn't come all the way over here to quarrel with each other," she doused the rising tension. "Besides Rylie, some totally unexplainable, truly outlandish things have been known to happen, especially to the Donovan clan," she murmured under her breath after the two had settled.

"Well, anyway," Rylie continued, "Once Colin opened the chest, that's when we saw the scroll with the "X" on it. The name of your shop was on the drawing, so we figured you must have seen the map too." Rylie's gaze on her aunt was inquisitive and expectant.

"Well, the truth is, I've never actually seen the scroll you're talking about," Aunt Molly tried to evade the question as she tried to figure out how much she knew and how much she should tell the kids.

"Then how did you come up with the name of your shop?" Colin asked, interrupting her train of thought and catching her off-guard.

She forgot just how clever Rylie and Colin were, and she

realized it was useless to try to hide things from them. "I heard the tale from Grandpa Marcus when I was a little girl. He told me the chest and scroll existed, but the chest disappeared years earlier. Grandpa Marcus encouraged me, but I never had an interest in actually hunting for the sea chest. The attic in the old Donovan house was huge and way too spooky with all those dark, little hidey-holes. The thought of crawling around in all the dust and cobwebs was just too creepy for me.

"As I recall, the tale was that not everyone who hunted the chest would be allowed to find it. The chest would only reveal itself to someone of its choosing. There was never any rhyme or reason for it."

She paused, looked around to see if someone was eavesdropping, and then gestured the two to come close and whispered, "Some say that is because the chest was conjured by very old Fairy magic.

"When I decided to open my shop, I remembered the tale, and thought <u>The Fairy Glen</u> would be the perfect name for my shop."

As he unrolled the parchment and laid it on the table, Colin said, "We brought the scroll with us and a sketch Rylie made of her dream Fairy. We thought you'd want to see them."

"I'd love to," Molly said as she accepted the drawing and studied the details. "This is absolutely stunning, Rylie, and so accurate. Tell me about the dreams you've been having."

Rylie filled her aunt in on the dreams, just as she had Colin earlier that morning. With each detail, Aunt Molly's eyes would grow bigger.

"I had several similar dreams when I was about your age, Rylie," Aunt Molly spoke when Rylie was done. She turned and looked at Colin, "What about you, Sport – have you had any odd dreams lately?"

"Ah, no," he said, drawing out the word. "Why would you think I'd be dreaming of Fairies? That's a girl's dream."

"Oh, I don't know, I was just wondering. Though you just might be surprised, Colin. What you think of as a 'girl thing' just might not be," she said with caution in her voice.

Colin felt a little uneasy. He looked at his aunt as if she'd lost her mind and, with a sneer, asked, "So, do you know why Rylie is having the same dream over and over again? You must admit it's really strange, don't you think? I mean, I've never had the same dream twice, and her dreams have so much detail in them, and they seem to continue like a mini-series."

Molly was about to answer when Josephine used the pause in conversation to make herself known. Obviously, she was feeling neglected and forgotten, and that just wouldn't do. With a light, graceful leap, she sprang up and landed squarely on Molly's lap. Then deliberately turned her head and fixed her golden gaze on the tray of donuts.

"Oh, you decided I needed to pay some attention to you, did you?" Molly murmured as she ran her fingers through Josie's soft orange and black fur and tickled her tummy. "You would like a taste of this jelly donut, wouldn't you? You always did have such a sweet tooth."

As Molly continued to stroke Josie with one hand, she offered tidbits of the donut with the other. Even though they had had a good helping of the donuts, the two never said no to another round. Josie contentedly purred and licked jelly from Molly's sticky fingers.

When she finished licking the last speck of jelly from the last finger, Josie curled up and instantly fell asleep.

"You are so spoiled, Josie," Rylie whispered. "You and Colin are always stuffing your faces." Then she began again, "Aunt Molly, in my dream, was the man I saw Grandpa Rylie? And who is Glory? " She stopped talking, seeing that her aunt didn't appear to be paying any attention.

"Aunt Molly, are you listening to me? You look like your mind just flew a million miles away."

"I'm sorry, Minx. I guess my mind wandered. I was definitely listening, and I heard your questions. It's just that those questions triggered some very fond memories for me.

"Yes, Colin, I believe I can explain Rylie's dreams. The man you saw in your dream, Rylie, was your Great, Great, Great - well, I don't know exactly how many greats - Grandfather Rylie Aiden Donovan. Glory is the Queen of the Fairies that adopted the Donovan family many, many years ago back in Ireland and who fell head-over-heels in love with our grandfather."

A little gasp escaped from Rylie as she stared at her aunt, wide eyed. Colin just burst out laughing.

"Yeah, right," he blurted. "She got you, Rylie," he laughed. But then he looked at Aunt Molly and saw that she wasn't laughing or smiling. Rylie too was looking at him sternly.

"Colin Donovan, whether you choose to believe or not is totally up to you," Aunt Molly said softly. "But I would think you would first hear me out and at least listen to the tale with an open mind before you mock me." Aunt Molly challenged.

Sheepishly, Colin stared down at his shoes as if he had suddenly grown another toe and it decided to poke its head out of the side of his worn tennis shoe. He knew better than to upset Rylie, especially when she was about to listen to the mystery of her family. He quickly straightened himself in the chair and resigned himself to listen..

Without missing another beat, Molly took a breath and began again. "I really hadn't planned to take this discussion quite this far, but I guess there's no time like the present to explain the mysteries of the Donovan legacy."

Chapter 6

Well, that got their attention. Both pairs of identical emerald-green eyes locked onto Molly, their intense gaze filled with quiet curiosity as she carefully lifted Josie. The sleepy feline let out a soft, disgruntled meow as Molly gently set her down on the floor, her fur slightly ruffled.

They watched as she stepped through the workshop door and quietly spoke to her assistant, Jenny. Closing the door behind her with a quiet click, Molly stood for a minute, giving herself some time to organize her thoughts, wondering just how she was going to explain a very fascinating, mysterious, and some might say unbelievable family heritage.

Funny, she thought with a wry smile, how it had never crossed her mind that the task of unveiling the Donovan Legacy might fall to her. If it had, she mused, she would have made a point of being far better prepared — perhaps even rehearsed the words she now struggled to summon.

Josie stretched and followed Molly to the doorway and sat looking up at her with a humorous expression on her face that simply said, "Oh, this is going to be good."

Molly bent, scooped Josie up again, cradling her in her arms and returned to her seat. Nuzzling Josie's neck, Molly mumbled, "Geez, Josie, I'm doing the best I can."

After much deliberation, she cautiously began, "What I am about to share with you should remain among us for the time being. You see, some Donovans do not believe in our family legacy. Or, for that matter, that Fairy magic even exists. And if you were to tell your friends, they would probably think you're crazy. So, until you learn which relatives or friends it's safe to confide in, you probably should only talk to me or your Uncle Shawn. Okay?"

Rylie exchanged a look with Colin, who then shrugged his shoulders and settled back in his chair. "Yeah, we're okay with that," she answered.

Aunt Molly took a deep, calming breath, exhaled slowly, trying to settle her jangled nerves, and began the tale the way it had been told many times over, by many different Donovans over the years.

"Your Great, Great, Great Grandfather, Rylie Aiden Donovan, had always believed in the creatures of magic that made their homes throughout Ireland. He steadfastly believed that just because he had never actually seen a leprechaun or an elf did not mean they didn't exist. He believed you had only to look about the forest to see proof their magic thrived there in abundance.

"Some of the folks from the tiny village of St. Bridget's Square, the place Grandpa Rylie called home, affectionately thought of Grandpa as rather fanciful and were thoroughly captivated by the tales he told in the pub. After a pint or two, Grandpa's tales became more extraordinary with the telling. Maybe, some would remark with a wink, even a little outrageous.

"But only a couple of his most loyal friends knew that the wildest of tales he spun were not tales at all but a depiction of actual events.

"You see, in Ireland, Grandpa Rylie owned his cottage and quite a bit of property. Pastureland spread from his cottage to the west, right up to the edge of a grand forest.

"It was his woodlands that Grandpa loved the best, and he took great pride in seeing to their care, especially a part of the wood that would later become known as the Fairy Glen.

"Now, Grandpa Rylie didn't know it was a Fairy glen when he first wandered there. What he saw was rare beauty in that part of the wood. The grounds that made up the glen were covered with a deep, rich green carpet of moss that felt like velvet to his bare toes.

"He often lingered on his visits just to inhale the heady perfume of the exotic wildflowers that covered every mound and created colorful borders around the trees. In all his travels, he had never seen anything as breathtaking.

"Grandpa felt deep within his heart that the glen was no ordinary place; it was a place of <u>magic</u>. He never could explain exactly how he knew magic thrived there, just that he could feel it deep in his bones.

"Often on his strolls, he caught glimpses of an unusual number of forest creatures that were drawn to that particular part of the glen.

"He spotted several families of bunnies tumbling and playing, totally carefree. There were bear cubs and wild hawks, a variety of squirrels and chipmunks, and on occasions, a silver fox and her three tiny kits would join the merriment."

"There's nothing unusual about seeing those animals in the woods," Colin scoffed.

Molly chuckled. "You're right, Colin. It's not that the animals were there that was so strange. They weren't just there; they were playing together—romping and frolicking as if they didn't have a care in the world. Deer and foxes chasing each other, squirrels and rabbits tumbling through the grass, and even a few curled up together, napping in the sun. Now, *that* was a sight to behold.

"As it was, it was quite by accident, or so Grandpa thought at the time, that he stumbled across some of Glory's Fairies playing hide and seek among the flowers in the glen on a warm, sunny afternoon.

"He stood frozen in place, half hidden behind a large oak tree while he watched, afraid if he moved an inch, they would vanish before his eyes.

"But I don't believe it was an accident at all," Molly confided. "If the Fairies, even the least of them, did not wish to be seen, they wouldn't have been. I think they revealed themselves to Grandpa because of his deep love for the glen, and they felt safe in his presence."

"So, then what happened," Rylie asked, her voice a whisper, her curiosity now a wildfire that couldn't be contained. She was truly captivated by the tale.

"Well," Molly continued, "the legend is that Glory, the Queen of the Fairies of the Glen, fell head over heels for Grandpa. Maybe not right from the very beginning because Fairies are not a trusting lot, especially of mortals. But it wasn't long before she found herself charmed. She developed a crush on him that lasted for centuries.

"It's easy to understand as our Grandpa Rylie was a handsome rogue. He was unusually tall, standing well over six feet tall and had the muscled physique of a man well acquainted with physical labor. Thick, coal-black hair hung almost to his shoulders, and he had the devil's own glint in his emerald green eyes – Donovan eyes.

"But Glory often confided that it was Grandpa's deep voice that lured her in and snared her heart.

"It seems Grandpa liked to take a walk to the glen at dusk when the fiery sun was sinking well into the night sky.

"He always chose the softest spot in the mossy glen to lie upon to rest while he waited patiently for the fireflies to begin their dance. He would watch the stars appear, one by one, in the evening sky, sparkling like diamonds.

"In the beginning, Glory would perch on one of the highest branches of the Sycamore tree where she made her home, well hidden from his prying eyes.

"Night after night, she would watch him enter her glen and make himself comfortable near her tree. She wasn't even sure when she began to think of him as a charming intrusion into her sanctuary.

"Usually, Grandpa would sing, and the rich timbre of his voice enchanted Glory. She was spellbound by the mellow sounds coming from the huge brute.

"Glory was surprised when she found herself eagerly waiting for the mortal's return each evening.

"One night, while Grandpa lay watching the stars and picking out his favorite constellation, Draco (the Dragon), he heard an incredible sound. Glory had decided to serenade Grandpa. Her voice was sweet and pure as it floated through the glen.

"Immediately, Grandpa sat up. Glancing from side to side, he looked around him, trying to pinpoint the source of the flawless voice. It was then he first set eyes upon Glory and the evening that changed his life forever.

"Glory was magnificent. A tiny gold crown encrusted with gemstones in every fiery color of the rainbow sat upon her silvery blonde curls. Gleaming hair spilled over her delicate shoulders and tumbled down her slim back, curling at her waist.

"Large violet eyes, fringed with long, dark lashes, dominated her delicate face and filled with mischief when she stopped singing just long enough to bestow a dazzling smile upon him before continuing her serenade.

"A turquoise gown of pure silk rippled around Glory, making her appear suspended in air, even though her gossamer wings were still.

"At first, Grandpa thought he had fallen asleep under the stars and was having an incredible dream, or perhaps some wood sprite, hidden in the evening mist, conjured the splendid vision just to play a trick upon him.

"He stared at the Sycamore for a moment, then slowly closed his eyes. He willed his heart to beat slower, and when he reopened his eyes once again, he fully expected the bewitching vision to disappear. But the little Queen remained.

"Seeing his befuddlement, Glory stopped singing. Once more, her smile lit up her face and a delicate pink blush stained her cheeks.'I am Glory, Queen of this Glen,' she said, regally inclining her head. 'Welcome, Rylie Aiden Donovan.'

"'How is it you know my name, my Queen?' Grandpa Rylie asked, jumping to his feet and bowing respectfully.

"Glory sighed. 'I know all I need to know about those that enter my glen. You have been coming here for quite some time, and I know thee well.'

"From that night on, the little Queen and Grandpa always made time to meet. Sometimes, their visits took place when the morning dew still glistened on the wildflowers; other times, they met at twilight, when Grandpa's chores were finished for the day.

"They quickly formed a close and eternal friendship. Due to their strange alliance, because it wasn't often you'd see a Fairy in the company of a mortal, some of the other Fairies, and occasionally a leprechaun, began to feel comfortable enough to visit with Grandpa, too.

"Years later, in a Shadow Harbor Pub, some of Grandpa Rylie's old cronies admitted that it was not unusual for Grandpa to boast that he had the good fortune to have known and befriended a leprechaun or two back home in Ireland. But Grandpa never spoke of Glory to an outsider. That secret, he kept to the Donovan clan. But I am getting ahead of myself, and I need to backtrack a little," Molly said.

"After a time, Grandpa grew restless with his life in Ireland and felt drawn to travel to America. He never really understood the persistent desire he had to leave his homeland and seek his future in a foreign land, but it hounded his every thought.

"He poured out his heart and dreams to Glory and they would talk for hours about the grand adventure he so desperately wanted to undertake.

"During their talks, Grandpa felt like he was being torn apart because the desire to travel to America was so overwhelming, yet he didn't know how he could go without Glory. He was at war with himself, and it was a battle he saw no conceivable way of winning.

"How could he ask her to abandon her family, her glen? After all, she was their Queen." Rylie asked. The answer was simple: he could not.

"Ah," Molly said with a grin. "The little Queen knew what was in Grandpa's heart. One night, she told him she had spoken with her family, and they all agreed to travel with him to his strange new land.

"Still, doubts plagued Grandpa. He treasured the love and bond of friendship he shared with Glory very much. So much that he was afraid if Glory left her beloved glen, and the home she had made in her Sycamore tree for more than a century, not to mention leaving her homeland of Ireland, she would come to regret her decision very much. And possibly, he could lose their friendship altogether.

"With a heavy heart, Grandpa knew he could not ask her to make such a huge sacrifice for him.

"So it was, as they said their goodbyes for the last time, Glory told him she had the power to grant wishes.

"As a parting gift, she offered to fulfill any wish Grandpa might desire; he had only to ask.

"Your Grandfather felt truly honored that Glory would make him such an offer. He really wasn't surprised Glory was capable of granting wishes because he had seen her do so many wonderfully magical things over the years.

"But Grandpa declined her generous gift, stating he already had everything he could want. Hadn't he worked and saved more than enough money to see to his needs on his journey? Wasn't he in splendid health? What more could a man ask for? But most of all, he felt just having befriended Glory was blessing enough.

"'You are a rare man, Rylie Aiden Donovan,' Glory said with awe. Then she kissed his cheek and bestowed the blessing of wishes upon his descendants. She told Grandpa Rylie she would pass down the gift to his children and to theirs for generations to come as it struck her fancy.

"The one condition she attached to the gift was that she'd only be granting it to those descendants who shared his belief in Fairy magic.

"So it was that Grandpa returned to his cottage. Already, he felt the ache building in his heart. He spent the next couple of days packing his trunks. One of which was the sea chest you found in the attic, a parting gift from Glory.

"Even though his hands stayed busy with the mundane task of packing, his mind seldom strayed far from thoughts of his little Queen. He honestly believed he was doing what was best for her and her family, but his heart was breaking.

"Grandpa had arranged with a friend to become the caretaker of his cottage and property. He had decided not to sell off his land but to keep it as a legacy for the family he hoped to have one day and to be able to preserve the Fairy glen.

"A tremendous thunderstorm rolled inland from the sea the night before he was to board the ship. Grandpa was finished packing and ready to make the long ocean journey. As he sat idle and alone in his cottage, tormented by his thoughts, the excitement he always felt for the upcoming voyage to America dimmed sharply in his grief.

"'Heaven forgive me,' he railed to the empty cottage. 'I'll not leave her behind.' With an oath on his lips, he grabbed up his tools and plunged out into the stormy night. Torrents of icy rain fell to earth, drowning the meadow as if even the heavens were unable to staunch their own flow of tears.

"Thunder boomed, and slashes of lightning flashed all around him as he ran across the sodden field. Raindrops pelted his face, and icy streams ran down his collar, thoroughly soaking his skin as he headed for the glen and his Glory.

"When he reached Glory's sycamore, he found her waiting for him.

"'Well, tis about time, ye stubborn brute,' she said with relief, a warm smile softening her words. 'I knew ye'd not leave me behind. Tis our destiny to make this journey together.'

"The rain showed no mercy and continued to pummel Grandpa's body, but he failed to notice anything but the sight of Glory as she stood waiting for him.

"'Glory, by all the Saints, get back inside where it's warm and dry. You have got a family to see to. I'll see to your home.'

"Fighting a surge of despair, Grandpa began the impossible task of digging up the Sycamore tree. He was determined to bring her home with them and transplant it once again on Donovan's soil when they reached their destination.

"The task, however, proved to be insurmountable for one man – Even a man as determined as your grandfather. So, Glory took pity on him and used a bit of magic to help him remove the tree and securely wrap it.

"She and her family said their goodbyes to those who decided to stay behind and accompanied Grandpa that night as they boarded the ship, _The Enchantress_.

"No one took notice of Grandpa carrying a huge Sycamore tree all by himself up the gangplank, his sea chest floating behind him.

"He left the tree bound in burlap upon deck, secured by Fairy magic. Neither the ship's crew nor the passengers found it odd when he walked to his cabin, apparently holding a lengthy conversation with himself, as Glory and the other Fairies formed a protective barrier all around him.

Chapter 7

"When the ship finally docked in Shadow Harbor, Glory led our grandfather to the perfect piece of land and the Sycamore was settled once more on Donovan soil. The Fairies were overjoyed to be returned to their sanctuary.

"With a slight nod of Glory's head, a small doorway suddenly appeared in the heart of the tree. Through the archway, the Fairies passed, one by one, following their Queen, happy to once again be on solid ground."

"That is so incredible!" Rylie exclaimed, delight dancing in her eyes. "I have been having dreams about Grandpa Rylie and Glory's adventure all along and didn't even know it."

Again, disbelief scrunched Colin's face as he looked from his aunt to his cousin.

"You guys don't believe all that really happened, do you? I mean, Rylie's dreams and Grandpa's tale are just some kind of weird coincidence. Right, Aunt Molly?"

"Well, Colin, as I said earlier, some Donovans believe, and then there are those who will never believe in the Fairies, even if Glory herself were to pop up right in front of them. It's something you have to decide for yourself. But this decision is not made in your mind. It's something you have to feel in here," she said, placing her hand over her heart.

"Well, I believe," Rylie said wistfully. "I just wish I could meet Glory for real, not just see her in my dreams."

"Be very careful what you wish for Minx because, in this family, strange things have a way of happening when we least expect it, and even stranger wishes are granted," Aunt Molly warned.

"Have you ever actually seen a Fairy?" Colin asked, his mocking tone clearly showing his skepticism."For real, I mean."

Smiling, Molly stared him straight in the eye and, without blinking, said, "As a matter of fact, Colin, I have."

"What? When?" Rylie squealed.

"No way!" Colin shouted.

Nodding her head, Molly said, "For me, it happened on my twelfth birthday. I already knew the family history from Grandpa's tales, but it was my mother who told me more about the gift of wishes Glory promised. But Mom also warned me that not everyone gets granted a wish, even if you do believe.

"Oh, let me tell you, I wanted to see Glory so badly. It was all I ever thought about, talked about. It was all I wished for. I remember sitting in my room on the afternoon of my birthday. I was wearing my party dress and sitting in the middle of my bed looking at the delicate Fairy figurine I received for a present. I'll never forget how I was begging out loud, pleading for Glory to visit me. I just knew my heart would break if it didn't happen.

"And suddenly Glory was there. She seemed to sparkle as she sat on my dresser, smiling at me. She was so tiny and beautiful that I just sat there, totally stunned. I could not find my voice for a full minute while I sat frozen, staring at her. That was when I heard her laugh – A musical sound like crystal chimes blowing gently in the wind. She sounded so delightful that I couldn't help but giggle. She raised her arms, and a shower of pink stars swirled all around me.

"I knew instantly that she was Glory. She looked exactly the way Grandpa had described her and how she appeared in my dreams. She was even wearing her tiny golden crown."

"Did she grant you a wish?" Rylie asked, bubbling with excitement. "What did you ask for?"

"I knew precisely what I would ask for if I was ever given the chance. I had been thinking about it for a very long time. So, when she asked me what wish she could grant for me, I had no hesitation.

"Thinking back, as gifts go, my request was rather unusual, especially coming from someone my age. I think I stumped Glory for a minute because she had the oddest look on her face, and all the stars she conjured winked out. She had to think about my request for a few minutes before granting it.

"You see, what I wanted more than anything else was to see into the future, to have the gift of sight. I was a very curious child, and I always wanted to know what was going to happen before it did. So, the gift Glory gave me is sort of a type of sixth sense.

"The way she explained it to me was that I would get a funny tingling feeling if something out of the ordinary were going to happen, and then a colorful picture would flash in my mind.

"It has been awesome over the years. It's kept me out of trouble more than a few times," she said with a chuckle. "And there have been many times when I was able to help other people. But knowing when to not interfere in other's lives has often been quite a challenge for me.

"But the strange thing is that my gift doesn't always work where our family is concerned. Oh, I still get a feeling if something is up with one of you, but I don't always know exactly what the problem is.

"As you both have a birthday coming up, my advice to you is this: start thinking about what you would wish for just in case Glory decides to make an appearance. But remember that responsibility comes along with the gift, so choose very carefully. I don't believe that wishes, once granted, can be reversed.

"Oh, and I better be the first one you tell," she laughed.

"Well, I hope Glory picks me," Rylie said. "I don't know exactly what I want from her, but I know I want something! I think my gift will have to be something unusual too. You do think she'll choose me and not Colin, don't you, Aunt Molly? After all, Colin doesn't even believe."

"Hey, I might not totally believe in Grandpa's story, but getting a wish granted by Glory would be awesome. Who knows, she could pick me. She'll take one look at this smile," he said, flashing a grin, "and she won't be able to resist."

"Well, Glory can be flighty, and she has been known to be very unpredictable. She grants wishes as the mood strikes her.

"They say she granted one of her wishes to your Uncle Jasper. That would be your Great Grandfather's younger brother, and rumor is he was a bit of a pirate. Not the kind you read about in books, mind you, but close enough. Everyone knew he wasn't much of a believer unless he was a bit tipsy.

"He always said that if there was a treasure to be had, he'd be finding his own; that it was lying out there on a beach somewhere, just waiting for him to come along and claim it.

"He spent many years sailing the open seas doing just that, searching for buried treasure. But good fortune always seemed to be just out of his grasp until one dark night. Having just returned from another unsuccessful voyage down-hearted and a wee bit crocked, he paced the backyard of the old Donovan house.

"With his head tilted back, his bleary eyes roamed the inky black sky that looked as if a giant had tossed a fistful of glitter high over his head.

"The more he stared at the tiny specks twinkling down upon him, the further back he tilted his head until he toppled over backward. He lay crumpled on the ground with his cap askew, looking up into the massive branches of the Sycamore.

"Uncle Jasper pulled himself into a sitting position and, in a smooth, practiced motion, swept his cap from his head, his gaze never leaving the great tree and called out, '*Glory, me darlin'*, if ye happen to be resting in that grand tree of yours and have a mind to, would ye be granting me one of your wishes? Just a wee one will do. Tis a treasure chest of gold I've been seeking for a very long time. I find meself discouraged and growing weary of the search and having no luck to mention. If ye could see your way clear to granting a wish and pointing me in the right direction, I would be eternally grateful.'

"To his astonishment, Glory appeared and kissed him lightly on his cheek. She hovered in the air close to his face, not uttering a word, studying him. Then she whispered something into his ear, and with a giggle and a flash of blue light, she was gone.

"Bedazzled, Uncle Jasper sprawled back into the grass and instantly fell asleep. When he arose at daybreak, it was with a spirit filled with anticipation that he headed back out to sea.

"His weary crew was baffled that their captain returned to the open sea so soon after hitting port. They were even more amazed that his bearings were so straight and completely astounded when an uncharted island suddenly appeared portside. On the deserted beach, rising up from the silky white sand, was a treasure chest brimming with gold coins that gleamed brightly in the afternoon sun."

Chapter 8

A solid knock on the workshop door cut through the buzz of questions swirling in the cousins' minds, ready to spill over like a shaken soda can about to burst. The sound stilled the room, drawing all three pairs of eyes toward the door.

When it swung open, a towering man with striking raven-black hair stood framed in the doorway, his sharp eyes sweeping over the trio with curiosity. He had the kind of presence that turned heads in any room.

"Hey, are you guys having a party without me?" he asked.

The questions tumbling around in Colin's mind were instantly forgotten.

"Hey, Uncle Shawn, what are you doing here?"

"I heard Molly was back in town and stopped by to say Hi. I'm glad I caught you guys, though. There's something I wanted to run by you."

"What's up," Rylie asked her uncle.

Shawn felt the electricity crackling in the air and looked at his sister, "Am I interrupting something, Molly?"

"No. We've just finished. Come on in and sit awhile. I'll get you a cup of coffee. Just let me run out and see how Jenny is surviving. She's been left minding my shop for quite a while now, while I've been in here visiting."

"Oh, yeah? So what have you guys been talking about," Shawn asked the cousins.

"Aunt Molly has been telling us about our Great, Great, Great Grandpa Rylie Aiden and Glory, and the wishes Glory grants," Rylie answered.

With a grin, Shawn said, "I guess you have had quite a talk."

Colin gave his uncle his best man-to-man look. "Uncle Shawn, do you believe that Glory really exists?"

Shawn's gaze slid through the open doorway to where his twin stood talking to Jenny, then turned to face Colin.

"Let's just say that I've seen a lot of peculiar things happen in our family over the years. Some of those things would be considered impossible to an outsider.

"I can't say that I've ever had the privilege of meeting the little Queen myself. But to answer your question, I would have to say I do. And it would sure be handy in my line of work to have a dose of that extra intuition Molly was gifted with." He winked.

"Ha," Rylie shouted. "I knew Aunt Molly was telling the truth."

"I never said she wasn't, did I?" Colin said defensively.

"Well, to be fair, Rylie," her Uncle said, "It's really hard to believe in something you haven't seen or experienced for yourself." He looked at Rylie for a reaction.

"It was easier for me to believe," Shawn began, a wry smile tugging at his lips. "Molly, being my twin and all, we've always shared more than just our annoyingly good looks. There's always been a connection between us—something unspoken like we're tuned to the same frequency. So, when she told me about receiving Glory's gift, I didn't doubt it for a second. I mean, how could I? It's Molly."

He leaned back in his chair, his voice taking on a nostalgic tone. "Now, your dad, Rylie — he never bought into it. He'd humor Molly when she tried to tell him about it, nodding along like he was listening. But you could see it in his eyes — he thought it was just a bunch of nonsense. He'd always chalk it up to a woman's intuition whenever Molly got one of her strange feelings. Dismissed it without a second thought."

Shawn chuckled, shaking his head. "But don't you dare try telling Hannah the little Queen is a myth? That woman will box your ears so fast you won't know what hit you. She's the fiercest believer of us all — and trust me, you don't want to get on her bad side.

"Not to change the subject, but I have something I need to talk to you two about. There's a new program being put together at the station. Deputy Chief Anthony Stone has dropped it in my lap, probably because I'm the only detective in town," he laughed.

"It seems the Chief's new pet project is to form a Junior Detective Program. The plan is to open it up to four or five students initially and see how it goes. So, of course, I thought you two might want to participate in the pilot program. If the pilot goes well, then we might include more students down the road."

Rylie didn't wait to hear anymore.

"Wow," she said, "I know I want to do it."

"Sounds cool to me, too," Colin added. "So what kind of stuff will we get to do?"

Seeing the gleam in Colin's eye, Shawn quickly said, "Nothing dangerous. The five of you would form a squad. You will be assigned an area of town, and you'll be taught how to become observant of your surroundings and what is happening in your assigned area.

"You will be instructed on how to spot potential problems and then how to write up a report on that problem. That report will then be given to your squad leader, who will report directly to me. Electing a squad leader will be one of the first tasks you will be asked to do at the initial meeting."

"Will we get to ride around town in a squad car?" Rylie asked.

"I think a ride could be arranged. You will find out more about the program at the first meeting, which will be next Wednesday at ten a.m. in my office.

"But before we go any further can you think of three more kids that would be interested in participating?"

"I know a couple of guys that would really like to do it," Colin offered.

"I think my friend Sam probably would, too," Rylie said.

"Why don't you two talk about it and call me tomorrow? In the meantime, I'll call your Dad, Rylie and run it by him. I'll talk to your parents too, Colin. This is a summer project, but like I said, we may extend it into the school year if all goes well.

"Once you know who else is interested I will need to call their parents and explain how the program works to them. Then all you'll need to do is show up at my office at the station. We'll have our first meeting, and I'm sure Deputy Chief Stone will want to say a few words to all of you. Be sure to dress sharp for the meeting and be on time. Deputy Chief Stone has no tolerance for tardiness. Oh, and no torn or dirty jeans, Colin," he added.

"This is going to be a great summer, Colin!" Rylie exclaimed. "I can't wait for next Wednesday to get here. Thanks, Uncle Shawn."

As Colin was adding his thanks, Aunt Molly returned to the workshop.

"Well, what's got you two all fired up?" Molly asked as she sat down at the table.

"I'll fill you in while you make me that cup of coffee you promised me, or did you forget," Shawn teased his sister.

"No, I didn't forget. I was just about to do that," Molly said as she popped back up and headed toward the coffeemaker, sticking her tongue out at her brother as she went.

"I guess we better be headed home," Rylie said. "It's getting close to lunchtime and Hannah hates it when we are late. Besides, I'm sure Colin is starving by now," Rylie said, rolling her eyes toward her cousin.

"Hey, I've only had three donuts, and everyone knows they aren't really food," Colin retorted while stuffing Rylie's drawing and the scroll back inside his shirt. He snatched up Josie, and the cousins headed toward the door.

"We'll call you tomorrow, Uncle Shawn," Colin said.

As she walked through the door, Rylie called back over her shoulder, "I'll have to come back to see your new elves, Aunt Molly. See you later."

"Don't forget what I told you." Molly's reminder trailed after the cousins.

Chapter 9

Late Saturday morning, the door slammed shut with a sharp bang as Rylie stepped into the treehouse, the wooden floor creaking under her weight. Sunlight filtered through the gaps in the planks, casting thin golden beams across the small space.

"How'd it go at Mrs. Pritchett's?" Rylie asked as she watched her cousin kick back on the sea chest. "Weren't you going to mow her yard this morning?"

"Yeah, I finished her yard. I was glad she closed off the doggy door, but I think she did it to protect Mr. Prickles from attacking the mower and getting hurt rather than keeping him from attacking me.

"When I was edging the grass near the front porch, I heard him growling and scratching at the door flap. It sounded like his paws were trying to tear it open. I swear he was body-slamming it with everything he had, throwing his whole tiny, furious self into the fight. The flap rattled, shaking so hard I thought it might pop right off its hinges.

"I just knew—*knew*——that at any second, the little demon would come flying through, teeth bared, eyes wild, launching straight for my ankles like some kind of possessed wind-up toy. My heart pounded as I braced for impact.

"When I finished, I dreaded having to knock on Mrs. Pritchett's door to get paid. With all the commotion Mr. Prickles was making, I did not think she would even hear me knocking. It took her a while to answer and when she finally did, she had Mr. Prickles tucked up under her armpit like a football. For a second, I thought she was going to lose her grip and Mr. Prickles was going to twist free and attack. But somehow, she managed to hang on to him.”

“So what did she say about your mowing? She couldn’t help but like the way you mowed. You always do a good job.”

“I don’t know. She marched around the whole yard inspecting everything. I just hung back, following behind her. All I wanted to do was keep away from the demon dog. I swear, Ry, that is exactly what he looked like, a pint-sized demon dog right out of the movies, his hair sticking out all wild, those tiny black eyes glaring at me, and his lips curled back, baring his ugly little teeth.

“I saw Mrs. Pritchett shaking her head back and forth a couple of times and heard her muttering something about how no one ever did the yard as well as Mr. Pritchett did in the old days. “She told me the job would have to do, and she handed me a ten-dollar bill. Then she pushed a fifty-cent tip into my hand, gave me one of her nods, and strode briskly back into the house, with Mr. Prickles snarling the whole way.”

“Well, at least you made it out of there in one piece. I thought for sure Mr. Prickles would have nailed you at least once,” Rylie teased.

Then, in typical Rylie fashion, she fast-forwarded to another subject and asked, “Did you think about who you wanted to ask to be part of the detective squad?”

Nodding his head, Colin said, “I called Stretch and J.D. last night. They’ll meet us here after lunch to talk about it.”

“No way. Why’d you have to ask Wade? He is such a jerk.”

"Come on, Ry, you're not still ticked at Stretch because he flew out at the last game, are you?"

"MAD – uh, yeah! I hit my first -- MY FIRST -- triple ever, and I was all set to score if Mr. Showoff had just hit a line drive between first and second, but oh no, he had to show off and try for a home run. He cost us that game and left me standing on third."

"Stretch really is a good guy Ry, and you know he's the one that usually wins our games for us. He just had an off day, that's all."

"Yeah, I'll say," Rylie snorted. "I sure didn't see him get a triple," Rylie grumbled to herself.

Ignoring Rylie's grumbling, Colin said, "I think Stretch would be good on the squad."

"Well," Rylie conceded, "at least J.D. will be part of it. He's pretty funny, and I already asked Sam, and she will be here in a little while, too. Besides, I think J.D. likes her."

"No way!" Colin laughed. Disbelief and an edge of panic sharpened Colin's tone. "There's no way J.D. likes Sam. I mean, not like that. Sam is just one of the guys. We've all hung out together since kindergarten."

"Well, you don't have to believe me, but I've seen the way he looks at her when he doesn't think you guys will see. Besides, girls just know these things," Rylie said smugly.

"Oh, now you're an expert on," Colin sputtered, trying to come up with a suitable word without actually having to say the "L" word. Love or anything close to it just wasn't a word he chose to use. Or think about for that matter, especially when talking about one of his buddies.

The bright, red flush that began on Colin's neck and crept up to his face had Rylie giggling. She just couldn't help herself and she burst out laughing. Unfortunately for Colin, the more she laughed, the more crimson he became.

"Oh, come on, Cuz. If you could see the look on your face, even you would laugh. It really is funny. I don't know why you hate to talk about mushy stuff so much."

"Man, Ry, give me a break. We're talking about Sam and J.D.," Colin groaned. "Can we just stick to talking about the Junior Detective Squad?"

"Geesh, I'm just teasing."

"Well, don't go talking about that stuff when the guys get here. Okay?"

"Alright, I won't," Rylie promised. She solemnly made a little 'x' with her index finger over her heart and raised her hand palm out. But she just couldn't quite keep herself from grinning.

"So what do you think we'll get to do on the squad?" Rylie asked. "I really hope we get to track down some bad guys and solve crimes. You know I have always wanted to be a detective, like Uncle Shawn, and this is kind of the same thing."

"That's probably why Uncle Shawn thought of us," Colin said. "But I doubt he'll let us get involved in any real crime-solving."

"I know, but it wouldn't hurt us to keep our eyes open and maybe snoop around for some clues if the time comes. Besides," she reasoned, "it ought to make Uncle Shawn look good if our squad does well."

Colin raised his hand and brushed a lock of hair out of his eyes. It was a habit he acquired when he started wearing his hair a little longer.

He watched his cousin's face and couldn't help but notice how the green of her eyes had deepened, and they took on a familiar gleam.

Oh man! he thought. He recognized that look. He had seen it so many times. Usually, right before she sprung her plans to pull a prank, one she was determined he would help her with. *Man, here we go again,* he thought, shaking his head.

A little past noon, the sun shone high overhead. Sunbeam and Moonbeam lounged on a branch of the Sycamore tree, enjoying the warmth of the sunshine while watching the comings and goings of the tree house.

Their attention was focused on the two figures noisily approaching the ladder. A tall, good-looking, athletic boy was first to begin the climb, taking the steps two at a time wearing a Boston Red Sox ball cap.

Sunbeam watched as the boy turned his head, looked back over his shoulder and laughed at something his friend had said.

The boy who followed was the complete opposite of the one leading the way, Sunbeam observed.

He was much shorter, with a round, plump face that gave him a cheerful, almost mischievous look. His quick, easy smile seemed to light up his entire face, crinkling the corners of his bright, eager eyes. There was an energy about him— — something warm and inviting, like the feeling of sunshine on a crisp morning.

"What do you think is going on in there?" Sunbeam whispered to Moonbeam.

"I don't know, but if we sit on the windowsill in the back behind the shutter, we can hear everything, and they won't be able to see us spying on them," Moonbeam told her excitedly, his voice getting louder with each word.

"Shush! Speak softly, or they'll hear us," Sunbeam scolded. Remember, we're not supposed to be obvious when we spy on the young mortals.

"You are not the boss of me," Moonbeam taunted. Lifting his hand and flicking his wrist, he showered Sunbeam with a flurry of fat pink and blue bubbles, then darted off toward the back of the tree house, with Sunbeam giving chase.

By then, the first boy had reached the tiny front porch, and just as he was about to open the door, he paused and looked up toward the higher branches. "Did you hear that, J.D.?"

"What? I didn't hear anything."

"I thought I heard someone talking. I guess it must have just been someone in the yard next door," he said, puzzled. Yet he peered back up into the branches for another second before opening the door and running smack into Rylie.

"Hey, Shorty, how you doin'?" Stretch asked. He reached out with one hand to steady Rylie and saved her from toppling over backwards.

Embarrassment and annoyance showed clearly in Rylie's expression as she looked up at Stretch, but before she could fire off the smart remark she had on the tip of her tongue, J.D. pushed his way into the tree house, leaving Rylie standing at the door.

"Hey, Stretch. J.D.," Colin greeted his friends. "We're waiting for Sam to get here then we'll have our meeting. I guess Rylie called her last night, too."

Rylie darted around Stretch at the last second, slipping past him with a triumphant smirk. Before he could react, she plopped down onto her favorite red pillow, sinking into its familiar softness.

"So what's the matter with you, Shorty? You look really ticked off," Stretch asked, looking from Rylie to Colin.

"I wouldn't mess with her if I were you," Colin warned.

Then, a thought struck him. Stretch grinned and asked, "You're not still sore about the game, are you Shorty? You know I tried to knock one home for you."

"You could have just grounded one, Wade, instead of showing off," Rylie snapped back, using Stretch's real name just because she knew how much it irritated him.

"Hey guys, you want to hear a new joke?" J.D. asked, trying to ward off another argument, even though he was beginning to think Stretch and Rylie really enjoyed fighting with each other.

"I hope this one is better than the last one you told us," Colin ribbed his friend.

"Yeah, this one will crack you up," J.D. laughed.

"What did one bug say to the other after he hit the windshield?"

"What," Colin asked, playing along.

"<u>Bet you don't have the guts to do that again</u>," J.D. said, laughing hard at his own joke.

"Ewe, that's terrible," Rylie said, scrunching up her face. However, the chuckle that escaped ruined the effect.

"Then why are you laughing?" J.D. asked, grinning.

"I'm not," Rylie said, letting another giggle escape.

"Do you want to hear another one? I have a ton of new ones you guys haven't heard yet."

Before anyone answered, there was a stomping noise on the stairs. All heads turned toward the door just as Sam poked her head in.

"Hi Sam, come on in," Rylie said.

Sam smiled and mumbled hi to the boys, then made Rylie scoot over and claimed a seat next to her on the pillow.

"I could hear J.D. laughing all the way up the ladder. What's so funny?"

"Please, don't ask, you'll just get him going again telling his Grandfather's joke," the friends all said in unison.

"Oh, right," Sam said. She looked at Rylie. "So, are you going to tell us some more about the detective squad?"

"Actually, Uncle Shawn didn't tell us all that much about it when we saw him yesterday. I just know there's going to be a meeting at his office next Wednesday and we all need to be there. He's supposed to go over the rules and stuff. I guess his boss will be at the meeting too." And then, as the kids were trying to make sense of what she had said, she added, "Oh, he said we'll get to ride in a patrol car."

Then Colin cut in, "Our main job will be to keep an eye on an area they assign us and pretty much just observe what's happening and report anything unusual to Uncle Shawn."

"Yeah, well, maybe we'll spot some trouble and get to report it," Rylie said.

"Uncle Shawn told us the program is really about observing and reporting, not getting involved in anything dangerous, Rylie," Colin warned.

"I wasn't thinking we'd actually do anything dangerous, Colin, but a little excitement would be cool."

"Sounds good to me," Stretch said, smiling at Rylie.

"At our first meeting, we have to elect a squad leader," Colin told the group. "Then the rest of us will report to that person. He or she," Colin amended, looking at Rylie and Sam, "will report directly to Uncle Shawn. So do you guys want to figure that part out now, and then when we go to the meeting, we'll already know who it will be?"

"Well, I know I don't want to be it," Sam quickly admitted.

"Yeah, me either," J.D. said. "I'm more like Robin than Batman," he laughed. "You know, the sidekick, only funnier."

"Yeah, that's how I feel too," Sam agreed, "just not about the funny part."

"Okay, then that leaves just us three," Colin said. "So, how are we going to choose?"

"Well, to be fair, you guys could put your names in a hat. And since I don't want to be it, I can pick out one of the names." Sam offered.

"That's cool with me," Stretch said.

Colin and Rylie agreed.

Stretch pulled off his ball cap and handed it to Sam. She took it, carefully folding the three small slips of paper with their names on them before dropping them inside.

Giving the hat a good shake, she let the papers tumble around for a moment. Then, without looking, she reached in and fished out a single slip, her fingers hesitating for just a second before pulling it free.

She slowly looked at each of her three friends while J.D. played a drum roll with his fingers on his knees. She unfolded the slip of paper and read the name.

"Come on, Sam, who is it?" Rylie asked impatiently.

"It's Colin. Colin's our new squad leader."

"Cool." Colin grinned.

"Dang," Rylie said, frowning.

"Well, Colin, since I didn't get it," Stretch said, "I'm glad it's you. It would have been real tough for me to have to report to Shorty."

From his seat on the old sea chest, Colin leaned back against the wall and tried not to show how glad he was to be the new squad leader. He knew his cousin well. She never could hide her feelings.

He clearly saw how disappointed Rylie was, and Stretch's remark only ticked her off more.

"Okay," Colin said. "I guess we all need to be at the station on Wednesday at ten o'clock sharp. Uncle Shawn said we have to be on time and we're supposed to wear decent clothes. He'll tell us about everything at the meeting. Oh, yeah, he asked me to call him and let him know who will be in the squad so he can call your parents for their permission. So make sure your parents know what's going on."

Later, as they were heading out, Stretch trailed behind Sam and J.D., his footsteps slowing as they reached the door. Something gnawed at the edge of his mind——a whisper of a sound, a feeling that wouldn't let go. He stopped abruptly, turning back toward the window. A flicker of movement had caught his attention.

Frowning, he stepped closer and peered through the narrow gap in the wooden shutters. His gaze swept up into the branches of the towering Sycamore, his ears straining for the faint voices he was *sure* he had heard just moments ago.

Then, out of the corner of his eye, a sudden blur of color streaked past——a flash so quick he couldn't make out its shape. His breath hitched as his eyes tracked its movement.

And then, in its wake, something even stranger——A delicate, shimmering cloud of pink and blue bubbles drifting lazily upward, catching the fading sunlight as they floated toward the highest branches.

Stretch blinked. "What the heck! Where'd those come from?!" Stretch wondered aloud.

"What are you mumbling about?" Rylie demanded. She had just risen from her seat on the cushion and was about to head out the door when the odd look on Stretch's face piqued her curiosity.

"It must have been a bird I saw fly by, but where did those bubbles come from?"

"What bubbles?" Rylie asked as she crossed the small space to elbow Stretch aside. Reaching around him, she pushed the shutters further apart and leaned out the window.

"I don't see anything." Rylie frowned, thinking Stretch was teasing her. Then, out of the corner of her eye, something fluttered.

Up among the highest branches, shimmering bubbles — pink and blue — drifted lazily in the air, catching the golden light that filtered through the leaves. They weren't just floating; they seemed to *hover* with purpose, their glossy surfaces reflecting the world in tiny, distorted swirls.

Rylie barely had time to process what she was seeing before— *pop!* One of the bubbles burst, releasing a tiny, airy giggle that floated down from the top of the towering Sycamore.

Then — —*pop, pop, pop!* — —more bubbles vanished, each one punctuated by another soft, mischievous laugh.

And just like that, the bubbles were gone, leaving nothing but the rustling leaves and the lingering echo of laughter in their wake.

Stretch and Rylie stared at each other. Neither of them said a word.

"Now you're making me crazy!" Rylie said as if the mysterious bubbles were totally Stretch's fault.

In a huff, she shoved past Stretch, barely sparing him a glance as she made her way to the ladder. Her footsteps were quick, almost stomping, as she descended the worn wooden steps with more force than necessary.

Once they joined the others on the ground, an unspoken pact was formed, securing that neither one would mention what they probably hadn't really seen anyway.

"See you Wednesday, Shorty. Colin." Stretch called out as he and the others said their goodbyes.

Chapter 10

Storm clouds, dark and heavy, churned in the sky like massive black bears locked in a ferocious struggle. They rolled and twisted over one another, thick and menacing, devouring the last traces of blue as they surged in from the ocean. The storm gathered strength with alarming speed, its inky masses looming over the small coastal town. Thunder cracked like the growl of an unseen beast, and mere seconds later, a jagged bolt of lightning slashed through the darkness, striking the beach with a blinding flash.

The air hung thick with humidity, clinging to the skin like a damp shroud, making the morning heat almost unbearable. The scent of salt and ozone filled the air as Rylie and Colin urged their bikes forward, sweat beading on their brows. Their destination—the police station—stood ahead, but the storm at their backs was closing in fast.

"We better get a move on it, or we're going to get completely soaked before we get to the station," Colin said, waving his hand toward the shirt and jeans he wore that were already lightly speckled with water spots. As they stopped at the red light, Colin had been looking at Rylie and did not notice the cloud of mosquitoes that swarmed him.

A big, fat mosquito buzzed past his ear, its whiny drone cutting through the humid air before it landed boldly on a sliver of his exposed neck. Without thinking, his hand shot up, smacking down with precision—but the little menace dodged at the last second, escaping unscathed.

Laughing, Rylie said, "Looks like they're using you for their morning feast."

"It's not funny. Why are they only biting me?"

"I don't know, maybe because you're pouring sweat and I'm not. Or maybe you just taste better than I do. It's probably all the donuts you eat."

"Yeah, right," Colin grumbled while he raced through the intersection. He glanced at Rylie. "Did your dad tell you our folks are planning to have our birthdays celebrated together again this year? Grandpa Marcus and Grandma Katie are coming from Ireland to be here for it. They're planning the party for next Saturday at your house; Hannah is baking our cake."

"Yeah, Dad said something about it when he left for work this morning. I can't wait to see Grandpa and Grandma."

Looking straight ahead, Colin tried to sound nonchalant when he asked, "With your birthday only a couple of days from now, have you decided what gift you would ask Glory for, if she pops in on you?"

"I thought you didn't believe in Glory or her gifts?"

"Geez, Ry, I don't know. I guess, maybe, there could be something to it," he admitted. "I mean, strange things have happened, like Aunt Molly said, like seeing the dragon's eyes move on Grandpa's sea chest. I didn't make that up. I know you don't believe me, Ry, but they really did move. So how is that possible? And heck, even Uncle Shawn said he believes. So I think maybe there could be something to it." Colin sighed. "All I'm saying, Ry, is that it couldn't hurt to be prepared. Right?"

Rylie searched her cousin's eyes, looking for any hint that he was actually mocking her. When she found no deception, she said, "Colin, I didn't tell you, but when Stretch was in the tree house, he thought he heard or saw something at the window, and when we looked out, we saw some large pink and blue bubbles floating up in the branches. When they popped, I know I heard a girl giggle, but the sound didn't come from down below. It came from high up in the tree. I can't explain that either. So, I guess strange things do happen. It's like, sometimes I think you have to stop thinking, and you just have to believe."

"Huh, Stretch never said anything to me about that."

"We sort of just agreed not to talk about it," Rylie said.

"So promise me you won't say anything to him. Okay?"

"Okay," he agreed. "So, have you decided what you'll ask for?"

"Well, kind of. I have a couple of ideas, but I'm still not sure which one I want the most yet." Then, as if looking for ideas, she turned to Colin and asked, "What about you?"

"I don't know. I don't think what I want is even possible."

"Oh, man, don't tell me you want Glory to let you play on the Red Sox, like that kid in that old movie we saw."

Colin chuckled. "No, that's not it. Just forget it. You'll just think it's weird anyway. Let's talk about something else."

Rylie knew Colin was not going to say any more about it, so she let the subject drop—for the time being anyway.

"Alright, but when you're ready, you have to tell me. You know we tell each other everything."

"Yeah, sure," Colin agreed. He was relieved that Rylie decided not to bug him until he told her what he was wishing for. Usually, she'd pester him non-stop until he caved.

"It's not like what I have in mind could happen anyway," he muttered to himself. They crossed Hillside Avenue, turning onto Main Street when the light sprinkle of raindrops began to take a serious turn, motivating the cousins to peddle even faster.

The Police Station was just ahead on the corner of Main and French Street. The ancient Victorian mansion was a cornerstone of the town. Originally built for the prominent Monroe family in the late 1700s, the mansion stood as a timeless sentinel against the harsh New England elements. Despite enduring countless storms and relentless coastal winds, it remained proud and unyielding, its three-story facade still exuding elegance and grandeur.

A steeply pitched gabled roof crowned the structure, while a wide, wraparound veranda embraced the mansion, offering a perfect vantage point to admire the sprawling estate. But the most striking feature was the Widow's Walk atop the third floor—an ornate, weathered platform that overlooked the restless coastline, where generations had once stood, scanning the horizon for ships that may never return.

Generations of Monroes had lived in the mansion until 1925, when the family donated the house to the town for the use of the newly formed Police Department. Up until 1925, the town only had a constable and a couple of volunteers to help enforce the law.

Tourists were delighted with the grace and charm of the mansion and were often seen snapping pictures while they wandered the lush gardens.

Colin and Rylie were the last of the squad to arrive at the station. They never even glanced at the gardens. They barely had enough time to say hi to the Front Desk Sergeant Polanski before dashing down the hall and racing up a flight of stairs to their Uncle Shawn's office.

As far back as Detective Shawn Donovan could remember, his goal had been to become a police detective. He couldn't believe his luck when Detective Rinaldi decided to retire. When he received his gold detective's shield and was given an office of his own, he had been thrilled.

To Shawn's way of thinking, the Deputy Chief had given him a fantastic office. One large enough to accommodate not only his pine desk and matching four-drawer filing cabinet but also a fairly large bookshelf, two visitor chairs, and a window with a view overlooking the east garden. It couldn't get any better.

Leaning against the corner of his desk, Detective Donovan looked up at the large silver and black clock on the wall and saw the hands inch closer to ten o'clock. He picked up the phone and dialed the front desk.

"Hey, Sarge, have my niece and nephew gotten here yet?"

"They sure have Detective. Just sent them on up to your office. They should get there any minute now."

"Okay, Sarge, thanks." He hung up the phone and looked over the rest of the squad; they all looked a little nervous. "Rylie and Colin will be here any minute."

He barely said the words when a light knock sounded on his door. The door swung open, and Rylie walked in, followed by Colin.

Once again, Detective Donovan's eyes slide to the clock. It now read ten o'clock straight up.

"Cutting it close, aren't you?"

The cousins mumbled an apology as they joined the other Junior Detectives crowded in what little floor space there was. When no one seemed to want to sit on the two available visitor's chairs and stood huddled in the corner, it occurred to Detective Donovan that his office wasn't quite as spacious as he thought.

"Well," Detective Donovan said, "I'm glad to see all of you could make it and on time too.

"I guess it's a little crowded in here so we're going to move down to the conference room where we have our staff meetings. Deputy Chief Anthony Stone will address us there."

Detective Donovan picked up a small cardboard box and left his office, leading the group down the hall. After everyone took a seat, the detective reached for the phone on a side table, sitting next to a small notepad and a canister of pens. He called the Deputy Chief to let him know everyone was assembled and ready for him in the conference room.

At the sound of approaching footsteps, every head turned toward the doorway. Stark silence blanketed the room when the large frame of Deputy Chief Stone filled the doorway. He stood surveying the group.

Chief Stone was a very imposing man, standing several inches over six feet with a stocky build. The expensively tailored charcoal grey pinstriped suit he wore matched his salt and pepper hair perfectly. He wore his hair short in a military-style cut that was a carryover from his Army days.

All five pairs of eyes looked wary as they stared back at him until his smile made an appearance and softened the hard planes of his face, adding a touch of warmth to his eyes.

The Deputy Chief walked briskly to the front of the room, addressing his detective while he glanced at each member of the squad. "Well, Detective Donovan, it seems you are to be congratulated. You have assembled a fine-looking group for your first Junior Detective Squad."

"Thank you, sir. Let me introduce you to the squad.

"Junior Detectives, this is Deputy Chief Stone.

"Deputy Chief, these two are my niece and nephew, Colin and Rylie Donovan. The big guy in the back is Wade Tyler, otherwise known as Stretch; the young lady next to him is Samantha Hunter, Sam for short. You know Sam's parents, David and Dani Hunter, they own Hunter's Sporting Goods; and that leaves J.D., Jesse Dillon to complete the team."

"Welcome aboard," the Deputy Chief said, his deep voice booming around the room. "I wanted to personally tell you how excited we are about this new project and to say our Chief is counting on it being a huge success. So, I'm sure all of you will work diligently with Detective Donovan to accomplish just that. Am I right?"

The Deputy Chief's eyes narrowed slightly when only silence greeted him in return, as all five of the team just stared wide-eyed, frozen in place.

"Yes, Sir, I'm sure my team will do their best," Detective Donovan quickly responded, filling the gap. And he was pleased when he heard faint echoes of 'yes sirs' from all of the team and saw their heads bobbing in unison.

"During this meeting, Sir, I've outlined an agenda that includes discussing the purpose of the Junior Detective Squad, what our department wants to accomplish by instituting this new program, having the squad elect a squad leader, and explaining how the squad will be representing the Shadow Harbor Police Department while out on patrol. Would you like to address the group on any of these issues?"

"No, that won't be necessary, Detective. Unfortunately, my time here is very limited. I have a meeting that I must attend shortly, and it is not my intention to steal any of your thunder. I just wanted to take a moment to welcome the squad members personally. Please continue."

"Thank you, Sir," Shawn said.

With a sharp nod of his head, the Deputy Chief turned on his heel and abruptly exited the room.

After closing the door behind the Deputy Chief, Detective Donovan said, "Well, that is probably one of the last times you'll ever see the Deputy Chief." Then, mumbling under his breath, he added, "Hopefully." As he walked back to the front of the room, he chuckled at the sighs of relief he heard.

"Our first order of business is for me to explain just what you're getting yourselves into. Of course, some duties or assignments may change along the way as you become more experienced, but for now, the plan is to keep things pretty basic.

"First of all, all of you," he said, glancing over at Rylie and Colin, "refer to me as Detective Donovan, or just Detective whenever we are around the rest of the police department. But if we are off duty, just Shawn will do.

"Good. Now, you all heard Deputy Chief Stone tell us how important this project is to our Chief. So it is vital we do our best to make this program a success.

"Something I want you to keep in mind is that you are not alone in this. If you feel unsure about what you should be doing or how to handle a situation, talk to your squad leader. Explain the situation and he or she will report back to me for my instructions. That procedure is what is known as 'following the chain of command.' Just as I report to the Deputy Chief, the Deputy Chief reports to the Police Chief. It is essential that we keep communication open between us.

"Is everyone clear on how the Chain of Command works?"

"Yes, Sir," the group answered.

"Basically, your squad will be assigned to one specific area of town to patrol. Your goal is to observe and become familiar with the residents and shopkeepers in your area. This part should really be easy because all of you have grown up here and know practically everyone already.

"You'll probably want to ride your bikes down to the wharf, then walk around your area and observe what's happening. You will be an extra set of eyes and ears for the department.

"Should you notice anything out of the ordinary, you are to report your observations to your squad leader, who will write a report and then give the report to me. I'll show your squad leader how the report is to be written a little later.

"At no time are you to get involved in any activity that could cause harm to yourself or your team.

"Fortunately, since we are a relatively small town, we don't have the amount or types of serious crime to deal with that the big cities do.

"Unfortunately, we do have the grifters and pickpockets that like to prey on our tourists, like any other tourist town, so you need to be careful and patrol with another squad member. Your squad leader will get with you to set up a schedule, and I'll review it.

"At the end of our meeting, you each will be given a dark blue tee shirt to identify yourselves as a member of the Shadow Harbor Police Department's Junior Detective Squad. Always wear it whenever you are on patrol.

"One thing the Department hopes to gain from the new program is that once the town gets used to seeing you patrol on a regular basis, they should start to open up and talk to you about problems affecting their area. It could be things they might not take the time to call the department and report but still have concerns about.

"After talking to the shopkeepers regularly, you will begin to spot potential problems before they become real problems.

"Then, when you make your report, I'll decide what action, if any, needs to be taken to provide the citizens with better community relations.

"Any questions so far?"

As she raised her hand, a grin slid across Rylie's face at the prospect of calling her uncle anything but Uncle Shawn.

"Detective Donovan, what if we see something important happening and there isn't time to contact our squad leader? Is it okay to call you directly and report the problem?" Then, plucking out and waving her cell phone from her pocket, she added, "We all have cell phones."

"Of course you can. There is always an unknown factor when you are in the field, which means that anything can happen at any time, and you'll need to use your best judgment.

"I will provide my cell phone number and the Front Desk Sergeant's phone number to program into your cells. So, if you can't contact your squad leader, or me, you can always reach the Sergeant for direction.

"But as I said before, it is important to use the chain of command first, if possible. It's unlikely that you will come across anything serious, and I cannot emphasize enough that you," He said, looking directly at Rylie, "are not to get personally involved in a potentially dangerous situation."

Snickering could be heard among the team because everyone knew that Rylie tended to jump head-first into a mess without always stopping to think it through.

Like the time they all went swimming over at Beaver Creek and discovered an old rope tied to a limb of a huge Oak tree. While the friends were still arguing about who should be the first to make the short, steep climb up the jagged face of the cliff, Rylie had already taken off running. Not once did she give any thought to the possibility that danger could be lurking up ahead.

She quickly climbed the cliff and, for just a moment, stood at the base of the old oak, deciding what her next move would be.

Then, raising her arms high over her head, she stretched as far as she could reach to grasp the rough knot tied in the thin rope. She bent her knees, pushed off hard with her legs, and swung out over the edge of the cliff. Instantly, Rylie's eyes sparkled with excitement and the thrill of being the first to try the rope, then just as quickly, the sparkle was replaced by terror as the brittle rope suddenly snapped, casting her down like a squirrel dropping a dried acorn from the tree top.

Rylie struck the rocky, muddy creek bank below, landing at the water's edge. Fortunately, the heavy rain that fell earlier in the week made the creek bed muddier and the water higher than usual, which helped to cushion her fall but wasn't enough to prevent Rylie from breaking her leg.

Then, before this shock could totally register, the kids were bombarded by another as bewildered paramedics came running through the woods toward the creek just seconds after the accident. Rylie's Aunt Molly was leading the way, tears streaming down her face and hollering Rylie's name. In all the excitement, no one had thought to ask Molly Donovan exactly how she knew the accident had even happened, much less how they all were able to arrive so quickly.

"Okay," Rylie agreed, staring back at her uncle. "I will only observe and report." Unless I have no other choice, she thought, I mean, geez, sometimes stuff just happens, and the rules get sort of fuzzy. It's not like I break the rules on purpose. Really!

"Have you given any thought to who'll be your squad leader?" Detective Donovan asked, looking over the group.

"Well," Colin said, "We already met in the tree house and talked about it. We put our names in a hat because three of us wanted to be the leader. Sam and J.D. opted out."

"Great, I'm glad to see you guys put some thought into this and did some planning on your own. So who won the draw?"

"I did," Colin replied.

"Good, we'll talk after the meeting and I'll show you how to write up your report. We like to keep the report simple, and you only need to turn in the activity report to me once a week unless something unusual needs to be reported sooner.

"The rest of you need to keep Colin informed of anything you notice on your rounds that strikes you as problematic. When in doubt, report it.

"On your first time out, we'll all go together so I can show you your route and break the ice for you with some of the shopkeepers.

"Basically, you'll be patrolling the marina area. You'll stop in and say hi to the shopkeepers and vendors. Get them used to seeing you around. You should also be available to help tourists with directions and information about our town."

J.D. elbowed Stretch in his side, and out of the corner of his mouth, he mumbled something to him.

Stretch, not being sure if he should raise his hand or just blurt out his question, ended up doing both at the same time. "When do we get to start patrolling?"

"Let's meet in my office tomorrow at ten o'clock, and we'll take a tour of the department first. Then we'll all head on down to the wharf. If the weather turns nice, we will walk down. There are tee shirts for each of you in the cardboard box on the back table, so grab one on your way out, and I'll see you guys tomorrow."

After saying goodbye, everyone helped themselves to a tee shirt and headed out the door.

"Colin, hold up a minute," Detective Donovan called out. "Let's go back to my office so I can show you how to write the report. It won't take too long. You can meet your buddies out front."

Thunder exploded and rolled over the town as the group stood together on the veranda, peering out at the charcoal sky through a sheet of rain.

"Shorty," Wade teased, "Maybe Colin will team us up on patrol."

"Yeah, you wish," Rylie growled, her eyes narrowing into little slits.

"I don't know what you are so afraid of! I think we'd make good partners. Just to show you that I can be a good sport, I'd even let you help me solve the crimes, then I'd let you take all the credit."

"First of all, I'm not afraid of anything. And second, you couldn't solve a crime if the crook ran right smack into you with the stolen goods in his hands," Rylie shouted as she stepped closer to Stretch, poking her index finger into his chest.

"Come on, guys, can't you two at least try to get along?" Sam pleaded. "We're supposed to be a team, and it really doesn't look too good with you two fighting on the Police Department's front porch," Sam pleaded as she wedged herself between Stretch and Rylie, pushing them apart.

"Besides," J.D. added, "since there are only five of us, and we have to work in pairs, I'm sure we will be rotated and we'll all have to patrol with each other at some time, so just chill out, okay?"

"Hey, I'm willing to call a truce if she is," Stretch offered, sticking out his hand for Rylie to shake, smugly challenging Rylie to refuse.

Embarrassed for letting Stretch get to her and not wanting to look like a schmuck, Rylie rolled her eyes, let out a long sigh, and muttered, "Okay, I guess I can, if he can." Then grasped his outstretched hand, shook it for exactly one second and dropped it.

Moments later, Colin joined his friends, totally unaware of the tension, and said, "Before I forget, Hannah wanted me to tell you guys that we're having a birthday party on Saturday, and you all are invited.

"Since my birthday is tomorrow and Rylie's is on Saturday, our parents are having one big party at Rylie's house. Our grandparents are coming in from Ireland on Friday, and they're pretty cool. Grandpa Donovan always has great stories to tell."

"I know I'll be there," Stretch said, his cocky grin back in place. "I wouldn't miss it for anything."

Only Colin heard Rylie snarl, 'Oh, great' because Sam and J.D. were talking at the same time. They both were trying to be heard over the thunder and pounding rain as it struck the porch roof, assuring Rylie they were definitely going to attend.

The five friends split up, disappearing into the misty, rain-soaked streets. Colin quickly tucked his new Junior Detective tee under the front of his shirt, shielding it from the relentless downpour. He yanked the brim of his ball cap lower, hoping to keep the rain off his face, and hunched his shoulders against the cold, biting wind.

It didn't help much. Within seconds, his shirt clung to his skin, heavy with water, and icy rivulets trickled down back, making him shiver. The storm had no mercy.

He let out a frustrated sigh as he swung his leg over his bike, gripping the handlebars with damp, chilled fingers. This was miserable.

"I'll be glad when this stops. I hate the rain," Colin complained as he mounted his bike.

Rylie sat astride her bike with her face tipped up, letting the rain splash over her, water streaming down her nose and running off her chin, oblivious to the dark stain it created on the front of her shirt.

"Not me; I love the rain. I love watching the lightning flash zigzagged streaks across the dark sky and then waiting for the boom to sound. It always reminds me of those huge cannons they shoot off in the park on the Fourth of July. Then, when the rain stops and the sun breaks through the clouds, everything just sparkles all around you, and the air smells great."

Disgusted, Colin stood crouched over the handlebars and pumped his bike, shooting past Rylie. He turned his head and shouted over his shoulder, "Come on, Ry, I'll race your crazy self home before your brain gets so waterlogged it completely turns to mush. Then what good will you be to the squad?"

Rylie responded with a tacky remark, or so Colin thought, but he couldn't be completely sure because most of her words had been whisked away in the wind and the rain as she raced after him.

Chapter 11

To Colin's great relief, the storm had passed, leaving behind a crisp, sunlit morning as the squad made their way from the Police Department down toward the Wharf District.

They were just a few steps from his Aunt Molly's shop when Detective Donovan suddenly veered off, heading straight into Lulu's Bakery, the warm aroma of fresh pastries trailing out as the door swung open.

"Morning, Lulu," Detective Donovan greeted as he walked into the shop.

"Sure is a fine day, now that the sun decided to poke its face out again, Detective Honey. What brings you into my shop with these pups tagging on your heels?" Lulu asked, letting loose with her booming laugh that always bounced off the walls of the tiny shop.

Detective Donovan was getting good at hiding the embarrassment he always experienced from Lulu's pet nickname for him, a name she seemed compelled to call him every time she saw him, no matter where that might be or whom he was with. The fact that he still managed to smile warmly at her said a lot about his character.

"Lulu, this is Shadow Harbor's new Junior Detective Squad. I'm sure you know all the members already, don't you?"

"Now you know I do. I've known these pups since they were in diapers, lying back in their mama's strollers, just waiting for me to give them a sweet treat." Lulu chuckled, her voice warm and familiar.

Lulu was one of those rare souls who always seemed to carry sunshine with her. Her creamy cocoa complexion glowed under the soft bakery lights, and her bright smile lit up her plump face, making her chocolate-brown eyes twinkle with mischief and kindness.

The team couldn't help but grin back, her warmth as irresistible as the scent of fresh pastries filling the shop.

"The Department has assigned their squad to the Wharf District, so you'll be seeing a lot of them this summer while they're on patrol." Detective Donovan then explained how the program worked and what Lulu could expect from the team.

"Well, now, this being their first day and all," she drawled, "we can't have them working this route on an empty stomach, now can we, Detective? Come on, come on over here and pick out a sweet. You'll need to be keeping your strength up for such an important duty; you too, Detective Honey. I'll not have you going back to the station and telling my friend, Sergeant Polanski, that I don't support my Police force."

The boys eyed the pastries hungrily, their gazes sweeping over the tempting array of flaky croissants, sugar-dusted éclairs, and golden danishes behind the glass case. Just as they were about to make their selections, a flicker of guilt and good manners kicked in, prompting them to step aside and let Rylie and Sam choose first.

With their treats in hand, the squad squeezed into one of the only two booths in the cozy little bakery, their laughter and chatter filling the air as they eagerly tore into their pastries. The rich scent of butter, sugar, and cinnamon wrapped around them like a warm embrace.

Detective Donovan, however, remained by the counter, engaged in quiet conversation with a customer who had just walked in.

Around a mouthful of lemon tart, Sam asked J.D., "So what part of the tour did you like the best?"

"I liked the fingerprinting. It's really hard to believe that no one in the entire world has the same fingerprints as anyone else," J.D. answered. "You'd think your brother's fingerprints would have to match your own, wouldn't you, since you're in the same family and all?"

"Yeah, you would," Stretch agreed. "I mean, if you had an identical twin, wouldn't you think your twin's prints would be the same as yours? Everything else is identical, so why not their prints? Like Colin's twin brothers? You would think theirs would match because they look identical. You can't even tell them apart. What would happen if one twin committed a crime and the wrong twin got arrested? The police wouldn't know which twin did it."

"But that's not the way it really works, Stretch," Rylie smirked. "Identical twins' prints don't match. According to the fingerprint technician we just met, twins' prints may be similar, but they are not exactly the same. She did say their DNA was the same, but not their prints. It's the swirls or loops and ridges that make each person's prints unique."

Continuing, Rylie said, "I thought the fingerprinting part was pretty cool too, J.D., so I asked her a few questions while she was doing my fingerprints."

"So, what else did she tell you?" Colin asked.

"She said that sometimes the criminals will wear latex gloves thinking they won't leave any prints at a crime scene. But one time, this guy dumped his gloves in the yard trash can at the back door of the house he was burglarizing. The police found them and were able to pull his prints from inside the gloves. It was just what they needed to nail the guy. I guess he wasn't too bright, leaving the gloves at the scene of the crime."

"Man, I almost forgot, with us doing the tour and all. Happy Birthday, Colin," Stretch said. "Are you doing anything special tonight?"

"I think my mom is making my favorite meal, but Hannah is baking my cake with Rylie's on Saturday."

"Well," Rylie said, "I'm giving you your present tonight, Colin. I have it in the tree house. Today's your birthday so I can't make you wait for your present until Saturday. So, meet me in the tree house after dinner, okay?"

"Okay, Ry, thanks."

Walking up to the booth, Detective Donovan asked, "Are you guys finished? We need to get moving. We have a lot of ground to cover today and lots of people to see."

They said goodbye to Lulu and walked next door to the Fairy Glen to say hello to Molly and explain the purpose of their squad. Their next stop was to call upon Molly's other neighbor, the Steeplechase Book Emporium.

Rylie knew the emporium well. She had spent countless hours within its walls, drawn to its quiet magic. The moment she stepped inside, the familiar pungent scent of old leather, ancient parchment, and the salty New England air filled her lungs. The shop was a maze of shadowed corridors, towering shelves, and hidden alcoves, where books whispered their secrets from dusty corners.

She had spent many hours wandering the maze of rooms, exploring every nook and cranny, or climbing the slim wooden ladders that lead up to lofts stuffed with over-crowded bookcases, in search of books on English lore, or her favorite, Irish castles and tales of Fairy creatures.

On occasion, Mr. Flannery, the proprietor, would seat Rylie in one of his overstuffed, high-backed leather chairs in front of the fireplace and present her with an ancient tome from his private collection, one that he'd brought with him all the way from England many, many years ago.

With extreme care, Rylie would turn the fragile pages, taking care to barely touch the edges. Letting her imagination soar, she saw herself roaming the halls of an old castle or climbing the turrets. She'd be dressed for battle, her bow in hand and her quiver of arrows slung high over her back, as she walked along the battlement, hoping to spy a hostile enemy lurking in the shadowed forest far below.

On a slow day, Mr. Flannery indulged both Rylie and Colin, weaving histories and magical tales about the castles Rylie adored, his deep voice carrying the weight of centuries past.

For over twenty years, Mr. Flannery owned and fondly operated the Steeplechase.

Rylie recalled Mr. Flannery telling them that he'd been on holiday while touring the eastern coastline of the United States and how he'd been charmed by the quaint little town of Shadow Harbor. Upon a whim, he decided to stay and make it his home. It had been the only spontaneous thing he had ever done in his entire solemn life.

Occasionally, melancholy would strike when he allowed his thoughts to travel over the pond to London, the bustling city of his birth, but all-in-all, he was quite content with the life he had chosen.

Mr. Flannery always wore a conservatively-cut dark suit. His warm, refined manner, paired with his silver-grey eyes, made him seem like he had stepped straight out of one of the very books he so carefully tended.

His only vanity was his thick head of lustrous white hair that he tended to wear rather long for a man of his advanced years.

Hearing the tinkling of the door chime, Mr. Flannery tipped his head in greeting and, in soft, cultured tones said, "Welcome, all of you, to my emporium. What brings you in today?"

Detective Donovan stepped forward, introduced the group, and briefly explained the purpose of their visit.

"It is certainly a pleasure knowing your team will be watching over the shopkeepers on the wharf," Mr. Flannery said. "I must admit, though, I am quite unaware of any particular problem anyone may be having, but then, I do tend to keep myself immersed in my books," he said with a shy smile.

"As for my emporium, it is extremely rare that any crime is committed within these premises," he said as he spread his arms encompassing his shop.

"You see, Detective Donovan, over the years that I've been proprietor here, I have come to realize that should someone be of a mind to pilfer, it generally isn't a book they'd be seeking," he said with a chuckle. "But be assured, should anything unsavory come to my attention, I will consider it my solemn duty to keep your team informed," Mr. Flannery said, a twinkle lighting his eyes.

Detective Donovan thanked Mr. Flannery for his time and taking their leave, the group headed deeper into the wharf district.

Most of the shop owners they spoke with had roots that sunk deeply in the community and had been for many, many years. Their businesses weren't just storefronts; they were family legacies, passed down from father to son, mother to daughter, each generation leaving its own mark while preserving the traditions of the past.

But no matter how different their trades were, they all shared one unshakable bond—their love for the wharf. Many of their forefathers had been seafarers, men who had braved the open waters, their lives dictated by the rhythm of the tides. And with that legacy came an inheritance greater than wealth—a deep, abiding love for the sea and the bustling harbor that had sustained their families for centuries.

As the squad walked along the boardwalk, many of the cart vendors wandered over just to say hello, while others had a need to satisfy their curiosity about the group. That is the thing about small towns: everyone wants to be the first to sniff out any tidbit of news and then pass it along over a cup of tea or mug of coffee.

Businesses like Rinaldi's Deli and The Crazy Cupcake felt it was their personal mission to keep the team well-fed. The boys sure didn't seem to have any problem scarfing down all the free food, but Sam confided to Rylie that she was going to barf if anyone else tried to give her anything more to eat.

Chapter 12

The sunshine held steady, gently warming the day and the sparkling ocean as the squad made the loop past the bustling Chowder Head Restaurant near the end of the weathered Sunrise Pier. They backtracked the short distance along the creaking wooden boardwalk to the sweep of rugged, salt-kissed rocky beach that led directly to where the old, long-forgotten abandoned medical yacht stood moored, like a weary, battle-worn sailor that had seen better days. Then, the group turned and headed back toward the familiar sight of the police station.

As they approached the quaint, weathered post office, Detective Donovan suddenly felt a spark of recognition—it was then that he recalled the customer from Lulu's Bakery, the one whose face had lingered in his memory like an unfinished puzzle waiting to be solved. Walking alongside Colin, he asked, "Did you notice me talking to Paul Pembroke at Lulu's?"

"Yeah," Colin replied, "Doesn't Paul work at the post office?"

"That's right. Paul told me that Sarge was missing, and he hadn't seen him for a couple of days. Sarge is Paul's boxer, and he's about a year old. He is completely tan except for a white mark on his forehead that resembles a crooked star. Oh, and he has two white dots on his front paws. Paul asked if your squad could keep an eye out for him. He was pretty upset.

"The last time Paul saw Sarge was a couple of days ago when he let him loose in his fenced backyard like he does every night before getting ready for bed. He said he received a lengthy phone call and talked for about half an hour. Then, when he called Sarge to come in, there was no response, only silence. Concerned, he searched thoroughly in the backyard and around his neighborhood but couldn't find him anywhere. Paul mentioned Sarge had never gotten out of his yard before, and he couldn't see how he got out this time; the gate was still latched when he checked it. Paul's been looking for Sarge every morning and evening since."

"Hey Colin," Stretch said, "I remember Sarge. He got away from Paul once when I was riding in his neighborhood. I helped Paul search for him back then.

"Paul told me that Sarge had too much energy and always wanted to run. I remember how frustrated Paul was, and he said he had his hands full trying to control Sarge whenever he took him for a walk. I guess Sarge would jump around trying to run and try to jerk the leash out of Paul's hand and that day, he got lucky.

"When I caught up to Sarge, he was pretty friendly for a big dog, and he came right over to me when I called his name. When I grabbed his leash, he just sat there panting and licking my hand. Everyone in his neighborhood knows him, so I'm surprised no one has seen him around and reported him."

"You know," Rylie said, "Janet Regan said Samson was missing last week, too. Remember Colin? When we were visiting Aunt Molly, Janet was talking to her sister, Silvia, and I heard her say that her friend's dog, Samson, was missing. Maybe someone is snatching them."

"Okay, hold on a minute, Rylie," Detective Donovan said. "This is exactly the sort of thing I don't want you to do, letting your imagination run away with you. Seeing a crime where there isn't one. This is just a coincidence, that's all," he said, shaking his head.

"All I'm asking the squad to do is to keep your eyes open and watch for Sarge while on patrol. You may spot him when you're headed to or from the wharf district, but I'm sure Sarge will wander home when he gets hungry enough, and I'm willing to bet Samson has returned home safe and sound by now, too."

"Alright," Rylie said, dragging out the word and letting loose a soft huff. "I was only," she started to say and broke off mid-sentence as she looked up and saw a frown crinkling her uncle's forehead. "Nothing," she mumbled.

Stretch quickly lengthened his stride, closing the gap until he was walking in sync alongside Rylie. She glanced over, and he met her gaze with a brief but reassuring smile and a slight shrug. Without a word, he lightly bumped her arm with his shoulder—a small, silent gesture of support that spoke louder than words.

"Detective, we'll all watch out for Sarge, and it couldn't hurt to look around for Samson, too, while we're at it. Right?" Stretch offered, hoping to remove the sting from the rebuke Rylie had received.

J.D. and Sam also seemed to close ranks around Rylie, their presence offering silent comfort. J.D. glanced at her and said, "You know, Samson lives next door to my Aunt Sarah. When I get home, I'll give her a call and see if she knows whether Samson has returned home."

"That sounds like a good idea," Detective Donovan said. He couldn't help but notice the unwavering loyalty Rylie's friends were showing by surrounding her, and it pleased him to see such genuine support among the friends.

Even Colin, usually more reserved, had silently stepped closer to his cousin—a small but telling gesture that didn't go unnoticed. "That should help ease your mind, shouldn't it, Rylie?" he asked.

"Yeah, sure, Detective," she said, trying to sound normal, but she was still miffed and not quite skilled at blocking the sulky tone from her voice. Then she said, "Thanks, J.D., that would be great. Let me know what she says, okay?"

The group had finally reached the bustling police department, and Detective Donovan asked everyone to follow him to his office, as they still needed to set up the patrol schedule.

As they passed the front desk, Sam hollered out to Sergeant Polanski, "Lulu said to say hi, Sergeant. She made some cream puffs fresh today and thought you might want to know." Seeing his face instantly brighten, Sam chuckled to herself, a giggle escaping as she followed J.D. up the stairs.

Everyone filed into Detective Donovan's office, and he took a seat behind his desk.

"Well, what did you guys think about your patrol route? Is everyone clear on where to go and what you'll be doing?"

"Seems pretty easy to me," Colin said, and the others echoed their agreement.

"Okay, then we need to get a schedule put together so you guys can get started."

"Uncle Shawn, ah, I mean, Detective," Colin stammered, "We all want to patrol as much as we can, but sometimes our folks have last-minute stuff for us to do, and it's not like we have any control over it. So, I was thinking, couldn't we leave the schedule open since our group is so small? Then, could any one of us patrol on any day? If we all show up, then we'll just split up and go different routes. Could we try it this way and see how it works out?"

"Well, it might be overkill if you all patrolled together, but if you split up, that should work out alright; just keep it to two or three of you patrolling together. If you know for sure you can't patrol, give Colin a call and let him know. We want to show a consistent presence on the wharf, but we don't want to overwhelm anyone. Just keep Colin informed and I'll check with him to see how it's going. Like you said, Colin, our squad is small, so we can start out flexible and see how it goes. Tomorrow's Friday, so who wants to take the first patrol?" Detective Donovan asked, looking around the group.

For a second, everyone just looked at each other and shrugged, not really sure if they actually wanted to be the first ones out.

"It would be better if Colin and I could start our patrol next week," Rylie said. "Tomorrow, our Grandparents are arriving from Ireland, and I know we'll have stuff we have to do at home for Hannah to help get ready for the party on Saturday."

"Sam and I could do it," J.D. offered, "I mean, if that's cool with you, Sam."

"Ah, sure," Sam replied as if she was used to having him make plans for them. She hoped no one noticed how surprised and excited she was. She'd been really looking forward to patrolling but hadn't counted on going with J.D. She was sure he'd choose one of his buddies to patrol with, especially Stretch, since they always hung out together.

"Hey, I'm not doing anything tomorrow I can meet you guys at Lulu's. We can start out from there," Stretch offered.

"Cool," J.D. said.

"Yeah, cool," Sam agreed, with a little less enthusiasm.

"I want you guys to take your assignment seriously," Detective Donovan cautioned. "No messing around while you're on patrol. Remember to keep your eyes open. Practice just observing your area. Watch for anything that doesn't seem to fit the usual activity for the wharf. Become a people watcher. Just don't be conspicuous doing it. We don't want to make our tourists nervous," he chuckled.

"It takes a little practice, but you'll get the hang of it. You might even spot a pickpocket who's still learning the ropes. Of course, a pro won't let you see anything, but a novice usually thinks he's pretty slick and won't get caught, so he tends to take more chances and show off more. His confidence outweighs his skill. His movements won't be as polished and flawless as they need to be. And he probably won't pay much attention to a couple of kids hanging around either.

"But the summer's young yet. Seasoned pros don't usually show up here for another month, when the tourists are more abundant and the spoils more lucrative.

"Keep in mind that our tourists become easy marks simply because they're on vacation. Their guard is down, and their minds are on shopping, or they have their hands full just trying to keep track of their kids who are running all over the place.

"If you are absolutely certain, without any doubt, that you have spotted someone shoplifting, or you see a pickpocket at work, call it in. We always have an officer assigned to the wharf area and he or she will respond right away.

"Don't make a scene or call attention to yourself. Calmly and quietly call the situation in.

"Always carry a small notebook and pen with you so you can accurately describe the suspect; jot down what was taken, who the victim was, and where the suspect hid or stashed the stolen property. The more details you have, the more credible you will appear to the responding officer.

"One of you needs to stay near the scene of the crime, make your notes, and report to the officer. Your partner's attention should stay discreetly on the suspect and try to see where the suspect is headed. At no time are you to follow the suspect. Remember, the suspect could possibly be carrying a weapon, so never do anything to draw attention to yourself or your partner.

"When you first start out on patrol, it's a good idea if you arrange between yourselves who will be the note-taker and who will keep an eye on the suspect should the need arise—less confusion that way in the heat of the moment.

"The tourist trade is essential to our town. We want to keep our tourists safe and happy and wanting to return next season. But we also have to serve and protect our businesses.

"Well, that's about it for today. Be careful on patrol, and I'll see you all at the birthday party on Saturday."

Chapter 13

"Hey, what are you doing up so early? We weren't supposed to meet until later. You always sleep late on Saturday," Rylie said, raising a curious eyebrow.

Colin walked into the treehouse and took a seat on the worn, wooden sea chest. "I don't know. I just woke up early and knew you'd be in the tree house, so I thought I'd wish you a happy birthday. That's all. Besides, with Grandpa and Grandma here, I figured Hannah would make a huge breakfast, so I came over early. No big deal." Colin mumbled, his voice unusually hesitant. But he didn't look her in the eye when he said it.

Rylie narrowed her eyes slightly as she stared at her cousin. It wasn't really what he said that had her eyeing him suspiciously, as much as it was the unusual sparkle in his eyes that he was trying to hide behind a poorly disguised casualness that aroused her curiosity.

"Well, something's up. You look different. What's going on, Colin? Tell me."

Colin jumped up, his eyes shining with barely contained excitement as he locked onto his cousin's. With a whoosh, he let out a deep breath and said, "Dang, Rylie, you're not going to believe me when I tell you!" In his excitement, his words collided, tumbling out of his mouth like a rushing river breaking through a dam. "I can hardly believe it myself!"

"She chose you, didn't she, Colin?" Rylie accused, her voice sharp with disbelief. "All this time, I just knew it would be me because, after all," Rylie's tirade halted only long enough for her to jump up and stomp around the tree house, her hands slicing through the air to emphasize her words while she continued to rant. "I'm the one that believed all along, not you. I'm the one that was having the dreams, but Glory chose you, didn't she? How could she choose you?" she cried in frustration, her voice cracking, tears stinging her eyes and threatening to spill over.

But as quickly as the spark of jealousy and disappointment flared, it fizzled out, leaving Rylie's face lit up with an expression of renewed anticipation. The overwhelming excitement she felt overpowered the momentary sting of rejection. "Well, tell me. What did you decide? What did you ask for?"

"Rylie, I don't know how to tell you. I guess I should probably just show you." In the blink of an eye, before Rylie could even gasp, Colin was no longer standing in front of her. The cutest black cat Rylie had ever seen was sitting on the top of the sea chest, his emerald green eyes staring up at her, unblinking, as if daring her to believe what she was seeing.

Rylie let out a squeal and clapped both of her palms over her mouth, positive her eyes were deceiving her. Twirling, she searched the room, half expecting to see Colin hiding in a corner, having played an outlandish trick on her.

"Holy cow, Colin, is that really you?"

"Yeah, it's me," he said, sounding bewildered, his feline tail flicking in mild annoyance.

"You can speak! I mean, I can understand you." Another squeal escaped Rylie's lips. "Does it hurt? When you change, I mean."

"No, it feels strange but cool at the same time."

"Wow, I can't believe it. Can you do any other animals?"

"I don't know. I've only thought about a cat so far. After all, I am new at this," Colin said with just a hint of sarcasm.

"Well, try it. Try something else. See if you can do a bird."

There was a slight shifting in the air currents, and suddenly, Colin the cat was gone. In his place, a plump bluebird flapped its tiny wings, hovering for a moment before landing lightly on Rylie's outstretched hand.

"Wow!" Rylie exclaimed, jumping up and down. "This is incredible. How long can you stay like this?"

"I don't know, Ry. I don't have a clue."

"Does everything look strange looking out of bird eyes?"

"Yeah, kind of, everything looks so much bigger from down here."

"Try flying around in here. Do you think you'll know how?"

"I've no idea, but here goes." Suddenly, Colin leaped off her hand, and just when Rylie thought he would crash onto the floor, there was a rapid fluttering of wings, and he soared around the room, diving and swooping around her.

"Open the shutters, and I'll try flying outside."

"Do you think you'll be okay? What if you change back while you're in the air?"

"I don't know, but I've got to try it. Just keep the shutters open so I can get back in. I can't change back in the yard where someone might see me."

"Okay. Colin, please be careful."

"Don't worry, Ry, I will be," he reassured her, his small, feathered chest puffing out with determination. He perched on the window ledge, his tiny claws gripping the wood as he summoned his courage to leap.

"Yeah, it sure looks a lot farther down when you're this little," Colin mumbled.

Biting her bottom lip, Rylie watched Colin fearlessly hop off the ledge. She couldn't help her sudden intake of breath when she leaned far out of the window and watched Colin suddenly drop. Then furiously, he flapped his wings, propelling him up into the Sycamore's highest branches, carelessly zooming in and out.

"Stop showing off," she hissed, "you said you'd be careful."

"Eh' lass, who's that you're scoldin'?"

Startled, Rylie looked down toward the base of the tree. There stood her grandfather peering up at her with a hand arched over his eyes, shielding them from the glare of the sun.

"W-what grandpa?" She stammered.

"Who were ye scolding lass?" her grandfather repeated.

"Ah, no one, Grandpa. There was a little bird on the ledge, that's all," Rylie said, crossing her fingers behind her back.

Curiosity was clearly etched in her grandfather's weathered face, causing his laugh lines to crinkle at the corners of his eyes, but he merely said, "Aye, Lass, I've been known to talk to the tiny creatures myself upon occasion. Hannah requested I summon you to breakfast and your cousin Colin, should he show himself. It's quite a feast Hannah's been preparing and should be ready shortly."

"I'll be there in a minute, Grandpa. When I see Colin, I'll tell him. He's always ready to eat, and I'm sure I'll see him pretty soon. Ah," she rambled, "we're meeting here this morning in the tree house."

Rylie knew she was babbling, but for the life of her, she couldn't stop herself and she hoped her grandpa wouldn't notice.

"As you wish, lass. I'll tell Hannah that you and the lad will be coming right along."

Once his grandfather moved a safe distance toward the house, Colin dipped back through the window.

"Boy, that was close!" Colin exclaimed. "But Rylie, it was totally cool. I can't tell you how much fun it was. I actually flew. I can fly, Ry," he repeated, flapping his wings.

"Well, you better change back, Colin and be quick about it. Everyone is waiting for us to come in for breakfast."

Instantly, Colin transformed back into his human form and stood in front of his cousin. Laughing, he grabbed her around her waist and swung her about. "It was completely amazing, Ry. Better than I ever thought it would be. I can hardly believe it really happened."

When he set Rylie back on her feet, she bent down and picked up a silky, soft, blue feather from the floor. Twirling the feather in her fingers, Rylie grinned and said, "I guess neither of us can deny it did, Colin." Then she gently placed the feather on top of the sea chest.

"Let's go, I'm starving. All this shapeshifting leaves a person extremely hungry," Colin said.

He followed Rylie out of the tree house, stopping her just as she was about to step onto the ladder.

"Ry, promise you'll keep this our secret, at least until I can get better used to it."

"Sure, Colin. Besides, who would ever believe me?" They looked at each other and said, "Aunt Molly." Then, they flew down the ladder toward the house.

"Ah, that went well," Sunbeam giggled, watching the cousins from her hiding place on the roof of the cottage.

"Looks like the lad caught on just fine, didn't he now?" Moonbeam said with a grin.

When the cousins entered the back porch, they were immediately bombarded by the sights and sounds of family. The warmth of home surrounded her instantly—the crackling laughter, the clatter of dishes, and the sweet, buttery aroma of biscuits mingling with the unmistakable scent of Hannah's famous cinnamon coffee cake.

Immediately upon passing through the doorway that led into the kitchen, each cousin was caught up and promptly hugged and kissed by the nearest grandparent.

"As sure as a leprechaun has his pot of gold, you'll be turning all the boys to mush, that you will, Lass," Rylie's Grandfather said with a wink as he hugged her tight. "But it's poor Daniel that I feel sorry for," He chuckled, turning Rylie loose.

"Aye," his wife agreed. "But have a look at the lad, he towers over me, he does. It won't be long before he passes you, I'm thinking, you old devil."

"I cannot deny I have a bit of the devil in me. But I was lucky enough to win you, Katie darlin'," He said with a roguish grin. "Just maybe it was that very devilment that lured you in," He said softly, "And helped me keep you all these years."

"No, it was a Fairy love spell you cast upon me with that silver tongue of yours that did it," Katie Donovan retorted. Lively sparks flashed in her indigo-blue eyes as she gave her husband a saucy grin.

Colin's grandmother hugged him to her once more before releasing him and said, "You have got the look of your Granddad, to be sure. Tis pity I feel for the young lasses hereabouts. They will surely need to be guarding their hearts, I'm thinking."

Seeing a blush creep into Colin's cheeks, his Uncle Daniel took pity on him and drew attention to himself.

"I don't know about the rest of you, but I'm being tortured, smelling all of this food. When do we get to eat?"

That was Hannah's cue. "Rylie, if you give me a hand, the food will be on the table in a jiffy."

Chapter 14

The table was quickly set, and everyone took their places. Grandpa Marcus sat at the head of the table with his wife to his right, just as it had been years ago when he was the head of the Donovan house.

Hot, flaky biscuits were just being passed around, and Hannah carefully set out pots of butter and honey on the table with a proud smile when suddenly the back door burst open, and Molly and Shawn sauntered in.

Another round of hugs and kisses was called for, and Hannah set about adding more place settings to the table.

"It does my old heart good to look around and see the Donovan clan together again and seated at this old table," Hannah exclaimed. "And there'll be more to come before this day is through."

"You've outdone yourself, Hannah," Marcus said as he surveyed the variety of tempting choices before him. "But I must tell you, I've sorely missed your pecan tarts. I've such a fondness for them, you know."

The calculating twinkle in his eye said he knew exactly what Hannah's response would be.

"I've tried making your recipe, Hannah, several times, but it just isn't to be. Mine never turn out like yours, no matter how carefully I follow your recipe," Katie groaned.

"Oh, Katie, I'm sure yours are just fine," Hannah said, and then she playfully patted Katie's shoulder lightly as she walked past her to place another hot biscuit on Marcus' plate. She bent down and loudly whispered in his ear, "If it is tarts you've been wanting, then it's tarts you'll be having."

Marcus let out a bark of laughter, his deep, hearty chuckle echoing around the room, and everyone at the table joined in as Hannah grinned broadly and returned the pan of biscuits to the stove, her eyes sparkling with satisfaction.

Molly loved watching her family and listening to the teasing that she knew set the mood for the day with everyone joining in.

Curiously, she found herself quietly observing her niece and nephew for any sign of a change in either of them.

She did notice that Colin seemed a little more exuberant than usual, but she thought that was due more to his grandparents' visit than anything else. But still, she couldn't quite shake the odd feeling that something was off-kilter. But she'd be darned if she could see a hint of what it was.

She would just have to corner them later and see what she could wiggle out of them. Or maybe she'd cut to the chase and pay a social call to Glory, she thought.

Her attention snapped back sharply from her musing when she heard her father clear his throat and address his family.

"Feels good to be back in this old kitchen surrounded by my family," Marcus began. He reached over and placed his wife's small hand between his and squeezed it tenderly, his eyes soft with affection. "We didn't realize just how much we missed seeing all of you every day."

"I thought you and Mom loved living in the cottage," Molly said.

"We do," Katie replied. "And the Fairy Glen is just as beautiful now as it was in all the stories we heard passed down through our family. But there is nothing like being in the midst of family. We found we missed the everyday drama and excitement of sharing your lives," she chuckled. "It's rather startling how everyone is growing up so fast, and visiting once a year no longer seems to be enough for us."

"So, what are you saying, Mom?" Shawn asked. A hush settled over the table. Everyone's eyes fastened onto Katie.

Katie looked up at her husband and inclined her head slightly. Marcus paused for only a second as he collected his thoughts and looked around the table. "We hadn't made a decision until, well, now, and we probably should wait for the rest of our family to be present to say what we've decided. But I'm sure the news will spread quickly enough.

"As peaceful and charming as the cottage is, we've found it can be lonely too. Sure, we have our friends in the village, but they are not a substitute for family, for blood ties. When we return to Ireland, it'll be close to the cottage. We've decided it's time to come home. We shall return to Shadow Harbor, where we plan to remain."

Everyone was stunned for the moment it took to digest the news. Then, total chaos broke the silence as everyone hollered out questions.

"Just wait until everyone hears the news," Hannah exclaimed, clasping her hands to her chest, her face glowing with joy as tears trickled down her cheeks. "What a celebration we'll be having today."

Daniel looked at his father and stated: "You and Mom will be living here of course."

Moisture gathered in his mother's eyes as she looked at her eldest son. "Donovan house has become your home now, Daniel. Maybe you should take a little time to mull it over."

"There's nothing to think over Mom. This house was yours and Dad's long before it was ever mine, and it will always remain so. This place holds too many memories to count. The only thing you need to worry about is how many tarts Dad will sweet-talk Hannah into baking." Daniel teased.

Rylie snorted. "You'll have to be quick, Grandpa, if you want to snitch one because Hannah doesn't miss a thing around this house."

"Oh, I think I still have a trick or two up me sleeve, lass," he said with a sly wink for his granddaughter.

"When will the move take place?" Shawn asked. His nature to want to know the why, when, and how of everything is what made him such a good police detective. His father already explained the why, so it was the when and how that he needed to know.

"We'll leave once we've rested, possibly in the next couple of weeks."

"Is there something I can do for you?" Daniel asked. "I can take a little time off, if that will help."

"Thank you, but no son. Most of everything will be left in Ireland at the cottage, especially since we will be living here."

"Well," Hannah said, "now that everyone is fat and sassy, perhaps you'll take a stroll around my beautiful gardens. Or you might have a notion to read the village news out on the porch, but I have a lot of work to do to prepare for this afternoon's celebration, and I don't need everyone underfoot in my kitchen!"

Looking from Daniel to Shawn, Hannah added, "If someone had a mind to set the picnic tables up in the yard, that would be a great help."

Everyone quickly scattered, some to the gardens and others to pitch in to get the party set up.

As the last Donovan filed out of the kitchen, Marcus turned back to Hannah and quietly asked, "Hannah, I was wondering if I might have a moment of your time?"

"Of course, Marcus. What can I do for you?"

"Hannah, I've noticed Glory is all aflutter lately. Any idea what she is up to?"

Hannah sighed. "I've not a notion. But I've been feeling it too. What with the cousins' birthdays happening, I am wondering if it has to do with them?"

"I am sure you are on to something. I will have to keep my eyes open," He chuckled.

Molly and her brothers followed their mother into the gardens. They took seats on the pretty stone benches, surrounded by blooming roses, to enjoy the morning sunshine and catch up on family news.

It won't be long before the rest of the Donovan clan descends upon us like a whirlwind, Katie thought, smiling. The calm before the storm never lasts long. There won't be any more quiet time once that happens, especially when the twins, Ryan and Rogan, arrive.

From what Hannah said, the two-year-olds were walking, babbling, commotion.

Rylie and Colin used the distraction to slip away and head back to the tree house. They knew they would only be able to hide out for a little while before Hannah noticed their absence and found stuff for them to do.

Rylie plopped down dramatically on the red pillow and stared at Colin as he twirled the blue feather. She felt her impatience rapidly building and she couldn't stand it another minute. She just knew she was going to explode if he kept her waiting any longer for the details of his visit with Glory.

Tons of questions bounced around in her head: How did Glory make her entrance? Was she wearing her crown? What did she sound like? Colin had to know she'd want to know every tiny detail. Why was he torturing her?

She jumped up from her pillow and paced directly in front of her cousin, glaring at him. She only stopped pacing long enough to fling her hands up in the air and shout, "Well."

Just when she was sure she was going to have to strangle him, Colin softly said, "Ry, do you realize what this means?" Not waiting for an answer he continued, "My life is changed forever."

Chapter 15

"All along, I thought of this . . . wish granting thing as just make-believe. Something fun. Something that would be totally cool if it could happen. But I never really expected it to happen to me. Now everything has changed.

"I mean, I have this power to do things that no one else alive will ever be able to do. It's kinda like having a superpower that I can never tell any of my friends about, not even Stretch. Not that they would believe me anyway unless I showed them, and then they'd just freak out.

"I keep remembering Aunt Molly telling us that with the wish comes responsibility. Do you remember her saying that, Ry? Well, I never gave that part of the wish thing any thought. What if I change and someone sees me? The next thing you know, they'll be locking me up and doing experiments on me," he groaned. "They will never believe a Fairy granted me a wish."

The flat tone of Colin's voice finally penetrated Rylie's anger and pulled her up short. She saw worry had transformed his face.

"Geez, Colin, why do you have to worry so much? First of all, you have always been responsible, and I can't ever see you not being that way, so I don't think that part of you has changed. You need to quit thinking so much and just enjoy your gift. Man, I can think of a gazillion things we can do to have fun with it," she said with a chuckle. "Believe me, I will be more than happy to help you think of stuff we can do."

Seeing the anxious look still lingering on her cousin's face, she knelt down in front of him and said, "I guess it wouldn't hurt for you to be a little cautious. And you know you can always talk to me or even Aunt Molly if it gets kinda weird for you. I can't say I understand how it feels to fly or to change into a cat, but you know I've always got your back."

"Yeah, I know. Thanks, Ry."

Rylie jumped up and stood in front of Colin. "Now quit stalling! Tell me everything you remember about how it happened," she commanded. "I think I've been patient long enough. When did Glory appear to you? What was she wearing?"

One question after another tumbled relentlessly out of Rylie. The flow seemed unstoppable. Colin groaned. He knew he couldn't answer all her questions even if he tried. Rylie's curiosity was like a runaway train — fast, loud, and impossible to stop once it gained momentum.

"Slow down, Ry, you're making my head hurt." Resigned, Colin waited for Rylie to run out of steam. When silence was finally all he heard, he looked at his cousin and grinned, "I'll explain everything, Ry, every last detail I can think of, if you'll just sit down and be quiet. Can you do that?"

Rylie merely stood glowering fiercely at him, but when she realized that wasn't going to work, she made a dramatic production of closing her lips into a hard, thin line, then mimed zipping them shut. For extra effect, she even pretended to throw away the key. Stiffly, she marched over to her pillow and plopped down.

It was rare that Colin ever got the last word with his cousin, and he felt like savoring his small victory. But he really didn't want to make her any angrier than she already was. Pushing his luck with Rylie was like poking a bear — risky and unpredictable. He also knew his cousin and her silence would definitely not last for long, so he let the incredible event of the night before unfold for her.

"It happened late last night while I was online checking out the Red Sox page. I wasn't even thinking about Glory or her gift anymore because my birthday was technically already over. Then <u>BAM</u>, there she was, just like that," he said. He loudly clapped his hands and watched Rylie jump. "She sat perched on the edge of my monitor."

Colin's eyes seemed to darken to a deeper shade of green as he searched his memory for the kind of details he knew Rylie was expecting to hear.

"She wore the tiny crown we heard about, and she had a ton of little flowers woven all through her hair. Some kind of long silvery dress seemed to shimmer all around her. But I can't say I really paid all that much attention to what she was wearing, Ry," he confessed.

"Her appearing suddenly like that kinda freaked me out, you know. Then she smiled, and her face sort of lit up. She had a tiny face, and her turquoise eyes sparkled like she knew some secret that I didn't.

"Her voice was pretty cool. When she spoke, she had Grandpa's Ireland in her voice, and at first, all she said was, 'Good evening, Colin, I'm Glory,' and regally nodded her little head. She acted as if it was normal for her to pop in and visit me like we were old friends.

"Then she asked me how I liked being in the detective squad. I know I must have had a dumb look on my face because she said, 'Oh, there's no need to be surprised, young Colin. I always make it my business to know what my Donovan's are up to . . . I always have.'

"We talked about my being a junior detective for a couple of minutes and, of all things, baseball. I guess even Glory enjoys catching a game once in a while.

"Then Glory stood and fluttered down to my desk. For a minute, I was scared she was going to leave, but she just took a couple of steps across the desk, sort of like she was twirling or dancing and forgot I was there.

"When she stopped, she turned around to face me and had this wicked grin on her face. She looked directly into my eyes and said, 'Something unusual, I'm thinking. What shall it be, young Colin? What does your young heart desire?'

"I was so surprised Ry, that I just blurted my wish out. Subconsciously, I think I was afraid if I hesitated for even a second, Glory would disappear, and I'd never get another chance.

"I told her that what I wanted more than anything was to be able to change into an animal. Then I quickly said, 'And back again,' just in case she misunderstood and thought the change was to be a permanent one.

"Then Glory murmured, 'Ah, I knew ye'd not disappoint. There's no mistake lad, ye've Donovan blood running in your veins. My Donovans have always been a clever lot. So, tis a shapeshifter you desire to be. I've not been asked for that bit of magic before. Very well, as you wish, so shall it be.'

"'H-how do I do it?' I asked her, stammering.

"She tipped her head to the side, 'Tis much easier than one would think, quite simple, really. Just close your eyes and clearly picture the creature ye wish to become and then simply command yourself to make the change. It really couldn't be any simpler than that, now could it?' She giggled. '*Magic*, Sweetling will see to the rest. Then, when ye are ready to return to yourself once more, merely reverse the steps you've taken.'

"A thoughtful frown crinkled her brow, and she added, 'You might find tis a bit taxing to do this shapeshifting frequently though, at least until you've mastered it. So pick and choose your transformations with care. You wouldn't want to find yourself in a situation where you need to change and be unable to do so.'

"Bewildered, the two little words, 'Thanks, Glory,' were the only words I could manage to utter.

"Glory fluttered her delicate wings, lifting herself lightly off the desk, and she hovered close to my face. The kiss she gave me felt like a flurry of butterfly wings tickling my cheek."

"'Aye, ye remind me so of your Great, Great, Great Grandfather. Ye've the look of him and ye possess his grand spirit too, I'm thinking.'"

"As Glory was about to take her leave, I finally found my voice and stalled her by softly saying, 'Your Majesty . .' my words hesitant but hopeful."

"'Is there something more you require of me?' she asked gently.

"I mustered some courage and said, 'My cousin, Rylie, has been wishing more than anything that you'd appear to her. I'm not even sure why you chose me instead of her because she's the one who has always believed in you. You see, her birthday is tomorrow, and I was just wondering . . .' I trailed off, not exactly sure how to ask the question that was hovering on my tongue.

"But before I could finish, she said, 'Aye, Colin, I am quite fond of your spirited cousin, but not even you, with all your Donovan charm and good intentions, can tamper with the fates, lad.'"

"There was no time to plead my case further because before I could even open my mouth to say another word, she was gone. The only thing left behind was a shower of tiny yellow stars floating over my desk."

Chapter 16

"Wow," Rylie breathed, her voice barely above a whisper. "You really said that? About me, I mean…?" Her wide eyes shone with surprise, hope flickering beneath her disbelief.

"Yeah. I know how much this wish stuff means to you, Ry, and I honestly don't know why she chose me instead of you, except Aunt Molly did tell us that Glory could be very unpredictable. Part of me feels kinda bad about it, but at the same time, it's totally cool getting my wish."

"It's okay, Colin. Really. It's not like it's your fault. I guess everything happened the way it was supposed to. It's just that I haven't thought about anything except what I'd wish for, and I know exactly what I'd ask Glory for. And now I won't ever get that chance."

For a moment, she tried to stay strong — but the weight of disappointment became too heavy to bear. Suddenly, her face crumpled, and the tears came, fast and hot. "I was so hoping," she sobbed as huge tears flooded her eyes, creating emerald puddles that shimmered and overflowed, rolling down her cheeks.

"Oh, man. Come on, Ry, don't cry."

It was so unlike Rylie to cry over anything that Colin felt completely out of his depth. Sarcasm? Sure. Bursts of temper? Absolutely — he knew how to handle those. But this — seeing his fiery, tough-as-nails cousin crumbling in front of him — left him clueless.

All he could think to do was lean down and awkwardly pat her shoulder, his hand hovering in the air before landing with a series of clumsy taps. "Oh, Ry, I'm sorry," he muttered, grimacing at how lame that sounded. Desperate to change the mood, he blurted out the first thing that came to mind. "What would you have asked Glory for?"

Hiccupping, Rylie roughly scrubbed away the tears that were dripping off her cheeks. "You've got to promise you won't laugh at me," she sniffled.

"I promise," Colin said, solemnly nodding his head in agreement. He took a seat on the floor and leaned back against the sea chest.

Rylie hesitated, searching her cousin's face for any sign of teasing. When she saw he was seriously waiting for her answer, she said in a rush, "I want to be able to disappear. Just think of the stuff I could do if I could be invisible . . . like, I could follow a suspect and find out all kinds of information and he'd never even know I was there. That's what I'd ask Glory for if I ever got the chance."

'D O N E,' a musical voice sang out, the words floating on the air and dancing around the room.

"Did you hear that, Colin?" Rylie asked, startled.

"Yeah, but where did it come from?"

Glowing in the wall where the heart of the Sycamore stood, a small archway appeared to take shape. The dark outline of the arch was surrounded by shards of brilliant yellow light waiting to burst through.

A tiny door silently swung open, and a very regal-looking Glory strolled into the room, trailed closely by Sunbeam, Moonbeam, and Violet.

The little Queen was adorned in a flowing rose satin gown encrusted with dazzling crystals that shimmered like tiny stars as they caught the sunlight. The gown swept elegantly across the floor, giving her an almost ethereal presence as she glided gracefully into the room.

"Happy Birthday, Darling!" Glory bestowed a beaming smile upon Rylie and took her hand into her own. "Aye child," she added with a twinkle in her eye, "your wish, too, has been granted."

For the absolute first time in her life, Rylie sat motionless — stunned, speechless, and wide-eyed — on her red pillow. It was as if time itself had paused, her breath catching in her throat.

Then suddenly, the room erupted with peals of giggles and laughter floating around the small room as the tiny Fairies danced around Rylie, their lively voices singing Happy Birthday.

Rylie looked around her and squealed in delight. Her cousin leaned back against the sea chest and watched everything in amazement. With all that had happened, he wasn't sure if anything would ever surprise him anymore.

"I don't think either of you have had the pleasure of meeting my family, but I do believe ye've heard them upon occasion," Glory said. A mock frown was directed at Moonbeam.

Sunbeam and Violet bobbed their heads in greeting, and Moonbeam bowed slightly with a cocky grin as Glory introduced them.

"The day with the blue bubbles — that was you?" Rylie asked Moonbeam.

"That it was," Moonbeam answered, his chest puffing out. "I thought I conjured those bubbles quite well that day," he boasted, his grin widening mischievously as he bestowed an impish smile on Rylie.

"We were to be quiet and just observe you and your friends," Sunbeam mumbled tartly, "but one of us has a bit of trouble in that area."

Seeing a kindred spirit and hoping to spare Moonbeam any further scolding, Rylie quickly asked Glory, "So, where do all of you live? Is that archway the doorway to your home?"

"It is and has been for longer than I can remember," the little Queen replied with a soft sigh.

"Then our Sycamore truly came all the way from Ireland?" Colin asked incredulously. "The Donovan legend and all of the stories are really true?"

"Aye, young Colin, they truly are. Your great, great, oh, I'm not really sure just how many greats," she giggled. "Grandfather Rylie Aiden was very dear to my heart," Glory admitted wistfully.

"But that, lad, was a very long time ago, and I believe your Aunt Molly is calling you, so we must take our leave. If ever you need me, just knock on the passageway to my home and one of us shall appear."

Shyly, Violet spoke for the first time as they prepared to leave. "We'll come and visit you from time to time, now that it's permitted. If that pleases you?" she shyly added.

"Wow, that'd be cool," Rylie stammered as she watched the little group vanish through the archway.

Rylie looked over at Colin. She was having trouble comprehending what had just happened when suddenly she realized she didn't know how her wish worked. She ran over to the little door and sharply rapped three times. To her delight, Glory answered the knock herself.

"Glory, I don't know how to make myself invisible."

"It's magic, Minx. Simply magic! I'm certain your cousin can explain how it works."

Glory evaporated in a cloud of pink mist, followed by a faint tinkling of giggles, and the door swung gently closed. It was a very dramatic exit, one that left Rylie feeling more than a little frustrated.

Rylie turned to confront her cousin. "What do I do, Colin? Tell me!" she demanded. "All this suspense is killing me."

"I don't know, Ry. I guess you just tell yourself what you want to do, and it just happens. That's what I did to change into the cat and then into the bird. It worked like magic," he said, snapping his fingers.

"But I don't think you have time to try it right now because I hear Aunt Molly calling us. It sounds like she's close."

The cousins hurried out of the tree house and spotted Aunt Molly as she was about to climb up the ladder.

"What's going on?" their aunt asked. "I could swear I heard some singing up there."

Colin climbed down the ladder and, shrugging his shoulders and looking clearly puzzled, asked, "Singing? Who'd be singing?" clearly puzzled. Then, before his aunt could quiz him further, he quickly added, "Does Hannah need us?"

"Actually, no. But the twins are here and it's your mother that could use some help. You'd better hurry. I've been calling you two for a little while, and the twins are rather rambunctious today."

Aunt Molly's eyes narrowed slightly as she looked from one cousin to the other. "Why do I have this feeling that you two are up to something?"

Rylie couldn't help herself; a mischievous grin spread across her face. "I don't know," Rylie smirked, "Maybe because we usually are." Laughing, the cousins escaped toward the house, leaving Aunt Molly staring after them, wishing she could get a clearer picture of the mischief that was about to take place. "Just," she told herself, "so I'll know what to expect, not that I'm being nosey, exactly. Besides, what the heck good is having the gift of sight if I don't get to see the good stuff before everyone else?"

Chapter 17

The twins giggled joyfully as they toddled after a bright yellow and orange butterfly that slowly drifted through the garden, just inches from their grasping fingers. The large, round blue dots on their wings looked like giant eyes, and every second or two, they would wink at the toddlers as if teasing them to follow.

Childish laughter drifted on the noonday breeze throughout the backyard and mingled with the familiar sounds of the sizzling barbeque and clinking dishes.

Ana was engaged in a lively conversation with her mother-in-law, Katie when she spotted her eldest son and her niece heading toward her across the lawn.

Frantically waving to draw their attention, Ana called out with a hopeful smile and beseeched them to keep an eye on the twins. "They're wearing me out already, and the day has hardly begun. You two do me a favor and take a turn. Please," she pleaded. "Do whatever you can to keep them entertained—play a game, chase the butterfly, I don't care what. Only until your friends arrive," she added when the beginning of a frown appeared on Colin's face.

With Rylie in the lead, the cousins exchanged a look and grumbled to each other as they headed toward the twins.

"Hummm, that's weird," Rylie mumbled. Stopping abruptly, she watched a butterfly hover and flutter its wings, just barely out of reach of Rogan's chubby fingers, as if daring the child to try and catch it. Then it drifted a foot or two ahead of the toddler before coming to a full stop once more, giving Rogan time to catch up.

Rylie barely noticed when Colin bumped into her. She was so entranced by the game that played out in front of her.

"Hey, watch it," Colin said, rubbing his shoulder with a frown.

"Shhhh! That's really weird," she mumbled to Colin. She stood and watched her nephews taking turns trying to capture the colorful wings. "I've never seen a butterfly behave like that. Do you see the eyes blinking on the wings? It's as if the thing's been bewitched or something..."

No sooner had she spoken the words when another thought took its place, causing her to turn away from the toddlers and scan the garden, searching.

There, tucked between the towering stalks of sunflowers, she spotted Violet, her eyes filled with mischief as she watched over the twins. Apparently, the shy little Fairy had appointed herself the toddlers' personal prankster, and she seemed to be thoroughly enjoying the task.

The mischief gave Rylie an idea. She grabbed Colin's arm and pulled him down to her height, then whispered in his ear, "Your mom told us to entertain the twins. Soooo, let's try out your new magic on them. It will be so cool, and I don't think anyone will notice. Besides, the twins are too little to tell anyone anyway. Come on, Colin, it'll be fun. And your mom did say to do whatever you could to entertain them, remember?"

Seeing Colin's lack of enthusiasm, Rylie decided to try a different tactic. Looking as innocent as possible, she hesitated for just a second before confiding, "I'd really like to try out my gift, Colin, but I think the sensible thing for me to do is wait and try it when we are alone the first time. Don't you think? But if you really don't want to do yours, I guess I could give mine a try. Hopefully, it'll work ok," she said with a shrug.

Rolling his eyes, Colin groaned. "Sometimes you are impossible. I just knew you were going to try and talk me into doing something." Before Rylie could open her mouth to defend herself, Colin gave in. "Okay, okay, I'll do it. But we must be careful. Do you see that patch of sunflowers near the back corner of the garden? Let's at least get the twins back over there so the flowers can block my change from anyone else seeing."

Excitement surged through Rylie as she tugged on his arm. "How about becoming a cat again? Ryan loves cats so that he won't be afraid, and it will be cool for Rogan, too, because he isn't afraid of anything."

The twins liked nothing better than to play games with their older brother and having Rylie there to play too was even better.

They cheerfully gave up chasing the butterfly to follow Colin and Rylie. Colin led them behind the patch of sunflowers that stood twice as tall as the twins and provided the perfect cover for a little magic.

Bending down on one knee, Rylie took ahold of each of the twin's hands and looked them both in the eye. "We're going to play a game, but it has to be our secret game, okay? Can you, little guys, keep a secret?"

Ryan solemnly looked to his brother Rogan to see what he would say, but Rogan was already bobbing his head up and down and telling his cousin, "We love secrets, Wylie. We won't tell anybody. We promise."

Rylie smiled at the way her nephew pronounced her name; He just couldn't master his Rs yet. It was one of the only ways she could tell him from his identical twin.

"Watch your big brother. I'm going to say a magic word, and Colin's going to magically change into a kitty. Watch, Ryan. Rogan, watch Colin."

Rylie noticed Ryan's attention drifted once more to the butterfly. He pointed, "Butterfly, Wylie," and giggled.

Rylie took Ryan's hand in hers once again.

"Ryan, watch closely. Here we go."

The boys' eyes were wide as they fastened on Colin and giggled when Rylie dramatically swooshed her right hand and said, "AlaKaZam!"

Instantly, Colin was gone, and in his place stood a sleek, black cat with shimmering emerald eyes.

Laughter rippled out of the twins, their faces lit with wonder as they jumped up and down, eyes sparkling with delight.

"Magic! Magic! Magic!" Rogan chanted, clapping his hands with glee.

Immediately, Ryan dropped to his knees to play with the kitty. Colin rolled over and then lightly pounced on Ryan, evoking a fit of giggles from both boys. Their giggles were so contagious they had Rylie joining in.

"Uh oh," Rylie said when she spotted Josie strutting their way. "Here comes trouble."

When Josie reached Colin, she sat back regally on her haunches, and for what seemed to be a full minute, her golden eyes searched his emerald green without blinking.

Then Josie stood and swished her plump calico tail in the air. She made a production of slowly strolling around the intruder, delicately sniffing. Abruptly, she stopped mid-stride, turned and lifted her gaze to Rylie, then slowly let it drift back to where Colin remained sitting.

Her curiosity satisfied, she sauntered off in the direction of the picnic tables and Rylie was certain she heard Josie snickering. Clearly, Josie dismissed the intruder as an imposter. The mocking expression on Josie's face had Colin bursting out laughing.

The familiar sound of Colin's laugh booming out of the black cat had the twins gasping and staring wide-eyed at him.

A thoroughly confused Rogan cocked his head and pointed a chubby finger at the cat and screeched, "Colin -- kitty."

"Shhhh," Rylie said, quickly placing her index finger on her pursed lips. "This is our secret, remember?" she frantically reminded the twins.

But the twins were no longer listening to her. They became more and more excited with each passing second and started jumping up and down.

"Colin, Kitty!" They both chanted at the top of their lungs while each one clumsily tried to bend down and pick Colin up.

Out of self-preservation, Colin started hopping around, too, doing his best to keep all of his body parts out of the reach of four grasping hands and hopping feet.

The more Colin jumped around, the more the twins' excitement grew, quickly becoming borderline uncontrollable.

At this rate, if the boys kept up the noise they were making, they were bound to draw attention not only to themselves but to Colin.

"You need to change back quickly, Colin!" Rylie snapped, her eyes darting nervously toward the adults. "Things are getting way out of control here."

"Yeah, I can see that! But I think you need to take the boys over to my mom first. If I change again in front of them, they'll really go nuts."

When Rylie took hold of the toddlers' hands and tried to turn them away from Colin, the kitty, the twins instantly dropped to the grass like falling dominoes.

Frustrated, Rylie tried pulling them up into a standing position, but their little legs turned to rubber, and they collapsed on the grass once again. Clearly, neither child was about to budge.

Abruptly, their laughter stopped, and they were on the verge of rebellious tears. Their bottom lips quivered, and their eyes shone with unshed tears. Their minds were made up. They were not going to leave the black cat.

Rylie knew if the boys started crying, without a doubt, their wails would bring every adult at the party over to them. It would cause more havoc than the fire bell screeching at the fire station. She knew parents and grandparents would come running and they definitely couldn't afford for that to happen.

Rylie broke out in a cold sweat and desperation seized her as she frantically looked around the yard, searching for anything, anything at all she could use to distract the twins.

Then she remembered Violet.

Hoping that Violet might still be close and watching the whole fiasco, she faced the nearest stand of pine trees and softly called out, "Violet, if you're here, we desperately need your help."

The tiny Fairy instantly appeared and hovered close to Rylie's shoulder. Carefully, she used the curtain of Rylie's hair to conceal herself from the toddlers' view as she listened to Rylie's plea. The very last thing they all needed now was for the twins to see a Fairy creature.

"You've got to do something, Violet. Quickly! We need some kind of distraction so Colin can change back without the twins seeing him do it," Rylie pleaded.

With a small command and a sharp flick of Violet's wrist, a cloud of silvery fairy dust spilled out of her tiny fist. Instantly, the sparkling glitter transformed into a flurry of tiny, colorful butterflies that zoomed in and out, encircling the toddlers.

"Wow! That sure got their attention," Rylie exclaimed, grinning in amazement.

Tears vanished. The twins jumped up and toddled after the blurry rainbow of color. In their haste, Colin the kitty was totally forgotten. Once the boys had their parents in sight, the wave of butterflies scattered in all directions. Disappearing like confetti in the breeze.

Colin, now standing on his own two feet, let out a sigh of relief and presented Violet with his most charming and grateful smile.

"Thanks, Violet. You are a lifesaver. That could have been a mega-disaster. It looks like I'm going to need to be more careful transforming around the little guys in the future. I'd have been sunk without your help," he confessed, once more flashing Violet a sheepish grin.

Violet was so flustered by Colin's profuse thanks that her face glowed as scarlet as one of Hannah's deepest crimson roses. He barely heard her softly stammer, 'You are most welcome,' before she darted toward the old Sycamore, her wings flickering in a blur of glittery pink.

Chapter 18

"Hey, Colin."

Rylie and Colin heard the shout and turned toward the side gate. There, they spotted Stretch flanked by J.D. and Sam.

"Oh, great!" Rylie muttered under her breath. "I thought at least today I'd be spared; after all, it's my birthday. Why, couldn't he at least have forgotten your invite, but no such luck! Man, I'd love to disappear right in front of him just to see the shocked look on his face," she ranted. "I bet Stretch wouldn't be so darn cocky then."

The picture her mind formed of Stretch's cocky smile melting into stunned disbelief brought a satisfied smirk to her own lips.

"Come on, Ry, it's our party, and like it or not, Stretch is my best friend. We've been friends forever, and that's not going to change. Besides, it looks like he brought gifts for both of us."

Even her annoyance couldn't completely stop Rylie from checking out the two brightly wrapped packages Stretch was carrying.

They could both be for Colin, she thought. But one was wrapped in light pink paper with a huge hot pink bow. That little revelation almost tugged a real smile from her lips, but she caught herself just in time.

"Well, I'm sure they're both for you, Cuz," she taunted as they reached their friends.

"Hi, guys." It was less annoying for Rylie to address the trio than to have to acknowledge Stretch's presence.

Rylie knew with all of her family around, she would probably have to be at least somewhat nice to Stretch, but she wasn't ready to be just yet.

"Where do we put the presents?" J.D. asked, tossing one of the ones he was carrying up into the air and catching it one-handed with a grin.

"Hannah set up a table near the picnic area," Rylie answered as she grabbed Sam's hand and hurried her away from the guys.

"What's going on with you and J.D.? Are you two going out?"

"No. Geesh, Rylie." Sam stammered. "It's no big deal. We're just friends." She hesitated for a second as if deciding what to do, then stuck out her arm and wiggled her wrist dramatically. "He bought me this yesterday when we were on patrol. You know, from that cart vendor near The Coffee Hut on the wharf. It's no big deal," she repeated.

"I couldn't very well say no and hurt his feelings."

Hanging on Sam's wrist was a delicately braided friendship bracelet—a trio of pastel-tinted silver strands woven together and secured with a tiny silver clasp.

"Wow, that's really pretty," Rylie squealed, genuinely impressed.

Her excitement caused Sam to giggle, and Rylie watched in amazement as a soft pink blush crept across her friend's tanned cheeks.

As long as Rylie had known her, Sam was always totally, a tomboy. Rylie never expected ever to see her wearing a bracelet, even a friendship bracelet. Sam had always said jewelry was too girlie for her, and she had no use for it. She would often sneer and say how she'd never understand why girls were always making a fuss over some dumb thing some boy gave them. *Well, I guess I won't be hearing her say that anymore,* Rylie mused, raising a curious eyebrow at the silver strands.

After depositing their gifts on the gift table, the boys took seats across from the girls and immediately helped themselves to the pitcher of ice-cold lemonade that sat in the middle of the table. Condensation trickled down the glass, and the clink of ice cubes echoed softly as they poured.

"Hey," Colin said, tilting his head, "It looks like they're about to start playing."

"Devlin's tuning up his fiddle and Uncle Shawn has his guitar," Rylie told their friends, nodding toward her uncle with a smile.

The words were barely out of their mouths when the music started. The pair began with an old Irish pub song that they knew would inspire Grandpa Marcus to start singing. The lively tempo had everyone taking part. Those who knew either joined in and sang the silly words or found themselves carried away laughing and tapping their feet.

That was one of the things Rylie liked best about her family, the way everyone was so boisterous and full of life whenever they got together.

It was a familiar pattern that went as far back as she could remember. The music would stop just long enough for Uncle Shawn and Devlin to eat. Then it would resume and last long into the night, with everyone dancing and taking their turn singing. Even their neighbors would find themselves irresistibly pulled into the noise and chaos, enjoying every minute of it.

Hannah knew how to please her Donovan clan well, as evident from the picnic tables that overflowed. Somehow, she always managed to have everyone's favorite dish, from Rylie's creamy potato salad to Colin's crispy fried chicken. Even Devlin's spicy baked beans had their place on the table.

The air was rich with mouthwatering aromas, as the scent of roasted meats and sizzling spices wafted across the backyard and mingled with the smoky goodness Daniel and Patrick created at the grill—all done under Hannah's ever-watchful eye.

"Don't you boys dare let those ribs burn," Hannah admonished as she rushed past to set freshly baked rolls on the table. "And don't be chit-chatting too much and getting yourselves side-tracked either."

"Hannah, my love," Devlin called out, jauntily flourishing his bow in the air and a teasing glint igniting the gold in his amber-brown eyes. "You'll never catch men chit-chatting. M-e-n," he said, drawing out the word, "Might chew the fat or have a lively debate, but they never, ever chit-chat."

Devlin's teasing caused a ripple of manly grunts and snorts among the men, even though the women rolled their eyes. They too, couldn't help smiling at his good-natured teasing.

"Oh, go on with you," Hannah retorted. "It's playing that fiddle of yours I think you should tend to, not trying to educate me on the ways of men at my age," she grumbled. But everyone heard her chuckle as she headed back into the house for the remaining platters of food.

Mr. Quigley, from next door, rested in one of the redwood loungers. Unconsciously, his right foot tapped a beat to the music while his fingers idly stroked the top of Duke's head as he lay sprawled in the grass beside him.

Duke appeared to be snoozing, but if you watched closely, you would see his nose twitching rapidly as puffs of barbeque smoke drifted past. His warm brown eyes were shuttered to half-mast, but he was totally on full alert as he continually scanned the area surrounding the grill, ready to pounce on any morsel that tumbled off.

The backyard overflowed with generations of Donovan's and a load of friends and neighbors as platters of food were passed around.

Colin glanced up from his plate when he heard his grandmother call his name and saw her walking toward him with her arm draped around the shoulders of a pretty, blonde girl bearing gifts.

He quickly swallowed the bite of crunchy fried chicken he'd just stuck in his mouth and set the chicken leg he'd been attacking back onto his plate.

Without thinking, he rubbed his greasy hands on his thighs, which fortunately were hidden under the picnic tablecloth.

He smiled and said, "Hey Shannon, I didn't know you were coming." When he saw confusion in her eyes, he quickly amended, "I'm glad you did, though."

"Rylie invited me. I thought you knew," Shannon said, returning his smile with one of her own.

"Ah, I think I might have forgotten to tell him," Rylie confessed, as she turned to greet her friend, but not before she saw the 'I can't believe you didn't tell me she was coming' look Colin shot her.

Rylie said, "With all the excitement of—Uhmm, I mean, all the meetings for the junior detective's squad and all, I must have spaced it. Sorry."

Inwardly, Rylie berated herself for almost spilling the beans about all the excitement of the Fairy wishes. *Man, I'm going to have trouble keeping all this inside,* she thought.

"Well, we are pleased to have you," Grandma Katie said warmly while she relieved Shannon of the two brightly wrapped packages she held tucked to her chest.

"I'll just be putting these presents with the others on the gift table. Go on now and squeeze in next to Colin and help yourself."

"Stretch, why don't you scoot on over here next to Rylie; there seems to be more than enough room for you on this side of the table."

As she walked away, she grinned as she heard her granddaughter grumble under her breath something about not even being able to eat in peace at her own birthday party.

Rylie continued grumbling to herself as she mindlessly stuffed a spoonful of potato salad into her mouth while the gift the little Queen granted her haunted her thoughts: *I can't believe I haven't been able to try it yet. Maybe I'll get a chance before my party ends; just a quick 'poof' to see if it really works. But how will I know if it worked if I can't do it around anyone? Man! Maybe I could just let Sam know. After all, she is my best friend. No, I better not, at least not here. Sam would probably freak out, and then I'd have a whole lot of explaining to do and Dad would probably forbid me to use it at all. I guess I'll just have to wait, even if it's killing me.* She groaned.

The slight sound barely escaped her lips when she noticed Stretch looking at her funny.

"What?" Rylie snapped.

"You okay? I thought I heard you mumbling to yourself."

Rylie so wanted to fling a sarcastic remark at Stretch or at least a spoonful of her potato salad, but she just couldn't think of anything caustic to say, which was totally unlike her.

All the talk of Fairies and magic was messing with her head. *I need to stop thinking about it and enjoy my party*, she thought.

"I'm good. Why wouldn't I be?"

The slight flurry of movement across the table gave Rylie the excuse she needed to go back to ignoring Stretch. She watched Shannon fill her plate and saw her friend sneak a peek at Colin, who was once again totally focused on eating, only this time, it was a barbequed rib in his messy fingers.

She listened to Shannon tease Colin, making him laugh and had everyone at the table joining in.

Then, the deep voice of Grandpa Marcus drew everyone's attention. "Tis glad I am to see all my family and friends gathered together. Too much time has passed between visits, I'm thinking. Although I sorely hate to admit it, the journey is getting a bit tough to make," he chuckled, "for Katie. But it's pleased I am that Katie and I have an announcement to make." Marcus reached out and tucked his wife's small, delicate hand into his own huge, callused one, tugging her gently to his side. "We've decided we sorely miss

Shadow Harbor, our family and dear friends. So, we shall soon be calling Shadow Harbor our home once again. And it seems it's Daniel's wish for us to return to Donovan House."

Stunned silence enveloped those of the Donovan clan and their friends who had yet to hear the good news. Once more Marcus and Katie were surrounded while everyone took turns clapping Marcus on the back and hugging Katie.

"Wow," Sam said. "It'll be cool having your grandparents here for good. I remember your grandfather telling some awesome stories about Fairy magic and leprechauns. The way he tells it, you'd think they really exist. And the magic tricks he performed were unbelievable."

"You have no idea," Rylie said as she rolled her eyes at her cousin, causing them both to burst out laughing.

The commotion around them was winding down, and Colin's attention was drawn to his mother and father as they stood next to his grandparents. He heard his mother laugh and saw her raise her hand to attract everyone's attention.

"Well, it seems today is the perfect day for sharing family news and making announcements. I, too, have something to share with all of you." Ana reached over, unconsciously mimicking her father-in-law's actions and took hold of Patrick's hand. She raised their clasped hands to her heart and shyly smiled out at the gathering. "Well, it seems Patrick and I are to be blessed with another set of twins."

Once again, congratulations were offered, and her family surrounded Ana. While her arms were wrapped around her mother-in-law, her eye caught Molly's. Molly had risen from her seat at the other end of the picnic table and was headed directly toward her. As she approached, she held up three fingers and slowly wiggled them, her eyes never leaving Ana's.

Ana caught the gesture, and confusion clouded her eyes when suddenly, her mother-in-law was replaced in her arms by Molly. Molly bent her head and whispered "three" into Ana's ear.

"Tell me it isn't so," Ana whispered back, a slight groan escaping her lips.

Molly smiled down at her best friend and sister-in-law and nodded her head.

"By all that's holy, Molly, not three more boys! What am I to do?" Ana asked, bewildered.

"Oh, no, Ana." Molly chuckled. "It'll be much easier than that. Tis wee lasses you'll be having," she said, mimicking her Father's Irish brogue.

"Girls," Ana gasped, "and I'm to believe that will be easier?"

"Well, maybe not easier, Ana, but it shall definitely be fun."

Ana wasn't the only Donovan groaning over the news of twins. Colin hung his head and sighed loudly, to the amusement of his friends.

"Oh man, are you in for it? Looks like you'll be watching two more cookie munchers pretty soon," J.D. laughed.

Chapter 19

"I thought the little guys were bad enough, and now there's going to be two more running around. At this rate, I'll never have any time to myself or even a place to hide out occasionally."

"Well, you can always fly away and hide out in the tree house," Rylie said, smiling sweetly. "You know, just fly the coop to escape."

"That's a weird way to put it," Stretch said.

Rylie tossed her head and flung her hair away from her face so she could glare up at Stretch. His comment instantly irritated her, but before she could start another one of their arguments, Sam elbowed J.D. in the ribs and asked, "Got any new jokes for us?" she asked, clearly trying to redirect the moment with some levity.

The shift in tone was subtle, but it was enough. Rylie's shoulders relaxed—just a little.

"Huh. Oh yeah. Rylie, did you know I once flew all the way to Florida?"

Rylie snorted. "No, J.D., I didn't."

"Yeah, I did, and boy were my arms tired."

No one could resist telling J.D. exactly how much his joke sucked. Even Shannon joined in the bashing. But the good-humored banter proved to be enough of a distraction to defuse Rylie.

Stretch looked at Colin. "What did Rylie give you for your present?" he asked. "Didn't she give it to you last night?"

Colin grinned, his cheeks turning slightly pink. "It was great. She gave me four tickets to see the Red Sox play. The only catch was that she said one of the tickets had to be for her. I guess my dad and Uncle Daniel are going to take us next week to the home game.”

Stretch looked smug. “That was really slick, Shorty – giving Colin a gift that includes yourself. I never thought to do that.”

Rylie just scrunched up her face and turned away to talk to Sam. Shannon smiled at Colin. “When are you guys going to open your presents?”

“Pretty soon, I think. It looks like my grandma and Aunt Molly are bringing our cake out now.”

Everyone turned to see a huge birthday cake aflame with twenty-four candles headed toward the table. Uncle Shawn strummed the opening cords to Happy Birthday, and everyone gathered around the picnic table and sang as the cake was set directly in front of Rylie and Colin.

Embarrassed by the attention focused on them, the cousins quickly blew out the forest of candles that were creating a small bonfire. They heard their Uncle Shawn holler, “Get ripping,” when Ana and Molly formed a huge pile of presents in the center of the table.

Rylie tore into her stack of presents, but it was the large one, tied with a hot pink bow, that Rylie kept sneaking peaks at as she reached for another present to open.

“Come on, Shorty, open mine,” Stretch said, pushing the large box toward Rylie. “I just know you’re going to like it.”

Resisting the urge to bypass his present for the small flat one sitting next to it, Rylie picked up the large box and was surprised to find it so heavy. Although she had ripped the paper off of all the other presents she had previously opened, she slowly pulled the hot pink ribbon and watched it unravel, then peeked up at Stretch for a second before peeling the paper off of the present.

In her hands Rylie held a wooden box stained a creamy golden color. Centered on the lid, Rylie's name had been stenciled in a deep blue script. When she lifted the lid, her eyes widened in surprise, and all she could say was, "Wow."

Neatly arranged in the box was an artist's kit, complete with a rainbow of colored pencils that had been sharpened to fine points. The small purple pencil sharpener had tiny fragments of colored pencil shavings still clinging to it. It was clear the kit hadn't just been bought—it had been prepared. Touched. Thought over. There were a dozen satiny smooth pots of paint and a variety of silky brushes in different shapes. A thick artist's pad had also been tucked into the bottom of the case. The pages were blank but full of promise, just waiting for her to bring them to life.

Rylie looked up at Stretch and whispered, "Thanks, Stretch. I love it. Really! But how did you know?"

"I saw your drawings when I was in your tree house. I thought you might like it. I did the stenciling myself."

"It's absolutely perfect," Rylie said as her finger traced the dark blue lettering.

Stretch watched as her dimple peeked out of the corner of her mouth when she smiled at him. There was something about that smile—unpredictable and rare—that made him forget every sarcastic jab she'd ever thrown his way. Then she had him laughing out loud when she sighed and said, "I guess we could call a truce, at least for the rest of the party."

With a little effort, Rylie managed to open the rest of her presents and even eat her cake without making one snide remark to Stretch.

Sam knew that Rylie loved the old Rock and Roll bands from the 70s, so she and J.D. gave her a Van Halen CD with the song 'Running with the Devil' on it and a CD of Heart playing 'Barracuda.' Both were favorites of hers.

Shannon gave Rylie a cool, silver Celtic warrior bracelet. As the cuff wrapped around her wrist, two dragons faced each other with their tails intertwined.

Rylie checked out the fielder's glove Colin received from Stretch and the CDs that Sam and J.D. gave him. When she sniffed the cologne that Shannon gave Colin, she absently reached down and stroked Josie as the feline rubbed against her legs. She still couldn't believe how perfect the present Stretch gave her was or that he took the time to stencil her name on the box. He was just so darn confusing, she thought. Every gesture, every word from him seemed to come wrapped in mystery.

The mountain of wrappings was cleared away, and the music grew louder and livelier as a couple of neighbors joined in the mix with their guitars. The warm twang of strings carried across the yard like laughter, uniting voices and feet in a loose rhythm. Little ones stumbled after fireflies that flashed through the night, their tired legs barely holding them up. Their giggles rose like sparks, fleeting and magical, as they chased the glowing lights weaving through the dark.

Uncle Shawn broke away from the musicians and joined his squad. Taking a seat, he asked, "So, how'd your first patrol go yesterday? The three of you hooked up, right?"

"Yeah. It was all good," J.D. mumbled in between stuffing bites of his second piece of cake into his mouth.

Sam shrugged. "Everything was calm on the wharf. No problems."

"We just walked around and talked to everyone, like you said," Stretch added. "I ended up leaving early, and J.D. and Sam finished the wharf off by themselves."

"J.D., did you get a chance to talk to your aunt about Samson? Has he returned home yet?" Shawn asked.

"She told me that Samson hasn't come home, and Kathy is worried. She said Samson had never been gone this long before. I guess Kathy put some flyers out around the neighborhood, but she hasn't heard anything yet."

Uncle Shawn frowned. "I talked to Paul last night and Sarge is still missing, too. I heard that the front desk sergeant received a few calls about other dogs missing. It's a little odd to have that many dogs go missing at the same time. I'll get their descriptions and let Colin know. He will notify each of you so you can watch for them around town. All the dogs reported had pet tags, and some were microchipped, so when we find them, they will be easily identified. But I still believe they will turn up sooner or later."

All the junior detectives turned to look at Rylie to see if she was going to mention her dognapping theory again. But with extreme effort, she remained silent.

Shannon broke the silence when she said, "It sounds exciting to go out on patrol. Is it dangerous?"

Colin glanced at his uncle and saw him grin. "We never know what we'll run into on patrol, but my squad has been trained to handle any situation." Colin noticed his uncle's eyes narrow at this embellishment and added, "Which means we know when to call in the big guys."

"Wow. Is it your squad? You're in charge of it?"

Shannon exclaimed. "That sounds dangerous to me."

"Nah, not really. We mainly just scout the area and report any suspicious activity. But it's kinda cool. I'm the squad leader, and I report to Uncle Shawn or, rather, Detective Donovan when on duty," Colin said, nodding his head toward his uncle. "Rylie, Sam, Stretch, and J.D. make up the rest of the squad. We all have shirts that identify us as part of the Shadow Harbor Police Department."

"So, where do you guys patrol?"

"We take turns patrolling the wharf district."

"I love the wharf. I can't wait to check out all the new summer stuff. Maybe I'll see you down there."

"Do you think you'd want to be a part of the squad?" Uncle Shawn asked. "If all goes well, we may increase the number of junior detectives in the fall."

"No way," Shannon laughed. "If I ran into a bad guy, I'd probably start screaming and scare everyone."

A short while later, Shannon's mother arrived to pick her up. When she left, the group was making plans for the coming week's patrol schedule.

"Okay," Colin said. "Rylie and I will patrol on Monday, then Stretch and J.D. will fill in on Tuesday; Rylie and Sam will go together on Wednesday. We all agreed that we should wait and talk on Wednesday afternoon to see who could do Thursday and Friday. Does anybody have any problems with the schedule?"

"Not me, boss," J.D. said, snapping to attention.

"Sir, no Sir," Stretch saluted, following J.D.'s lead.

"Come on, you guys," Colin said. "What's going on?"

"Oh, please. Our great squad leader ought to be able to figure it out." Rylie taunted.

"For a minute there, I wasn't sure what you needed us for," Sam teased.

"Well, it looks like you guys have the schedule worked out, so I'm outta here." Pushing himself up from the picnic table, Uncle Shawn shook his head. He looked at Colin and smiled. "Having your squad turn on you is an ugly thing," Shawn said, chuckling.

Rylie and Colin barely managed to dodge their Aunt Molly the rest of the night. Every time she headed in their direction, they ducked out of sight or had one of their friends intercept her and ask her something about her shop. The cousins were trying hard to avoid answering the questions they knew she was dying to ask. Not that they expected to avoid her forever, but they wanted to face her when they were ready. Rylie definitely did not want to have to admit she received a gift from Glory before she at least got a chance to try it out.

It was late when their friends left, and the cousins were finally able to sneak off to the tree house.

"Come on, let's go," Rylie hissed. "Aunt Molly finally sat down and is talking to your mom, and I've waited long enough."

Curious, Josie followed Rylie and Colin into the tree house. She looked from Rylie to Colin, searching their faces, and then sat back on her haunches as if waiting for the show to begin.

"Okay, now what?" Rylie asked. "Should I just try it?" she asked with a slight tremor in her voice. Rylie knew her voice shook a little, but she didn't know if it was from the excitement she was feeling or from fear of attempting to disappear.

Colin plopped down on the sea chest and watched Rylie fight her panic.

"I don't think we have a lot of time in here Ry. It's getting late, so if you're going to try it, you'd better get started. Just think about what you want to do and do it," he coached. "It's really not that ..." Before he finished his sentence, Rylie was gone. As he looked around the room, no trace of her remained. Little goosebumps crawled up and down Colin's arms. Suddenly, he felt a sharp tug on his hair, and he jumped a foot off of the chest.

"Hey," he yelped as he collided with Rylie, causing her to stumble backward and land on her backside.

"What are you doing?" Rylie shouted.

"I don't know. Your being gone like that sort of freaked me out, and talking to an empty room is kind of weird, too."

"Well, talking to you as a cat isn't exactly normal either, but it didn't freak me out," Rylie said, climbing to her feet.

Then, standing a foot in front of Colin, she made herself reappear again just to jack with him.

"Man, Rylie, you've got to quit doing that."

Rylie looked at her cousin's pale face and felt a tiny stirring of guilt. But unable to help herself, she burst out laughing.

Between laughs and gulps of air, Rylie said, "I'm not laughing at you, Colin. It's just so amazing. I did it! It really worked!" she exclaimed. "I felt this little tingle, and I knew I was gone. Poof! It is so cool. This was the best birthday ever!"

"Yeah, well, you better remember not to get too close to someone when you're invisible because I just knocked you on your butt by accident," he clarified when Rylie glared at him.

"But you're right. It really is cool," He admitted. "So, how do you feel? Are you tired or anything? Do you feel weird?" He asked, wiggling his eyebrows.

"Not really, I feel normal." Then she blinked out again.

"Ry, you really need to stop doing that. At least, let me know first."

"Okay," she said. "I'mmmm back." Then instantly, she popped back, startling Colin again, and giggled. "We are going to have so much fun with this," Rylie exclaimed.

"Ry, we both need to be cautious using our gifts. If anyone sees us, we could be in big trouble."

"Don't start spoiling it, Colin," Rylie snapped. Then realizing her cousin really was worried, she softened. "It's okay, Colin. I'll be careful and responsible. I promise. But I want to have some fun with it, too, you know."

"I know Ry. I do, too. This is all so unbelievable, and I just don't want anything to go wrong."

"You have to stop worrying and try to enjoy it." Rylie sighed. "I guess we better go down before Aunt Molly comes up here looking for us. We've done a pretty good job of avoiding her so far. I really don't want us to be alone with her tonight. I have a great idea of how we can tell her about our gifts tomorrow."

"That's what I'm afraid of," Colin admitted, shaking his head. But Rylie knew when she saw him grin that he'd go along with her plan.

Rylie stayed a step behind Colin as they headed toward the music. She watched her grandmother rise, her face flushed with anticipation when Uncle Patrick pulled her to her feet and drew her out into the small clearing used for dancing.

Seeing that her grandpa was now sitting alone, it occurred to her that she could have a little fun with her gift and probably not get caught. Without giving it another thought, she ducked behind a row of shrubbery and carefully peeked out to see if anyone noticed. No one had. Colin didn't even realize she was no longer following him.

Between the darkness of night and the dense shadows cast by the shrubs, she felt completely concealed. She hovered behind the thick branches and then slowly made a small opening and watched Colin talk to their grandfather. Taking a deep breath, she let it out slowly to steady herself and thought it was now or never. Cautiously she left her sanctuary, being careful not to disturb any of the branches. She stopped directly behind her grandfather. *Oh, cripes! she thought.* I forgot about Josie. Josie had followed her into the shrubbery and was now sitting right next to her, intently staring directly into her eyes or where her eyes would be if she were visible. Rylie nudged Josie with her toe, trying to distract her, but all it did was annoy Josie, and she started bumping into Rylie's leg. Fortunately, since Rylie was standing behind her grandfather, Colin didn't seem to notice, so Rylie decided just to ignore Josie and hoped she would just go away.

Well, here goes, she thought, and reached out and lightly tickled her grandfather's neck. She pulled her hand back and smiled as her grandfather reached up to brush the nuisance away. When his hand was once again resting on the arm of the lounge chair, she did it again. But this time, her grandfather turned his head and looked straight at her, and she froze. When she pulled her hand back, she was a little slower than she should have been and lightly brushed his fingers causing Rylie to gasp at the exact moment the band stopped playing.

Hearing the slight sound, Colin's head whipped around. Realizing Rylie was not with him, he choked. His Grandfather looked at him with mild concern and asked, "Are you alright, lad?"

"Uh, yeah. I'm okay."

"Where might your cousin be? I've not seen much of her this evening."

"Oh, I'm sure she's around here somewhere. She has a way of disappearing when you least expect it," Colin said.

Looking over Colin's shoulder, Grandpa Marcus said, "Ah, there you are, lass. Come here, sit next to me. As sweet as you are, you're bound to keep the pests away from me. They seem a bit busy tonight."

"I'll do my best, Grandpa," Rylie said sweetly.

Colin coughed again. "Oh, I'm sure you will, Ry. Now that Rylie is here in the flesh, I doubt you'll be bothered anymore, Grandpa."

"Lad, you may want to have your grandmother have a look at your throat."

"Nah, it's nothing Grandpa, I'm okay. Really."

Chapter 20

The small cluster of garden elves lounged on the gleaming wood floor near the front door and watched as Colin strode to the back of the Fairy Glen in search of his aunt, with Josie prancing behind him. Aunt Molly spotted Colin and frowned as she emerged from the back room.

"Well, if it isn't my elusive nephew. I couldn't help but get the impression you and your imp of a cousin did your best to avoid me at your party. I believe you even commandeered your friends to run interference for you. It was really starting to annoy me. But later that night the thought occurred to me that just maybe there was a reason you two would go to so much trouble just to avoid talking to me. Could it be you weren't ready to share? Is that it, Colin?" Her voice rose with excitement as each word came spilling faster than the one before. "You have something to tell me, don't you?" She glanced suspiciously around her little shop and asked, "Why are you here alone? I thought my brother said you and Rylie were patrolling together today." Colin could guess Aunt Molly was eager and might have spent the night wondering and guessing what the two little miscreants would have been up to.

Aunt Molly was so wrapped up in firing off all the questions she had been storing up that she didn't notice she wasn't giving Colin a chance to answer any one of them. But Colin thought it better than to interrupt. When she finally ran out of questions and stopped to take a breath, it was Josie who caught her attention.

"And what are you doing, Josie?" Aunt Molly asked as she watched Josie arch her back and weave a figure eight. The only answer she received was a low, throaty purr. Shaking her head, Aunt Molly looked at Colin and bent down to pick up Josie. She had her fingers almost curled under Josie's arms when Colin shouted, "Aunt Molly, no!"

Thinking Colin might have been warning her against Josie, Aunt Molly crooned, "Silly girl," and almost lifted Josie in her arms when her hand bumped into something very solid. Her fingers loosened on Josie who flopped out of her hand, twisting her body in the famous cat-like fashion, landing on all fours.

"What did I ju…" she shrieked, but before she could complete the question, she heard a familiar voice, which was clearly not Colin's. She looked around but couldn't see anyone else. *Clearly, Josie cannot speak*, she mused to herself as she stared around.

"It's just me, Aunt Molly," Rylie said as she popped into sight. Unfortunately, Rylie was talking to herself because her aunt had fainted dead away the moment Rylie appeared.

"Oh, no!" Rylie remarked, and the grin she was wearing quickly faded into a worried look when she saw her aunt collapse.

"Quick, Colin, do something!" she ordered a panicking Colin.

"I don't know what to do!" was all Colin could respond with. He wanted to say, "I told you it won't be a good idea!" to his cousin, but he knew now wasn't the time.

"Go lock the front door and pull down the shade before anyone comes in here. I'll go get a wet towel," Rylie commanded, thinking quickly because she knew Colin wasn't up to it.

Colin obliged and ran through the shop, dropping all shades and securing all windows and doors. When he returned, he found his aunt cradled in Rylie's lap. She was pressing a dripping wet handtowel to her forehead. "Come on, Aunt Molly, wake up," Rylie pleaded.

"Maybe we should call 911," Colin suggested.

"And just how are we going to explain what happened?" Rylie squeaked.

"Rylie," Colin pushed, we have to do something.

The idea was risky as the cops might ask questions Rylie was sure she didn't want to answer, but she also knew her favorite aunt could be at risk.

"Okay. But just give her another minute," Rylie begged. Biting her lip and feeling desperate, Rylie smacked her aunt's cheek.

"What are you doing?" Colin yelled, grabbing Rylie's hand before she could assault her aunt again.

"Let go, Colin. I saw them do that in one of those old Westerns. It worked," Rylie said defensively as she tried to pry loose her hand and land another smack on her aunt's face.

"That was on TV, Ry. Everything works on TV," Colin said as he gripped her hand tighter. When he was sure Rylie wouldn't smack Molly again, he let go, reached into his pocket, and removed his cell phone. He quickly pressed the buttons. "Well, I'm calling."

Before he could hit "send," Molly twitched, showing signs of consciousness.

"Wait, I think she's coming around," Rylie stopped Colin.

They both stared at their aunt as she slowly opened her eyes and focused her gaze on her niece. Relief washed over the two, but they knew they weren't out of the woods yet.

"W-what happened?" Aunt Molly asked, her mind and eyes clouded.

Rylie was about to make something up, but she could think of nothing that would explain what happened. Luckily, she didn't have to, at least for the moment. Not waiting for a reply, her aunt started babbling.

"You, you weren't here." Aunt Molly's eyes widened as it all flooded back to her.

"I remember feeling something, but there wasn't anything there. Then I heard your voice. And you just appeared out of thin air. Josie was acting so strangely."

"Easy, Aunt Molly." Colin soothed. "Are you alright? Should I call 911?"

Aunt Molly couldn't drag her eyes away from Rylie's face, but shakily, she said, "No, Colin, don't call. I'm okay. I think. Just help me up."

Shaking off the grogginess and keeping her stare locked on Rylie, she got back on her feet. Her head felt clearer. Unconsciously, she wiped away some of the water that was trickling down her cheek, and Colin led her into the workshop and sat her down at the table.

She looked at Rylie and asked, "You were invisible? How is that even possible?" But the answer came without Rylie having to explain. More accurately, it slammed into her like a punch to her gut. *THE GIFT!* She thought, and suddenly, her eyes and everything around was crystal clear. She was now alert, and her previous excitement seemed to be returning. "That's what you asked for? Glory granted you invisibility?! Good heavens!" she groaned, dropping her head into her hands.

"I am so, so sorry, Aunt Molly," Rylie said sheepishly. "I never intended that to happen. But you did say you wanted to be the first to know," she reminded her aunt with a small smile.

"So, I thought showing you would be better, er, more fun," Rylie reluctantly admitted with a grin.

Her Aunt's silence had Rylie searching her face for some sign of how much trouble she was in. And she was becoming very uncomfortable as some real guilt slithered its way into her conscience.

"You scared ten years off of my life," Aunt Molly murmured, but she didn't sound angry, which was a relief for the two.

"You did look pretty spooked," Colin said. He tried to maintain a straight face, but he couldn't help himself. He laughed, breaking the tension.

"Well, I certainly wasn't prepared for that," Aunt Molly admitted, shaking her head. "All Saturday night, I kept trying to get a clear picture of what was going on with you two, but all I got was fuzz and a slight headache. Glory certainly is getting more creative with her gifts these days."

"She did say my request was unusual," Rylie admitted, "but I have the feeling I'm not the only Donovan to receive an unusual gift." She nudged Colin under the table, grinning mischievously.

"Uh, Aunt Molly, are you up to another surprise?" Colin asked his aunt. He, too, was now wearing an ear-to-ear grin that spelled trouble to Aunt Molly.

"You're going to have to give me a minute." She took a deep breath and let it out slowly, trying to calm her rattled nerves. She had envisioned all sorts of gifts the cousins might ask for, but none as fanciful as invisibility.

Rylie handed her aunt a glass of water, and Aunt Molly sipped slowly, giving herself time to absorb everything. Sensing her anxiety, Josie softly leaped into her lap and began licking her arm, offering comfort.

Aunt Molly stroked the chubby calico. "It's okay, Josie, I'm fine now. But I can't believe you played a part in this charade," she admonished.

With a wobbly grin and her sense of humor restored, she cautiously said, "Please, don't tell me Glory gave you a second gift, Rylie."

"Actually, I got mine first," Colin said a bit smugly.

"Oh, thank goodness," Aunt Molly exclaimed with relief. She quickly glanced over at her niece and winced, "Sorry, Minx, but giving you the chance to request two outrageous gifts goes beyond what even the Donovan clan can endure."

Aunt Molly looked at her nephew. "I don't know why, but I had a feeling it would be you Glory would honor with her gift. Okay, sport, what did you ask Glory for?"

"Well, I guess I need to show you Aunt Molly. Close your eyes, and I'll tell you when to open them," Colin chirped, excitement sparkling bright in his eyes.

"Oh no, not again," Aunt Molly whispered as she clasped her hands around Josie and crushed her to her chest. But despite feeling exceedingly wary, she did as she was asked and tightly closed her eyes.

"Okay, open your eyes," Colin ordered without wasting another minute.

Sitting at her feet, swishing his tail, was a green-eyed, coal-black cat. Molly gasped the moment she opened her eyes and saw the feline looking up at her. Josie hissed.

"It's just me, Josie," Colin said, and Josie jumped out of Molly's arms and circled him, sniffing.

"Colin is that really you," his aunt asked with disbelief, as she looked around her workshop trying to spot where her nephew was hiding. She was sure they were playing a trick on her this time.

"Yeah, it's me. Watch. I can change into anything I want to." In the blink of an eye, Colin, the black cat, changed into a small, yellow parakeet and flew up onto the table next to his aunt. He realized his excitement might have gotten the better of him as he kept his eyes fixed on Josie in case she decided to pounce on the bird. But that didn't last long, and the excitement returned as he fluttered around his aunt.

"Incredible!" Aunt Molly exclaimed. This time, she prepared herself for the unexpected and was able to laugh instead of fainting. "Oh, my," she said, rubbing her fingers across her forehead. After admiring and musing over Colin's gift for a little while, her expression changed to a serious one. "You had better change back Colin, and we need to talk. But first, I need to put out the closed sign on the front door. I don't think we want this discussion to be overheard. I should have thought of that earlier."

"Oh, I already took care of that. Before, when you fainted," Colin grimaced.

"Aunt Molly, before you say anything, I want you to know that Colin and I have already discussed it. We know we have to be sensible and cautious when using our gifts. We don't want to freak anyone out by being seen."

Rylie blushed furiously when her aunt replied, "Like you did me, you mean?"

"Yeah, but that was different. We thought you were made of stronger stuff," Rylie defended. "That you could easily handle the weird."

"I know you guys are going to want to have fun with these new abilities, but please, you have to be very, very careful," Aunt Molly stressed. "And definitely no more playing tricks on me," she added.

"Trust me, you're safe. You scared me too when you fainted," Rylie said, hugging her aunt. "But we better get going. We need to go on duty, so we'll pick Josie up later, okay?"

"Actually, I'll drop her off at the house; I want to see Mom and Dad after I close up shop."

Reaching the front door, Colin turned to his aunt and asked, "You won't tell anyone, will you?"

"Cross my heart, I'll not say a word unless I'm asked directly. I'll not lie to you. But I can tell you that Hannah has her suspicions.

And I'm sure your grandfather will be seeing Glory, so if she doesn't spill the beans, I imagine Violet might. But we'll deal with it if the time comes—together."

The door chimes jingled softly when the cousins left the little shop. A whiff of fresh sea air surrounded Molly as she lingered in the doorway, watching the next generation of Donovans make their way to the wharf. "And it begins," she whispered to the Garden Elves, a grin spreading over her face.

Chapter 21

The clip-clopping of horse's hooves echoed along the shoreline as a horse and buggy clattered over the century-old cobblestone path carrying a couple of tourists to the Wayfarer's Inn that sat nestled at the edge of the wharf.

Rylie and Colin had just finished making their rounds of the wharf district when they darted behind the remote rest station located on the far end of the beach. When they emerged, Rylie was accompanied by a huge furry beast. Clearly, they weren't done experimenting with their newfound gifts.

Half amazed, half confused, Rylie asked, "What the heck are you? You look like a very large wolf and part something else?"

"I'm not exactly sure," Colin confided. "I tried to focus on becoming a wolf, but my thoughts kept jumping around, so I guess I'm some sort of a mixed breed."

"Yeah, you got that right. You look pretty cool, though. Scary but cool," Rylie admitted. "What's the plan?"

"Let's patrol down toward the old ghost ship, and then I'll change back. We shouldn't run into anyone we know down there this morning."

Colin padded alongside Rylie as they patrolled the beach looking for anything that seemed out of place.

"Oh, no, Colin," Rylie whispered.

"Yeah, I see him. But you want to hear something funny, Ry? I could actually smell him coming way before he appeared."

"Yeah, it is. Right now, think quickly. He is almost here. What are we going to do?" Rylie asked, her voice filling with dread.

"Well, don't panic, just stay cool."

Approaching from the water's edge was Melvin Putsney, wearing his normal scowl; his caterpillar eyebrows scrunched up so that they formed one single dark furry slash across his forehead. His puffy face was as red as a summer tomato and slick with perspiration. Thick, short, pudgy arms swung at his sides, his fingers stroking the leather noose that was attached to a long wooden stick hanging from his belt. At least you assumed he was wearing a belt somewhere under the huge roll of belly flab. His eyes scanned the area to find his catch of the day. No stray missed his wicked gaze. Waves of menace flowed from him as he stalked along the beach. He obviously was just looking for and hoping to find trouble.

Rylie and Colin barely shifted direction, choosing a path that angled away from Shadow Harbor's one and only Dog Catcher when an angry shout stopped them in their tracks.

"Hey, you," Melvin yelled, "Stop right where you are." The dog catcher huffed and puffed his way over to stand directly in front of Rylie, invading her personal space and causing her to gag. Rylie quickly stepped back when he snarled, "I know you. You're that Donovan girl. You Donovans think you run this town."

A greasy smile slithered across his face when he glimpsed Rylie's flush of anger. He also noticed she stepped closer and tightened her grip on the wolf's fur. "Yeah," he sneered. "I know your uncle, but this is my territory and that mutt you're walking don't have no tag. And you don't get a leash on him either. So, I'm running him in."

Grinning evilly, he slowly unhooked the noose and drew it out like he was an old cowpoke drawing a gun, then cautiously, he edged toward the wolf.

Colin, who was already grimacing more at Melvin's body odor than the anger boiling within, let loose a rumble of warning deep in his throat, the hair on the back of his neck standing on end.

Rylie yelled, "Don't Colin! Run!"

Melvin was so focused on the wolf's snarl that he never heard the name Rylie yelled.

The wolf hesitated a second too long and Melvin was quick. He had the loop out, and he flung it like a lasso toward Colin's head. A high-pitched giggle escaped Melvin's lips in anticipation of catching and controlling such a beast. Surely, he had done it many times before.

But Colin was both quick and lucky. The huge wolf barely shifted his massive head in time, and the noose fell short, landing in a coil on the ground. Melvin let out a grunt and dashed to retrieve the noose. In a flash, the wolf was streaking toward a small stand of trees, warm sand splaying out behind him.

"Hey!" Melvin screamed, shaking his fist and his noose in the air.

"I'll get you, you wild-eyed mongrel. Believe me, I don't miss often. I'll get you," he bellowed, his face such a mottled red he looked like his head was going to explode. His stubby nostrils rose and sank as he huffed, his nails digging into his palm as he balled his fist and slammed it on his own thigh.

Melvin turned his hate-filled gaze on Rylie and glared, angry waves pulsing from him. She hadn't budged from her position as she had all her attention on helping Colin, the wolf, evade this despicable Dog Catcher. She was even devising a plan to jump at Melvin should he manage to catch Colin in his noose.

"That mutt of yours is in for it when I catch him, I promise you that," he sputtered, spittle flying from his thick lips. "And don't think you're escaping so easily. I'm writing you a ticket," he sneered.

As he jerked the ticket pad out of his pocket, Rylie snapped, "You can't do that. I don't own him."

"You were walking mighty cozily with him. I saw you. Don't bother trying to deny it."

"He just popped out of nowhere and started walking with me. That's not my fault," Rylie said, trying to stay as close to the truth as possible.

Melvin was searching for his pen when a piercing screech was heard. Startled, Melvin looked up in time to see a blue jay execute a perfect arc and dive-bomb, pulling up only inches from the bald spot that sat directly in the center of Melvin's head. Melvin dropped the ticket pad, flailing his arms, trying to protect his head.

"What the heck! That bird is crazy!" Melvin hollered as he ducked and looked up toward the sky, anticipating another attack. His eyes bulged like huge muddy brown balloons, and his mouth gaped open as he watched the blue jay circle back and swooping down for another pass. Melvin quickly gathered himself up, tightening the grip on the stick with the noose, readying himself to catch the bird, but he didn't know the blue jay had other plans.

As the bird neared its target, Rylie heard a soft "Bombs away" floating in the air. This pass, Colin left a nice runny package square in the center of the bull's eye on top of Melvin's head.

Rylie's eyes widened, and her hand flew to her mouth to stifle her laughter. It really wouldn't be wise to anger the ogre any further, she thought.

Melvin spun around, his flashing eyes pining Rylie. "What's so funny? You find this funny?" he screeched as he ran his stubby fingers through the goo on top of his head, all thoughts of writing a ticket forgotten.

"No. I mean, kind of," Rylie stammered. "Ah, I need to go. I'm supposed to meet my cousin," Rylie said. Not waiting for a reply, she practically flew to the cover of trees where she'd seen Colin retreat. She heard the words, "Wait, you little brat, I'll get you and your mutt!" trail behind her, but she knew better than to turn and respond to Melvin.

"Colin, where are you?" she called softly.

"Over here."

Rylie found her cousin resting beneath a large Oak tree, leaning his back against the rough trunk.

"Holy crap Colin, what were you thinking?"

"I don't know. He's just such a jerk to everyone."

"Are you okay?" Rylie asked, concerned. She noticed Colin's face was looking a little pale.

“I just need to rest for a second. I guess double changing and flying so far wears me out.” Even though his face beamed with the excitement of his heroics, Colin looked visibly drained.

“Do you think anyone saw you change?” Rylie asked. “You really need to be careful changing in public. Geesh—and everyone thinks I’m irresponsible.”

“There wasn’t anyone around and I was quick. Trust me. I’m getting rather good at this, Ry.” Colin smirked.

“Well, we were going to finish our patrol over at the ghost ship. Do you still want to go there?” Rylie asked.

“Yeah, but man, am I hungry.”

“You’re always hungry,” Rylie said, shaking her head.

Cautiously, they left the shelter of the grove, watching for any sign of Melvin lurking about. Rylie walked alongside Colin and grinned at him. “It really was funny when you bombed him. I tried so hard not to laugh that I thought I was going to choke.”

“Well, I wouldn’t have done it, but he goes out of his way to be mean. It was kind of fun to get him for a change. And besides, I had to find a way to get you away from him.

“Thanks, Colin.”

“It’s cool,” Colin grinned. “I really can’t stand that guy. Do you remember when that tourist’s little Chihuahua got loose? Melvin caught the little pup in his noose and dangled it all the way back to the lady. The poor thing was howling and kicking all the way. Melvin had a huge, sadistic grin on his face when he returned the little guy. The lady’s daughter was in tears. I remember the lady said she didn’t want any trouble, so she didn’t report him. She just took the ticket, packed her little girl and their dog up and left the beach. I've never forgotten that Ry. I think Melvin hates dogs. And everyone else."

"Why doesn't someone report him?" Rylie asked, her eyes shooting angry green sparks.

"I heard he was the mayor's wife's nephew, so he never gets into trouble. I guess he'd been reported before, but I don't think anything ever happened. Reporting him seems to be a waste of time," Colin said in disgust.

The ghost ship, used and discarded, bobbed in the inlet like an old elephant waiting to die.

Colin stopped and leaned on the weathered fence, bleached white from the salt air and sun, and stared at the beautiful site. At least to his eyes, the old, dry-docked ghost ship was a beauty.

"Do you know why they call this old yacht the ghost ship, Ry?"

"No, I never really thought about it," she admitted.

"Well, back in the 1860s, there was this old ship called the USS Red Rover and they were a hospital ship that roamed the sea and aided the wounded soldiers of both sides during the American Civil War. Then, later on, passenger liners and even private yachts were converted by the Navy for use as hospital ships during World War I. Back then, firing on a hospital ship was generally considered a war crime. See that faded red cross painted on the side in that white patch?"

"Um-hum," Rylie mumbled. She knew better than to show too much enthusiasm when Colin was in his lecture mode, or they would be there all day talking about his favorite subject, ships, unless, of course, he was talking about baseball, which was also his favorite subject.

"That was the symbol they used to designate the yacht as a hospital ship. When the ship was no longer needed, it was returned to its owner and, in some cases, dry-docked. This one, 'The Angel of Mercy,' is named after Mathew Beebe's wife, who was a Navy nurse—served two years at sea before they decommissioned her. They say she saw a lot of death and devastation on board. Lucy Beebe died just before the ship was returned to Shadow Harbor, and Mr. Beebe couldn't bear to see the ship again. So here it sits. They say it's filled with the ghosts of the departed sailors that were lost at sea. Sometimes, tourists that walk the beach late at night claim that they hear the moans and cries of the wounded."

"That's creepy." Rylie shuddered. *By far, this might be one of Colin's most interesting lectures*, she thought. She looked up at her cousin and asked, "You don't believe in all that stuff, do you? They're probably just hearing the old ship creaking."

"You know what's funny," Colin laughed. "You're asking a guy who believes in Fairies and magic if he believes in ghosts?"

"Well, do you?" Rylie persisted, her gaze fixed on Colin, demanding a response.

"Nah, not really," Colin admitted. "But it's a pretty good story."

Colin cocked his head when a gust of sea wind blew past. "Did you hear that?" he asked.

"Oh, come on, Colin. That's pretty weak. Did you really think I was going to fall for that? Ooh…" she said, pretending to shiver.

"No, seriously, Ry. You didn't hear the barking?"

"What barking? I didn't hear any barking."

Colin looked around and then turned back toward the ghost ship. "I could swear I heard barking coming from the ship."

"I think you better be careful turning into a dog anymore. It's messing with your head," Rylie teased.

"I know what I heard," Colin muttered. But he decided it wasn't worth arguing about. "We better head to your house, Hannah will be watching for us."

Chapter 22

Hannah was up to her elbows in soap bubbles when the telephone rang. "Colin, please answer that; I'm in the middle of washing dishes," she said. "Just tell whoever it is that I'll call them back in a little bit."

"Hullo. Oh, hi, Mrs. P," Colin said. Colin had recently started calling Mrs. Pritchett, Mrs. P., and she didn't seem to take offense. In fact, she seemed to be okay with it. In one of her softer moments, she told him that it reminded her of her deceased husband because that was his nickname for her.

"No, I'm not doing anything. What, he's missing?" Colin was a bit alarmed. "Oh, great," he mumbled under his breath.

"What did you say," Mrs. Pritchett asked sharply.

"Ah, nothing, Mrs. P."

"Well, you just might want to remember that I have excellent hearing, young man."

"Yes, Ma'am. Sorry, Mrs. P."

"Well, are you going to help me or not?" Not waiting for a response, she continued. "I would appreciate it if you would take a look under that horrible porch on that old Garcia house. You know the one I am referring to, the one that Mr. Garcia abandoned some time ago. What a shame that was, too," she complained.

"It used to be a fine property back when the Goldbergs owned it."

"Mr. Garcia didn't abandon it, Mrs. P.," Colin interrupted. "He died, and his wife was ill and had to go live with her children somewhere down south."

"Humph," Mrs. Pritchett grunted. "Well, that's neither here nor there. What I want to know is, do you intend to look under the Garcia porch for poor Mr. Prickles or not young man? You might even ask your cousin, Rylie, to help you. I believe Mr. Prickles took quite a shine to that girl."

"Ah, sure thing, Mrs. P.," Colin snorted, "Rylie will be happy to help look for the little guy." It took supreme effort not to burst out laughing right then and there. "I'll get Rylie, and we'll head straight over there."

"If you don't have any luck finding him, be sure to let me know; don't keep me wondering. But I am confident you will find him napping under that porch. For the life of me, I will never understand why he is so partial to that dilapidated old building when he has a perfectly good bed right here," Mrs. Pritchett grumbled.

"Well, I better get started, Mrs. P. and I'll let you know what happens," Colin said quickly, cutting her off mid-sentence in a polite attempt to end the conversation.

But Mrs. Pritchett, true to form, wasn't about to let him have the last word.

"See that you do," she snapped, her tone sharp and final. "I don't relish sitting here worrying about my little angel."

Then Colin heard a loud click as Mrs. Pritchett disconnected. "Rylie," Colin bellowed, dragging her name out, "We have to go."

"Where?" Rylie asked, entering the kitchen.

"Mrs. P. called and said Mr. Prickles ran off. She wants us to check out the old Garcia place. I guess the demon dog likes to nap under their porch. He sneaks off and runs over there, but this time, he's been gone longer than usual, and Mrs. P. is worried about him."

"Not another one," Rylie mumbled. Then, after thinking about it for a second, she said, "He probably is under the porch because if anyone did snatch him, they'd turn him loose pretty quickly."

"Yeah, you got that right," Colin agreed.

The Garcia porch loomed in front of Rylie like a gaping mouth waiting to devour her. "This is the place he likes to take his nap?" she asked skeptically as she stared at the paint-chipped, sun-bleached, sagging porch.

"According to Mrs. Pritchett, the little demon seems to like it under there. I think it ticks her off." Colin said. "See those broken boards? I bet Mr. Prickles probably goes under through there," Colin said, pointing to the gap along the front of the house.

"I guess that's where you'll have to crawl through," Colin calmly explained.

"Me?!" Rylie screeched, looking at Colin like he was crazy. "I am not going under there."

"Well, I can't do it, Ry, so you're going to have to crawl under and see if Mr. Prickles is there. If he is, he'll need to be coaxed out. It's not like he'd come out with us just calling him."

"Why do I have to do it? Why can't you," Rylie asked stubbornly.

"Because," Colin said slowly, as if explaining the situation to his two-year-old siblings, "if I change into any type of animal, the little demon will attack, and if I go in as me, he'll attack. It's going to have to be you. What's the big deal anyway? Don't tell me you're afraid to go under there?"

"No, I am not afraid. But it's got to be totally gross under there, and besides, Mr. Prickles doesn't like me any more than he likes you."

Colin smiled. "Actually, Mrs. P. said Mr. Prickles is fond of you."

"What, has she lost her mind?!" Rylie exclaimed.

Hoping to defuse the eruption he knew was coming, Colin said, "Relax, Ry, you won't actually be going under there as yourself. Think of it as a chance to use your gift."

"How's that supposed to help get him out—if he's even under there?" Rylie snarled.

"I believe it's called planning ahead," Colin smugly replied.

"When Mrs. Pritchett called and asked us to check under the old house, I put my plan together. Do you know those special dog bones that Dog Bakery sells? Well, I snagged one from Hannah's stash of dog treats she keeps for Duke, one of those big bones with white chocolate stuff on the end and topped with colored sprinkles."

Rylie rolled her eyes. "That's not chocolate. Dogs can't eat chocolate. It's some kind of yogurt coating."

"Well, it looks like chocolate," Colin mumbled. "Anyway, I have one in my pocket. Duke goes crazy for these bones, so I figured even as ornery as Mr. Prickles is, he won't pass one up."

"Okay, so I still don't see what that has to do with me," Rylie said.

"Simple. All you have to do is vanish, and I'll hand you the dog bone. Then you crawl under and wiggle it in front of him like a worm on a fishing line. Once he takes the bait, you just keep scooting back toward the opening. Then, when he's chewing on the bone, you can hook this leash on him, and I'll run the snarling beast home."

"You have it all worked out, don't you?"

"Uh, in theory," Colin said. "What do you say?"

"It looks like I don't have much of a choice. But what if he bites me."

"If he goes crazy, Ry, just drop the bone. I'm pretty sure he'll go for the treat instead of some phantom he can't even see."

Rylie walked behind the nearest hedge, grumbling, "Well, he better. I can't believe I let you talk me into doing this. It's probably so nasty under there that I'll catch some weird disease."

"Quit complaining, Ry and just do it."

"I am doing it. It stinks under here, and it is really dark. Oh, gross, there's piles of cat poop everywhere. I am never going to get this stink off of me. You owe me big time," Rylie threatened.

"Well, do you see him or not?" Colin whispered.

"Why are we whispering?"

"Because I don't want him to know I'm out here," Colin admitted.

"Well, I think it's a little late for that because he's waking up and looking this way."

Colin knelt and quickly glanced in the opening. "Here's the bone, Ry; I'll toss it to you. Just show it to him."

The bone landed near Rylie's right hand with a soft thud. It wasn't your average chew toy—it looked more like a fancy, overpriced, bone-shaped sugar cookie you'd find at a specialty dog bakery. She carefully picked it up with two fingers and wiggled it as she slowly inched closer to Mr. Prickles. Her elbows scraped along the rough boards, dust clouding around her face. The ground felt like it hadn't seen sunlight—or sanity—in decades. When she was about a foot away from him, she froze.

She held her breath, partly because it stunk so badly under the porch, like something had recently died under there, and partly just out of fear. She was afraid to move a muscle and her thumb and index finger were starting to cramp as she held the bone out straight in front of her. She hoped Mr. Prickles would soon start to move forward and take the bait.

Mr. Prickles did not move forward. What he did do was let loose a low, threatening growl, causing Rylie's stomach to churn.

He can't see me, he can't see me, he can't see me, she chanted inside her head.

Mr. Prickles twitched his nose, and his beady eyes searched the area where Rylie crouched. He looked confused. Clearly, he could smell and see the tempting morsel that suddenly appeared before him, but there was also another scent that was slightly familiar to him but he couldn't locate the source. It was this other scent that was making him nervous. Slowly, he stretched out on his belly and crept forward an inch at a time, drawing closer and closer to the treat.

As Mr. Prickles neared, a slight tremor started in Rylie's hand, causing the bone to quiver. Mr. Prickles sensed Rylie's unease and stopped, but instead of growling, a slight whimper escaped. He really wanted the bone, but the smell of fear hung in the air.

Rylie knew she had to calm herself, or they would never get Mr. Prickles out. Slowly, she took a breath in through her nose and blew it out through her mouth. After repetition, she was surprised. She actually felt her heart rate slow. Mr. Prickles must have sensed it, too, because, once again, he was creeping forward. Now, Rylie thought, *all I need to do is crawl backward toward the opening and I can get out of here.*

With deliberate care, she edged backward, her movements slow and measured to avoid the jagged bits of debris scattered across the ground. The foul-smelling piles nearby exuded an air of menace, and she forced herself not to dwell on their grim, unspeakable contents. The mere thought was enough to churn her stomach. Trying to think positively that she was actually going to pull it off, she stopped her retreat, leaving only her head and right arm under the porch. She waited. Finally, Mr. Prickles snatched the bone. Once he was lying down, munching it, she signaled to Colin to hand her the leash.

This is going to be the tricky part, Rylie thought. She managed to keep the leash out of Mr. Prickles' line of sight, then quickly snapped it onto his collar and held onto the leash with both hands.

Hearing the click, Mr. Prickles gulped the last smidgeon of cookie and headed out from under the porch at a full run. Rylie was pulled off balance at the front of the porch, her hands slipping loose, but fortunately, Colin reacted quickly and grabbed onto the leather leash.

Colin followed Mr. Prickles at a full run directly to his house. He needn't have worried about Mr. Prickles biting him because the demon dog fled as if the gates of Hades had opened and he was summoned home.

Mr. Prickles never once slowed, even when he reached the safety of his own front porch, not even to turn and consider who he was dragging behind him.

Gulping for air, Colin came to a dead stop. He barely had time to release the leash before Mr. Prickles' tail disappeared in his doggie door. *For such a little dog, he raised enough racket to wake the dead*, Colin thought.

The uproar brought Mrs. Pritchett to her front door, soothing a frazzled Mr. Prickles. Who had just moments earlier jumped into her arms and, believe it or not, was licking Mrs. Pritchett's neck and clinging to her arm.

She detached the leash and returned it to Colin, shaking her head. "For goodness sake, I asked you to bring my pumpkin home not scare the daylights out of him. My poor angel," she cooed.

"I guess something spooked him," Colin hedged.

"At least he's back home. Right?" Rylie asked, rubbing the stitch in her side that she got from trying to keep up with Colin.

Chapter 23

Mrs. Pritchett stood stiffly stroking and cuddling Mr. Prickles. "Well," she sniffed, "he does appear to be unharmed. Thank you, both of you, for seeing him home." With a curt nod, she dismissed the cousins, turned and closed the door with a sharp thud, the sound lingering like a warning.

Not wanting to linger near the threshold of the demon's lair a second longer, the cousins quickly walked to the corner. Once they were out of sight of the Pritchett house, they stopped.

Finally, having caught her breath, Rylie looked up at Colin, and a fit of giggles seized her and had Colin busting up, too. "I don't know why I'm laughing," Rylie struggled to say. "It was darn scary under that porch and nasty." The reminder of just how nasty it was brought a shudder to Rylie's slender shoulders. "But I guess for a first adventure, it wasn't that bad. But next time, Colin Donovan, you're doing the dirty stuff," she snapped.

"No problem," Colin agreed. "For a minute there, I didn't think Mr. Prickles was going to take the bait."

"Yeah, me neither," Rylie agreed. "I was terrified just being that close to the little monster," Rylie said, gesturing dramatically with her hands to indicate the foot or so distance she had stopped in front of the dog.

"You should have seen him, Colin. He was growling and looking all around him like he was searching for something. I was so close I could smell his doggy breath and it was not pleasant. Then he looked straight at me, and his whine was almost scarier than his growl because he looked so scared. He almost had me feeling sorry for him.

"That's when I realized he was sensing my fear. It took a lot for me to calm myself down. I swear my heart was pounding like a drum in my chest. I kept telling myself over and over that he couldn't see me. But I was lying right smack in front of him with nowhere to go if he decided to make a run for it. He would have crashed right into me, and that would have been disastrous. I knew I had to make myself relax. I remembered something Aunt Molly taught me about breathing to calm yourself, and it seemed to work because Mr. Prickles quit whimpering and focused on the dog bone. It's a good thing you thought of that bone, Colin, or we'd still be there, stuck under the porch with him pacing around like a time bomb, it worked great. Now, all I want to do is get home and take a shower."

As if emphasizing her point, she reached up and picked a long string of some unidentified substance from her hair and flung it into the street. "Oh gross," she muttered, shaking her head in disgust.

"Yeah, I was hoping you were headed for a shower," Colin said with a grin. "Ah, Ry, would you do me a favor?"

She glared at him. "What now?"

"Would you stand downwind till we get home; you're making my eyes water."

Rylie's screech of indignation had Colin darting off in the direction of home with Rylie following in hot pursuit. Rylie was gaining on him, barely two feet behind. As Colin made a sharp left and ducked behind a hedge, Rylie didn't anticipate the sudden turn. It took her a couple of quick steps to spin around and follow, her breath coming in quick, shallow gasps. She reached the bush and skidded to a halt, realizing there was no sign of Colin. A flicker of movement above her head caught her attention. Her gaze shot upward, and there, perched on the lowest branch of the oak tree shading the hedge, was a little blue bird. Its bright, mischievous green eyes locked onto hers, sending a curious shiver down her spine. Then one of the eyes winked at her.

"No fair," Rylie yelled, jumping up and trying to swat the little bird, but Colin easily dodged her attempt, the bird flapping its wings in a quick escape. His laughter carried behind him on the wind, a mocking sound that only made Rylie more frustrated.

When she finally stormed into the yard, she found Colin, his long legs stretched out in front of him, resting on her back porch steps when she finally charged into the yard.

"About time you got here Ry. You are kind of slow, aren't you?" He taunted, a smug grin playing on his lips.

"That's not fair, Colin," Rylie grumbled, her face blotchy and sweaty.

Even though Rylie was short, she was usually very fast. She really hated losing a race, and that feeling quadrupled if she felt the other guy had taken unfair advantage of her. Seeing Colin's smug smile and watching him shrug his shoulders shot a mega dose of self-pity shooting straight through her.

Tired, dirty, and feeling pretty much miserable, Rylie mumbled, "Maybe I asked Glory for the wrong gift."

"Nah, your gift is cool too, Ry. There's a lot of stuff you'll be able to do that I won't, like today. If you hadn't been able to blink out, we never would have gotten Mr. Prickles to go home."

"Yeah, I guess you're right, but going under that porch really sucked. If we have to search for Mr. Prickles again, I am not going under there. You're just going to have to let him chase you out next time."

Rylie stomped up the steps, the frustration boiling inside her. She pulled open the screen door with a sharp motion, too tired to argue any further. "Well, I have to go clean up. I'll see you later."

Wearily, Rylie walked into the kitchen, fully expecting to run into Hannah and she wasn't looking forward to receiving her lecture. But to her surprise, luck was on her side. The only one she found was her grandfather sitting at the table preparing a cup of tea.

Grandpa Marcus looked up from stirring a bit of sugar into his tea, and his welcoming smile faltered. "Well, now, lass, what happened?" He spread his arms, and Rylie let him hold her close, his chin resting on the top of her head. "Did you fall in a dung heap, lass?" Wrinkling his nose, he added, "I've got to say you have that smell about you too. Did you and the lad have a tussle, then?"

"No, Grandpa," Rylie giggled. "Actually, we had to rescue a demon dog from the devil's lair," Rylie told him.

"Well, tis a mite fine job ye must have done, eh? Because although you look a bit worse for wear, that isn't blood I'm seeing you covered in. But perhaps you should tell me the whole of it right from the beginning after you wash up," he chuckled, releasing her.

Seeing how cautious Rylie had suddenly become, Grandpa Marcus gave her a conspirator's wink. "The rest of the family will be away for a couple of hours yet, so we've plenty of time. Now go on with you, darlin'. I'll be waitin' to hear this magical tale of yours when you return all sweet smellin'."

Rylie ran upstairs to her room, grabbed a handful of clean clothes, and rushed into her bathroom. She stood in the steamy shower and let the hot water cascade over her as she rinsed the soap bubbles off for the second time. I guess I'm clean enough now, she thought, looking at her wrinkled fingers. But what am I going to tell Grandpa?

For a minute she thought about calling Colin to see what he thought she should do but decided not to. She was still a little miffed with him. She would just start the tale and hope for the best. After all, if anyone understood the gifts, it would be her grandfather. "Wouldn't it?" she wondered aloud. Sighing, she whispered, "I hope this works." She crossed her fingers on both hands for good luck and headed downstairs.

"I'm glad you decided to join me." Grandpa Marcus teased. "I'm already on my second cup of tea. But from the flowery smell of you, the wait was worth it."

Rylie took a seat across the table from her grandfather and solemnly said, "I've been thinking, Grandpa, before I share my adventure, well, I think we need to make a pact."

Grandpa Marcus returned her serious look and nodded his head. "Aye, lass. I thought you might."

Biting her lip, Rylie looked her grandfather in the eye, trying to see if he was teasing her. But she saw only his clear, steady gaze.

"You were right, Grandpa; my tale does involve magic, and oh, heck, wait just a minute."

Rylie jumped up and, rushed over to the phone and dialed. "Can you come over for a minute? Yeah, it's important. No. I'll tell you when you get here. Okay, just hurry." She hung up the phone and took her seat once more.

"I think Colin needs to be here too Grandpa."

"Do you now?" was all Grandpa Marcus said. But his sharp, emerald green eyes were twinkling.

Barely a couple of minutes passed when Colin flew through the back door.

"What's going on, Ry? You sounded kinda funny on the phone. Oh, hi, Grandpa."

His Grandfather smiled warmly and nodded his head. "Have a seat, lad."

"Well, I was about to share our adventure with Grandpa," Rylie said, raising her eyebrows, her eyes opening wide. She stared hard at Colin, hoping he'd get what she was trying to tell him and secure his support.

"Oh, okay." Colin looked from his grandfather to Rylie and then stammered, "Ohhh, you mean all of it?"

"Yeah, but Grandpa agreed to make a pact, Colin. I didn't feel right making a pact without you. I thought the three of us should be part of it."

"Wow, you're cool with doing a pact, Grandpa?" Colin asked, impressed by the seriousness of the gesture.

"Aye, lad, whatever you say shall remain among the three of us. That is the sort of pact ye sought?"

Rylie looked at Colin, and they both nodded in agreement. Then, to the surprise of the cousins, Grandpa Marcus spat on his large, calloused hand and held it out for Rylie to shake. Rylie mimicked her grandfather's action and then grasped his hand firmly, feeling the weight of the promise. Colin did likewise, placing his on top, binding the three together.

"So it shall be," Grandpa Marcus said. "Now go ahead, lass, begin this tale of yours."

Now that she was free to reveal their secret, she wasn't exactly sure where to begin or how much to explain. She looked at her grandfather hesitantly.

"Just start at the beginning, lass. Tis the beginning that always seems to be the hardest. It will all fall in place after that."

So it was that Rylie told her grandfather about the dreams. She saw the surprise on his face, followed by pride when she explained how clever Colin was to find the solution and unlock the chest. She even found herself confiding to him how upsetting it was for her that Glory appeared to Colin first.

Rylie liked it when her grandfather chuckled when Colin bombarded the scoundrel dog catcher. But when she saw the worry on his face, she was quick to reassure him that she'd been pretty safe when she crawled under the Garcia porch, even if it was horrifically gross under there.

Her grandfather listened intently to her amazing tale, with Colin jumping in occasionally to put his spin on the events.

"Well, it appears Glory has become rather fanciful these days." Grandpa Marcus said. "Oh, she always was flighty. Everyone knew there was neither rhyme nor reason to her granting a wish, but now it seems the wishes she grants have become even more wild and wonderfully extraordinary, as well."

Grandpa Marcus scratched his head. Looking thoughtful, he said, "But then, I do believe that started with your Aunt Molly's request. Donovan used to ask for simple things like gold or land and occasionally a love match."

"You knew about Aunt Molly?" Rylie interrupted.

"Aye, lass, and I cannot say that I was really surprised by my daughter's request. The lass always had to know everything that was going on from the time she was knee-high. When she received her grand gift, she was bursting to tell someone. She confided in me then, and it seems she has in you as well."

Grandpa Marcus cautioned gravely, "You'll need to have care using your extraordinary gifts. You don't wish to cause a stir in our tight-knit little community."

Colin and Rylie assured him that they'd already received that speech from Aunt Molly and once again promised to be careful. The cousins also confided that it was a relief to be able to talk to someone else about the magic and finally share the excitement together.

"So, would ye be up for a wee demonstration of these fantastical gifts of yours? Or have you both just been having a bit of sport with me?"

Colin looked at Rylie. "Ladies first."

Rylie grinned broadly and vanished.

"Glory be." Grandpa Marcus slapped the table and laughed. "Are ye there lass?"

"I'm here, Grandpa," Rylie whispered in his ear and lightly tugged on the hair at the nape of his neck before reappearing.

Her grandfather startled slightly but instead of getting angry as Colin had done in the tree house, he laughed. He grabbed Rylie up and twirled her around. "Amazing, truly amazing."

Then he said, "Ah, twas you the night of your party. I had a feeling there was magic afoot, but I laid the blame upon the garden Fairies."

"Nah, it was me," Rylie confessed, slightly embarrassed at having been caught. "It's just that I wanted to try out my gift so badly, and you were sitting there all alone, well, except for Colin, so I thought, why not?"

"Now then, what about you, Colin?"

Colin moved away from the table and his grandfather to give himself a little more room. Then, in a flash, a beautiful black and grey wolf appeared, its fur shimmering in the dim light.

"So, what do you think, Grandpa?" Colin asked, his voice filled with anticipation.

It was the fact that the wolf could talk that shocked Grandpa Marcus more than the fact that his young grandson had become a shapeshifter.

"I'm speechless," Grandpa Marcus croaked. "You're able to speak. Amazing! The little Queen has truly outdone herself. But then she has had centuries to perfect her craft."

"You look great, Colin. I guess you got it right this time, huh?" Rylie teased. "He was part wolf and part something else when he changed at the wharf," Rylie explained to her grandfather, her eyes widening with the memory.

"Well, I was kinda new at it. This time, I was more focused," Colin admitted.

"Ye make a fine brute of a wolf," his grandfather praised. "But it's gettin' on, and the family shall be returnin' shortly. Perhaps ye best shift back, lad."

"So, Grandpa, what gift did you ask Glory for?" Rylie asked once Colin joined her at the table.

"Ah, I was wonderin' when you'd be gettin' around to askin' me that. My wish was not nearly as imaginative as yours. I'd always had a fascination for magic ever since I'd heard the first Donovan tale. But I was not content to merely hear about the magic. I wanted to be part of it, too, to be able to perform magic myself. So that's what I asked Glory for. Do you remember all those magic tricks you grew up thinking were so amazing? Well, in fact, they truly were magic. I can make small items disappear and reappear with just a snap of my fingers."

Grandpa Marcus produced a coin from his pocket and tossed it up in the air in front of Rylie, and the cousins watched as it disappeared the moment it touched his fingertips. "I always got such a thrill at your squeals of delight."

"Yeah, at my birthday party, Sam mentioned how much she loved your old stories and magic tricks," Rylie said.

Yawning, Colin said, "Well, I better head for home. I'll see you tomorrow, Ry. 'Night, Grandpa."

Rylie continued to sit with her grandfather at the table while they waited for the return of her father and the rest of her family. Rylie enjoyed having her grandfather all to herself, and it didn't take much coaxing to get him to share some of his captivating tales of living in Ireland, painting pictures of the past with his words.

Chapter 24

The sun was brilliant, sparkling off the turquoise blue ocean, its warmth wrapping everything in gold, coaxing tourists from antique featherbeds to come out and sit at one of the outdoor cafés that graced the wharf and sip a cappuccino or stroll along the boardwalk. It wasn't quite midmorning and already the wharf was buzzing with early shoppers, women oohin' and aahin' over summer purses and colorful beach bags on display.

A light breeze ruffled Shannon's blonde hair when she and her friend stopped at a yellow and white striped cart to admire a display of shimmering silver toe rings.

"I just have to have this one," Shannon exclaimed to her dark-haired friend showing her the delicate ring with three deep blue stones woven into slim strands of silver. "Don't you think the stones look exactly like the ocean?"

"I think they're the same color as your eyes, Shannon and it's really cute. You should definitely get it," her friend Ashley coaxed.

Shannon paid for the toe ring and absently tossed her wallet back into her purse. Neither girl took any notice when a man in mirrored sunglasses bumped into Shannon, mumbled 'sorry,' and turned back toward the entrance to the wharf, Shannon's wallet now cleverly tucked under his baggy tank top.

"Let's go check out the sandals at Nina's. I heard she got some cute ones in the other day." Ashley had just grabbed Shannon's arm to tug her away from the jewelry display when she spotted Stretch walking with Rylie and Colin a couple of carts away. Ashley waved frantically and called out loudly to catch Stretch's attention.

Shannon winced at the over-the-top extremes Ashley shamelessly went to, trying to get Stretch to notice her.

A huge smile lit up Ashley's face and in a loud whisper, asked Shannon, "Don't you think Stretch is really cute?"

"Yeah, I guess." Shannon grinned. "But Colin has the greenest eyes I've ever seen."

"Hey!" Rylie shouted. "Did you guys see that?"

"What?" Stretch scanned the boardwalk to see what triggered Rylie's alarm.

"That guy in the black tank top just bumped into Shannon and swiped her wallet."

"You sure?" Colin asked.

"I'm positive! Shannon's wallet is pink. I saw him stash it under his tank top, and he's going to get away if we don't do something."

Frantically, Rylie issued orders: "You guys should go talk to Shannon and take down her statement; get a description of her wallet and how much money she had. Oh, and don't forget to call it in. I'll keep my phone ready, and I'm going to follow him."

"Wait a minute," Stretch said, "that's not a good idea, Shorty."

Rylie glared at Stretch while trying to keep an eye on the escaping thief. She shot a quick glance at Colin and said, "It will be like I'm invisible, just a shadow. He'll never know I'm following him. Trust me."

"Okay, Ry, but be very careful. Once you see where he's going, call me. Just don't take any chances, and don't follow him too far," Colin cautioned.

"What! I can't believe you're letting her go alone." Stretch wasn't happy having Rylie tail the guy by herself, but worse than that, he definitely didn't like being left out of any possible action.

"It'll be okay, Stretch. She'll keep her distance. I'm sure the guy will never see her."

Before Stretch could argue further or insist on going with her, Rylie melted into the crowd and, to a baffled Stretch, seemed to just disappear. He stayed where he was and craned his neck, searching the crowd, but he completely lost track of her. He had seen her slip behind a display of pirate flags that flew next to the Snow Cone Shack, but she never reappeared. Frowning, he shook his head in frustration and let out a slow, irritated sigh, then closed the distance to where Ashley and Shannon stood, still laughing and chatting, blissfully seemingly unaware that anything had happened.

"Hey guys," Shannon said, flashing a pretty smile at Colin. Her smile faltered when Colin didn't smile back. "Is something wrong?"

"Shannon, look in your purse and see if your wallet is there," Colin requested.

"Of course it is. I just bought this cool toe ring a minute ago," she said, holding up a tiny yellow and white striped bag.

Calmly, Colin asked again, "Would you please check Shannon? It's important."

"Sure, but I know it's right here," Shannon assured him while reaching into her purse. Confused, Shannon looked up at Colin. "I just put it in my purse. I know I did." Panic was quickly replacing Shannon's confusion and she frantically searched through her purse. Not finding her wallet, tears welled in her blue eyes and threatened to spill over as she looked around her on the ground, hoping it had simply fallen out nearby.

"Maybe it fell out," she stammered, "it has to be here somewhere."

"I don't see it anywhere," Ashley said as she tried to peer around a rather large woman and her bundle of packages.

Colin pulled his cell out of his pocket, dialed headquarters and quickly reported the situation. While on hold, he asked Stretch, "Why don't you get a description of Shannon's wallet for our report?"

Stretch knew he needed to distract Shannon and keep her panic from escalating. He also noticed that some of the tourists were turning and giving their little group curious looks. He wanted to avoid drawing any more of the crowd's attention, so he gently took Shannon's arm and asked her to move away from the booth with him. She looked hesitant but let him guide her quietly. Ashley followed, sticking close to Stretch's side, casting glances at the people gathering nearby.

Stretch flipped back the cover on his notepad and wrote the date, time, and location at the top of the page. By the time Colin joined him, Stretch had finished adding the few details he could recall about the suspect Rylie was following. With Colin's help, he was able to add a few more details to the man's description— including a faded tattoo on his forearm and a limp.

Looking up from his notes, he asked Shannon to describe her wallet for him. Although Stretch had been the one to ask her the question, it was Colin Shannon who looked up at them when she asked one of her own instead. "What's going on? Do you think someone stole my wallet?"

"First, give Stretch the description of your wallet, Shannon, then we'll explain what we think happened. Okay?"

"Alright," she said, nodding her head. She turned to Stretch, "My wallet was a pink camouflage with my name printed on the front in large white letters. My aunt sent it to me from California last Christmas. I had over a hundred dollars of my babysitting money in it—all the savings I've been holding onto for weeks."

"Did you get all that Stretch?" Colin asked.

"Yeah," Stretch mumbled as he continued jotting in his notebook.

"Do you remember a man bumping into you, Shannon?" Colin asked.

Shannon looked at him blankly and shook her head no. Colin prodded, "When you were standing at the counter, Rylie saw a man bump into you, and it looked like the man swiped your wallet. Rylie was sure she saw him put it under his shirt. So, try and think. Do you remember seeing a man standing next to you—someone close enough to brush your arm or block your light?"

"What, man? I didn't see any man, Colin." Shannon said, shaking her head. Bewildered, she turned to her friend and asked, "Did you see anyone, Ashley?"

"No, I didn't see anyone either." Ashley shrugged. "I guess I was looking at the toe ring."

"Where is Rylie?" Shannon asked, looking around.

"Rylie is following the guy. She should be calling me any minute to let me know where he went," Colin replied. *At least she better call soon, he thought.*

"You guys let her follow the thief by herself?" Ashley asked, her eyes widening in shock.

"Well, it wasn't my idea," Stretch mumbled.

"I can't believe my wallet's gone," Shannon said, a sinking feeling churning in the pit of her stomach. "So, what do we do now?" she asked quietly.

"We were instructed to wait here and meet the wharf patrolman. He should be here any minute," Colin said as he searched the area for any sight of an officer headed their way. "Don't worry, Shannon," Colin soothed, patting her shoulder. "We'll find this guy and get your wallet back."

No sooner had he spoken when a tall, uniformed officer with bright red hair stepped around the far end of the vendor cart and headed their way.

Spotting the two junior detectives, the officer hurried over to them. "Morning, I'm Officer Hudson, and you are detectives . . ."

"I'm Colin Donovan, and this is my partner, Stretch Tyler," Colin said. "I don't think you know Stretch, but I met you before with my Uncle Shawn, ah, that is Detective Donovan. But I've seen you around the wharf."

"I thought you looked familiar," Officer Hudson said. "You and your cousin, what was her name, Rylie, wasn't it? You two are always running around here. I can't say I ever met Stretch, but I've seen him around," he said with a friendly nod toward Stretch.

"Shannon is a good friend of ours, and she had her wallet lifted."

Colin introduced the girls and explained what happened. Officer Hudson was impressed with the way Colin reported the incident and with Stretch's notes.

"Well, it looks like the wharf rats are starting a business early this season," Officer Hudson sighed. "You have a pretty good description of the suspect. I'll ask around; it could be some of the regulars know who this guy is and who he hangs with. We'll start with the vendor where you bought your jewelry. Maybe he noticed the guy hanging around."

Office Hudson turned his gaze to Shannon. "You'll need to have one of your parents come down to headquarters so we can file a report." Recalling something Colin briefly mentioned earlier caused a slight frown to crinkle his forehead.

"You say you have another junior detective following the suspect? That couldn't have been part of the procedure you learned in Detective Donovan's training class."

In Colin's initial telephone report, he sort of slid over the fact that Rylie was the other partner patrolling today and that she was in the process of following the suspect —a detail he had hoped wouldn't raise too many eyebrows just yet.

Colin's face turned pale. "Well, not exactly, Sir," he mumbled. "But she, I mean, Detective Donovan is staying pretty far behind him, and Rylie said she'd call me when he got wherever he's going."

"Sounds like too many Donovan's for me," Officer Hudson laughed. "Let's just skip to first names. I don't think that Rylie," Colin's phone rang, interrupting Officer Hudson.

"Hello," Colin said. Relieved to hear his cousin's voice, Colin fired questions at her. "Are you okay? Where are you?" He paused for a second, listening, and then said, "You're kidding me."

"Where is she?" Stretch asked anxiously.

Colin waved his hand, telling Stretch to hold on a minute and listened as Rylie filled him in, then disconnected.

Well, what did she report?" Officer Hudson demanded.

"Rylie is outside the comic bookstore. You know the one Stretch, The Comic Cellar."

"Yeah. It's on the corner of Boston and Main," Stretch said.

"I know the place. Kinda rundown since the Wilson kid took it over. It used to be a nice place back when his old man ran it," Office Hudson said. "What's going on?"

"Rylie said that the man in the black tank top went into the comic bookstore. She said there wasn't anyone else in the bookstore so Tank Top walked up to the counter and lifted his shirt, showing him the wallet. Tank Top talked to the counter guy for a couple of minutes and then they both went into the back room—like they'd done it a dozen times before, easy."

Officer Hudson removed his communicator from his waist and pushed some buttons. Colin heard dispatch confirm they were sending a car immediately. He could feel the tension spike around them.

In the excitement, Colin almost forgot that Shannon and Ashley were still standing there, frozen in place, their eyes wide and unblinking.

"Shannon, why don't you call your dad? He works downtown and can meet you at the station. We're going to head there now and make our report so you can walk over with us. The Comic Cellar is only a couple of blocks from here, so we'll hook up with Rylie on the way. The police will handle everything now. That is," Colin hesitated, "if you're finished with us," Colin asked Officer Hudson.

Officer Hudson grinned. "I heard we had some help on the wharf this summer. I have to say, I never had a case wrapped up quite as quickly as this one. You kids are fast, clever, and surprisingly coordinated. Your team did a great job, even if it wasn't quite by the book. Thanks. I'll see you back at the station and give you a hand with your report, Colin."

"If you'll get your father on the phone, Shannon, I'll explain everything to him. The responding officers will need to take Rylie's statement, too. That's one thing we do in abundance around here: paperwork."

While Officer Hudson was speaking to Shannon's father, Colin's phone beeped, indicating he was receiving a text message. His pulse quickened.

Wary, Colin quickly stepped away from Officer Hudson to read the message from Rylie.

"Went in back room. Pile of wallets. Cash. Credit cards. Hurry.".

219

Chapter 25

It was difficult for Rylie to keep Tank Top in sight when she left Colin and followed him through the crowded wharf, and it annoyed her. He moved like a ghost through the chaos, slipping between tourists and vendors with maddening ease. She didn't want to get too close to him and spook him. She was looking for any place that would give her the cover she desperately needed to allow her to blink out without having any witnesses. Timing was everything—blink too soon, and she'd blow her cover. Too late, and she'd lose him. She knew she could only spare a second or two, or she would lose track of the suspect. The air was thick with salt and grilled fish, the shouts of street hawkers and the laughter of children ringing around her. Every distraction gnawed at her focus.

She frowned when she glanced back over her shoulder to make sure neither Stretch nor Colin was following her and saw Stretch staring after her with a scowl on his face. His expression wasn't just suspicion—it was concern. Or maybe suspicion wrapped in concern, which was worse. From his height and vantage point on the wharf, she knew he would have a clear view of her all the way to the end of the boardwalk, and the last thing she wanted was for Stretch to see her disappear.

Well, it's now or never, she thought. She detoured around a spyglass cart and ducked behind a display of huge pirate flags. They rippled in the breeze, casting shifting shadows that danced like wraiths. Her heart pounded. One breath. Two. When she re-emerged into the wharf traffic, she was no longer visible. "Let him figure that out," she smirked.

She was careful not to bump into anyone and freak them out in her haste to catch up to Tank Top. She caught him just as he stepped off the pier and headed up the sidewalk leading away from the wharf.

Rylie was relieved that he did not choose to cross over the beach area. Sand would've been a problem. She had no idea if her blink left tracks—and she wasn't in the mood to find out with Stretch still watching from a distance.

Tank Top was smart enough to walk at a steady pace, not moving too fast so he wouldn't draw unwanted attention. He looked like a guy trying very hard to look like a guy who belonged—relaxed shoulders, measured steps—but the constant tension in his jaw gave him away.

Deep frown lines made his mouth appear as an ugly slash, and his icy grey eyes darted nervously from side to side as he frequently looked back over his shoulder and scanned the area looking for any sign an alarm had been sounded. There was a haunted look to him now, like he was expecting shadows to leap out of doorways.

Twice, Rylie saw him flick his hand over the back of his neck as if he were brushing tiny hairs that were standing at attention.

It seemed he sensed someone was following him, but he could not figure out who or where the person was. Rylie was giving the guy the willies, and she had to tighten her own lips to keep from giggling. If he only knew she was barely six feet behind him, slipping through the crowd like smoke.

After following Tank Top deep into the second block leading her further away from the wharf than she had intended to go, Rylie started to get a little nervous. She was wondering how much further he planned to travel when he suddenly stopped in front of the Comic Cellar. Luckily, she was a couple of steps behind, or she would have crashed right into his back.

Tank Top casually looked around him. He looked across the street and up and down the block. Seeing nothing out of place, he turned and peeped in the shop window. He shifted his position to peer back and forth through the small openings left between the painted comic characters of Wolverine, Batman, and Spiderman that were plastered all over the window, trying to view every angle of the shop. The characters grinned in exaggerated poses; their bright colors faded and cracked from too many summers of sun. Satisfied that no customers were shopping or hanging out in the store, he flung open the door.

His lips curled back, exposing scummy green teeth in what Rylie thought had to be a smile. She shuddered and was extremely glad to be invisible.

Tank Top gave the counter guy a thumbs-up but hesitated in the entryway for just a second, waiting for the counter guy to return his signal. It was subtle—a nod, a twitch of the hand—but it was enough. They knew each other. When he did, Tank Top sauntered over to the counter, lifted the front corner of his black tank top, and revealed the camouflaged pink wallet tucked into the waistband of his jeans.

His smile grew as he bragged about how easy the job had been and how stupid the girls were giggling over some jewelry they bought. His voice carried, greasy and smug, through the thin glass like oil over water. Rylie had not followed Tank Top into the store but stood outside, peering in through the dirty window that Tank Top had previously looked through. Smudges and streaks blurred her view, but she could still make out the smug tilt of his chin and the triumphant wave of the stolen wallet. When she saw him reveal the wallet to his partner, she retreated to the corner of the building and ducked down the side alley. Using the large trash dumpster as her cover, she reported in to Colin.

After concluding her phone call, Rylie fully intended to become visible and wait patiently across the street for Colin and the police to show up. She even picked out a spot—a quiet patch of shadow near the mailbox, perfectly boring and perfectly out of the way. But both her insatiable need to know what was going on in the shop and the anger she felt for her friend getting ripped off got the better of her. Her pulse was still hammering from the sight of that pink wallet. Her good intentions slipped away, and she found herself walking back to the front of the shop. She paced back and forth in front of the door and peered into the window. When she saw the two guys walk to the back of the store and enter a back room, she said, "It's now or never."

Rylie eased open the front door. She wasn't worried about any door chimes, like the ones her Aunt Molly had over the front door of her shop, because she would have heard them when Tank Top entered. But what she didn't know was that a soft buzzer sounded in the back room when someone opened the front door. Barely two steps in, she froze. Rylie had barely closed the door when the counter guy stuck his head around the back corner.

"I'll be there in a minute," he said but stopped short when he didn't see anyone in the room. His brows furrowed, and he took a tentative step forward.

Rylie stopped moving and held her breath, waiting to see what Counter Guy was going to do. She watched him walk further into the room and heard him call out, "Anyone here?" She watched him glance up at the ceiling corner and check the mirror he had installed there; it gave him a clear view down the tall aisles. She watched the puzzlement cross his face and saw him shrug his shoulders. "Guess they just opened the door and left," he mumbled.

Holding her breath, Rylie quietly trailed him down the frayed carpet aisle that led to the back room. The carpet was old and threadbare but still offered enough naps to muffle any sound of footsteps. She moved like a shadow, slow and deliberate, her hands brushing along the edge of the nearest display for balance.

Fortunately, Counter Guy left the door open when he re-joined his buddy, allowing Rylie to hover in the doorway. She watched Tank Top place Shannon's wallet on a table and pull out a cardboard box stashed underneath. He dumped the contents onto the round lunch table and sat down. What she saw gave her a start. In front of him was a pile of wallets in a variety of shapes and sizes, male and female styles. Counter Guy joined him and together they started to sort through the wallets, pulling out the cash and credit cards.

"You actually waited to go through all the wallets I scored," Tank Top said.

"Yeah, well, it's not like they were going anywhere," Counter Guy shrugged. "Besides, you were ticked off the last time I emptied them without you being here. Like you thought I was going to rip you off or something."

Rylie had seen enough. Her jaw was clenched so tight it ached, her fingers curling into fists as she stepped away. She turned and hurried from the room. In her haste, Rylie didn't notice the litter box sitting in the hallway close to the door. She caught the edge of the plastic box with her foot and tripped, spilling litter and cat poo everywhere. The smell hit her first, then the sound—a sharp crack of plastic and the gritty crunch of litter scattering across the tiles. Rylie frantically jumped up but slid down again when her foot skidded on a large chunk of poo. The noise she was making had Tank Top and Counter Guy scraping back their chairs and rushing for the door. Rylie barely had time to find her footing and flee into the front of the store before both guys came crashing around the corner wild-eyed, searching for the intruder.

Not caring if she made any more noise at this point, Rylie flat-out ran for the front door. She flung it open and sailed through. She never even noticed the skinny Siamese cat calmly sitting at the end of the aisle, curiously watching her. Its blue eyes blinked slowly, unimpressed by the chaos.

Rylie flew across the street and stopped when she spotted the bus bench. She plopped down on it and tried to catch her breath and steady her breathing, afraid if anyone walked past, her panting would freak them out. She bent forward, elbows on knees, willing herself to slow down. Her heart was still racing, her face flushed hot with adrenaline and embarrassment. But she had what she needed.

Chapter 26

From where she sat, Rylie had a clear view of the Comic Cellar. She watched Tank Top and Counter Guy frantically search the street for the person who had just escaped their shop. They looked like a couple of cartoon villains who'd been outsmarted by a ghost.

Rylie covered her mouth, stifling a laugh as she watched the two guys look at each other, their eyes bugged out from the bizarre invasion. Not seeing anyone, they ducked back inside and closed the door. The moment the glass door clicked shut, she allowed herself a full grin.

Rylie looked around and spotted a large van parked in the alley next to the side door of a florist shop just a little way from where she was sitting. She darted around the van and, used its bulk as cover for her reappearance, and quickly left the alley to return to the stone bench.

Rylie sniffed and wrinkled her nose, glancing around, trying to find the source of the offensive odor she smelled. She'd taken two more steps before she realized the stench was following her. Then with a groan, she remembered the cat poo fiasco and grimaced.

She stopped, lifted her left foot and inspected the bottom. The relief she felt at seeing a clean shoe only lasted the length of time it took for her to check out her right shoe. To her horror, she spotted the stinky smear clinging stubbornly to the sole of her shoe. She darted to the small patch of grass running along the curb and scraped her foot back and forth, desperately trying to dislodge every brown speck that stubbornly clung to the sole of her sandal. Each scrape made her more desperate, more determined to erase the humiliating reminder of her stealth gone wrong. The more she scrubbed, the more the odor seemed to blossom. Determined to rid herself of any trace of the foul crud, she vigorously dragged her foot all along the grassy curb. A passing jogger gave her a strange look, but she didn't care—there were worse things than looking weird, like smelling like cat poop.

Finally satisfied she no longer reeked, she returned to the bench and sent a text message to her cousin. Rylie knew she was still too shaky to talk to Colin. He would definitely hear the nerves in her voice and probably overreact. She knew a text message was safer. She would explain everything to him later when they were alone.

It seemed like only seconds had passed when two police cars pulled up to the curb in front of the Comic Cellar. Their sirens turned off, but their strobe lights flashed red and blue streaks across Spiderman's face, giving the superhero a sinister look. It was oddly poetic justice in comic book colors.

Rylie watched as one of the officers headed down the short alley toward the rear of the shop, and the other officer cautiously entered the front door.

Neighbors living above the row of shops opened their windows and leaned out to see what was going on. Even some of the shopkeepers began to gather on the street wondering what all the commotion was about. None of them, however, seemed surprised when they saw the Comic Cellar was the focus of the ruckus. Apparently, the Comic Cellar had a bit of a reputation.

Rylie was glad to see Colin coming up the street, and for once, she didn't even mind that Stretch was with him. She felt relieved knowing they were finally here. When she noticed Shannon and Ashley were walking with them, she gave the girls a little wave.

Rylie felt a tiny flutter in her stomach when she looked at Stretch, and he smiled at her, looking relieved. The flutter caught her off guard. "The flutter is just from my nerves," she chided herself, "that's all."

"Hey, Ry," Colin called out, "Are you okay?"

She shrugged. "Sure, no problem."

"So, what happened, Ry?" Stretch asked anxiously.

Being the center of attention suited Rylie, and she recited a colorful but edited version of her detective work. She added just enough drama to make it entertaining without giving too much away. Smugly, she watched Stretch's face relax when she explained how cautious she'd been. Unfortunately, she couldn't brag that she had no problem at all remaining invisible the entire time she followed Tank Top, even when she was sliding around in the cat litter.

Stretch watched Rylie's face closely as she gave her report. Something just didn't ring true, but for the life of him, he just couldn't figure out what she was leaving out. Her words flowed a little too smoothly, and her smile held a little too long. He'd seen that look before—usually when someone was skating just above the truth.

Colin also suspected that there was probably a lot his cousin wasn't telling, but he didn't press it. He'd wait and get the unaltered version later.

Shannon and Ashley held their breath while they listened, fascinated by Rylie's bravery and quick thinking. Their eyes were wide, hanging on every word like it was straight from an adventure movie.

"I can't believe you followed that man all this way," Shannon exclaimed.

"I'd have been scared to death," Ashley said.

"So, do you think I'll get my wallet back?" Shannon asked Colin. "And my money?"

"No problem, Shannon. Your money's still in it." Rylie answered without thinking.

When all eyes turned to her in surprise, Rylie realized her blunder. Her stomach dipped like she'd missed a stair. Quickly, she stammered, "I mean, I'm sure it must still be in your wallet because the police showed up so fast. Right? I watched Tank Top talk to the Counter Guy for a couple of minutes before they went into the back room. It's not like they left with it."

Rylie's explanation seemed to satisfy the girls, but both Colin and Stretch clearly weren't satisfied with her answer. Their expressions didn't shift—they just watched her a little too carefully now. But before Stretch could quiz her further, Ashley tugged his arm, drawing his attention and rattled off several questions.

Colin used the distraction to move closer to Rylie and whisper in her ear. "You have to tell me what really happened, Ry."

"I'll tell you everything later. I promise," she whispered back.

"We'll meet in the tree house."

"I think Stretch has a problem with your story."

"Too bad," Rylie grumbled. "It's not like he's going to figure it out. And besides, I don't answer to him anyway."

"No, I guess not, but you need to be a little more careful, Ry, especially when you talk to the officers in charge. If they see any hole in your story or you make a slip, they're going to pounce on you."

"I know. I know," Rylie said, her lips tightening. "I'm not perfect, Colin."

"Don't get mad, Ry. I just don't want you to accidentally say something you can't explain your way out of. Okay. The less you say, the better."

Rylie sighed. "Okay, I'll try really hard to think before I speak," she said with a grin. A shaky grin, but a grin nonetheless.

Their attention was drawn to the commotion across the street when the two officers hustled Tank Top and Counter Guy, handcuffed, into the backseat of the squad car. The two guys were hollering something about the shop being haunted, and them having no idea how the wallets got there.

Rylie felt a surge of satisfaction when one of the officers placed a cardboard box in the trunk knowing quite a few people would have their money and credit cards returned to them. Justice, sealed and packed.

"This was so cool," Rylie whispered to Colin. Despite everything—the stink, the stumble, the close calls—she felt a spark of pride burn warm in her chest.

When she spotted an officer headed their way, she said, "Looks like I'm up."

Chapter 27

Stretch was the last to enter the tree house. Rylie quickly claimed her pillow and sat down with a sigh.

"Man, I didn't think we'd ever get finished with all the paperwork at the station," Rylie complained. She flopped back against the wall, her voice equal parts relief and exhaustion.

"We decided to meet up with you and do the paperwork afterward. But it was worth it. Just knowing Shannon will get her wallet back soon is cool," Colin said as he kicked back on the sea chest. The wood creaked beneath him, familiar and comforting.

Stretch stretched his long legs out on the floor. "You really did do a good job Shorty. We never would have caught those guys if you hadn't spotted Tank Top stealing Shannon's wallet. It's cool being part of the team. J.D. and Sam are going to hate they missed all the action." He grinned, proud but casual, like giving credit was no big deal—even though for Stretch, it kind of was.

Rylie blushed at Stretch's praise and the fact that she kind of liked it was making her a little uncomfortable. Her stomach fluttered in a way she wasn't used to, and she quickly looked down, brushing imaginary lint off her jeans.

"Well, I heard your report to Officer Hudson was great, too. If he hadn't taken you guys seriously, it could have ended differently," Rylie said.

Colin smiled. "Shannon's father told Uncle Shawn he was grateful our team did such a good job. That ought to make the Chief happy."

"Man, I almost forgot to tell you, Shorty. When I stopped in to say hi to Mr. Flannery this morning, he said he'd taken a *stroll* (that was his word, not mine, Stretch clarified) down near the old ghost ship and saw a man dragging a couple of dogs toward the far side of the ghost ship. He said that the guy looked rather disreputable and a little dangerous. Mr. Flannery thought about reporting it but later, when he'd returned to his shop, he thought he might have been overreacting."

Rylie perked up. A ghost ship, a shady guy, and dogs? It sounded like something out of a creepy campfire story.

"When did he take his stroll?" Colin asked, snickering. The word itself seemed to amuse him more than the story.

"Hey, I'm just telling you what he said. Mr. Flannery told me he was out very early this morning, probably around six a.m."

"The other day when Rylie and I were over there, I thought I heard some dogs barking," Colin said. "Maybe we should check it out tomorrow. Ry and I have to cover for J.D. and Sam. They both have something they have to do and can't patrol."

"Sounds good to me," Rylie agreed, "but we really need to be careful if the guy is as bad as Mr. Flannery thinks."

Both Colin and Stretch looked at Rylie and snorted. "Now you're talking about being cautious?" Stretch teased. "Never thought I'd see that."

Rylie reached down and grabbed a paintbrush that was lying next to her on the floor and launched it like a mini paint-covered missile at Stretch's head.

Stretch jumped up, easily dodging out of harm's way. "Well, it looks like I better get going unless you need more target practice, Ry."

Rylie squealed with outrage and searched her area for anything to throw that would do some damage. The only thing she saw was the little jar of water she used to clean her watercolor brushes. She was about to grab that and douse Stretch with the dirty water when Colin stalled her by yelling, "Run Stretch!" and then grabbed the jar at the same time Rylie did.

Rylie gave up and quit struggling with Colin over the jar when she heard Stretch's laughter and the thump of his feet pounding down the ladder.

Rylie just frowned at Colin, her glare half-hearted at best.

"Look, I'll make it up to you. How about you and I go check out the Ghost Ship tonight after dark? I know how you like scary stuff, so I'll tell my folks I'm staying here tonight. Then, after moonrise, we'll ride our bikes down to the wharf and see what's going on aboard the ship. What do you say?"

"Really?!" Rylie exclaimed. "You're not going to chicken out later, are you?"

"Nope, I promise. I want to see what's going on down there too, and if anything is happening, we can always use our gifts to check it out." Colin said. He gave her a conspiratorial wink, and the old thrill of adventure sparked instantly between them.

Their tiff completely forgotten, the cousins set about planning the strategy for later that night.

Chapter 28

The eerie echo of pounding waves crashing against the hull of the ship reverberated like a drumbeat of doom, intensifying through the thick blanket of fog enveloping the ghost ship.

The fog's ghostly tendrils stretched out and coiled around the low wooden fence that was meant to provide a small measure of security for the ancient ship. They clung like spectral fingers, creeping with an unnatural sentience. Silently, it slithered and swirled around the stone benches scattered along the crushed sea-shell path, obscuring them from view and turning every familiar landmark into a sinister silhouette, making the once well-worn path feel more like a trap than a trail— treacherous and disorienting.

The path the cousins followed lead not only to the entrance of the ship, but it was intended to lead a curious tourist to the weathered stone pillar bearing a small tarnished brass plaque detailing the decommissioned ship's name, The Angel of Mercy, her dates of service and a brief history of her life at sea. That simple marker, once a point of interest and education, now stood as a ghostly sentinel in the darkened night—its presence ominous rather than informative.

In wolf form, Colin's keen senses and sharpened eyesight gave him an edge against the murky elements. He could easily, soundlessly, run through the night, leaving Rylie far behind, his dark black and grey coat blending with the shadows, rendering him as invisible as his cousin. The only trace of him was the unearthly green glow emanating from his eyes.

Although Rylie was invisible, she still had the restraints of a mortal body and had to move cautiously through the thick fog, feeling her way around the wooden fence. Unable to navigate as soundlessly as Colin, she quickly muffled the squeak of surprise that escaped when her left arm collided with the corner of the stone pillar.

Colin immediately stopped in his tracks. His pointed ears were alert and focused on the slight sound, causing his massive head to turn in her direction. Rylie couldn't suppress the chill that ran down her spine as she stared into the green orbs.

"Are you okay?" he growled.

"Yeah," she whispered back, rubbing the tender flesh on her arm. Rylie purposely kept her voice low as she recalled Colin's earlier warning about how sound carried through the night.

"There's a bench directly to your right, why don't you wait there, and I'll try to locate a safe passage onto the ship. As soon as I find a way in, I'll come back for you."

Before Rylie could protest, Colin blended with the night mist, disappearing completely. Frustrated, she stumbled onto the damp bench and plopped down in a huff.

Rylie's common sense tried its best to smooth the sharp edge of irritation prickling beneath her skin. She reminded herself—again— that they were partners, and Colin's plan did make logical sense. But knowing that didn't make it any easier.

As she waited, she concentrated on calming down. When she was no longer thinking of ways to get even with Colin, she realized she was totally alone in the darkness.

The stillness of the night flowed over her. The prevailing sound was the crashing of the waves and the eerie foghorn echoing its warning in the distance. She searched her surroundings and realized that the fog had become even thicker as it rolled in from the sea, making it impossible for Rylie to see anything around her. She felt the dampness cling to her face and arms and seep through her summer clothes, chilling her.

Rylie had never been one to scare easily and really enjoyed being out at night; the fog was just a bonus, so it irked her that she couldn't quite block out the tiny threads of fear that slithered through her mind. She fought the icy prickles and drove them back by telling herself there wasn't anything in the dark she hadn't seen during the day. She bolstered her courage by doing what she did best. By going on the offensive, she put all of her senses on alert and concentrated on separating any sound that wasn't part of the night.

She listened to the waves and the deep, throaty sound of the foghorn. She caught a scraping sound, but the fog rendered it impossible to pinpoint the source. Holding her breath, she strained to listen, her eyes darting from side to side. Not hearing anything more, she slowly released her breath.

Again, the sound floated in the fog, like someone was shuffling their feet through gravel.

Rylie knew what she heard wasn't caused by Colin's return because he would be silent in his approach. She was aware that sounds could be deceptive at night and had no way of knowing how far away, or for that matter, exactly what was making the sound.

When she heard an incoherent mumbling, her blood froze. She watched a tall, inhuman shadow emerge and realized how vulnerable she was sitting on the bench. It couldn't be human, she thought. No one is that tall. Then she realized what she was seeing was a blending of man, shadow and fog that played a trick on her.

As the man shuffled closer, she was able to pick out a few fragmented words of his mumbling. She watched with frightened fascination as the menacing figure loomed ahead of her and then came to a stop directly in front of the stone bench.

As if in slow motion, a distorted foot rose out of the fog, and instantly, Rylie realized that if she didn't act quickly, he was going to stomp her. Without a whisper of sound, Rylie slid to the far side of the little bench, barely missing being struck by the descending boot.

A silent puff of breath escaped when Rylie finally realized the man hadn't seen her. He couldn't intentionally have been trying to harm her because he had no way of knowing she was sitting on the bench, Rylie reminded herself.

Being invisible was going to take some getting used to, she thought. The man had just been swinging his foot, trying to make sure it landed squarely on the bench while he fished for his pack of cigarettes.

Rylie watched the match tip flare and stared hard at the distorted reflection of the man's face as he lit up. The cherry red glow of the tip of his cigarette looked like a fiery hot coal burning in the night.

Rylie quickly clamped a hand over her mouth and nose, stifling the inherent need to cough, when a plume of bitter white smoke drifted past her face. The acrid smoke burned her eyes, but she stubbornly refused to shut them, leaving herself in total darkness even for a second. Sheer self-preservation demanded she keep the man firmly in her sights.

Rylie recalled Hannah telling her about a man she'd once had the misfortune to meet who seemed to radiate pure wickedness. At the time, Rylie simply thought Hannah had been exaggerating because no one could be so bad that you could feel the evil surrounding him.

But that is exactly what Rylie felt as she sat half a bench away and shuddered just being that close to the man. She sincerely hoped Colin would return soon.

"Plain crazy having to come down here, in this fog, in the middle of the darn night," the man ranted.

"The boss always wants everything done late at night. The guy gives me the creeps, the way he stares straight through me, never blinking. Talks to me like I'm a moron. 'Just get it done,' he demands, 'I don't care how you do it.'"

"If he doesn't know, he can't be blamed, can he?" the man grumbled.

"He lets me and Ol' Melvin take all the chances and for what? A few bucks. Well, I ain't as dumb as Doc thinks I am. I'm getting my share of the money tonight and calling it quits. This place creeps me out. Melvin can stay if he wants to, but I'm outta here tonight."

Afraid to move a muscle, Rylie sat on her end of the bench and listened to the man grumble to himself about someone named Doc and someone else he called Melvin. She was doing her best to commit to memory as much of his conversation with himself as she could for the report she would make later.

Both Rylie and the man jumped when a deep howl pierced the night. Startled, the man dropped what was left of his cigarette.

Rylie watched him spin around in a circle, trying to locate the wolf. Clearly, it unnerved him to feel so exposed, for him to become the prey. Automatically, he crushed out the glowing ember and tugged his cap tighter on his head as he rushed toward the locked gate. He was afraid to run the short distance to the gate because he was certain the sound and motion would draw the beast's attention.

Rylie rose and cautiously followed the man. She stopped when he stopped. She heard the lock click and saw the gate swing open in front of him. Where did he get a key? She wondered.

In the man's haste to seek sanctuary aboard the ship, he failed to secure the gate. Rylie decided not to wait for Colin and quickly followed the man through the gate toward the ramp.

Seconds later, Rylie felt the brush of fur along her leg and was relieved that the crashing waves swallowed her squeal of surprise. Colin fell into step alongside her, but this time, Rylie took the lead. The man they followed was so intent upon getting aboard that he never once looked back over his shoulder, or he would surely have died from fright at the sight of the massive grey wolf, with his *eerie,* glowing eyes silently stalking him.

The man hastened up the ramp, easily swung his long legs over the railing and headed across the deck straight for the steel door. When he tugged the door open, the squeak of seldom-used hinges masked Rylie's soft thud as she landed awkwardly upon the rocking deck. Colin simply glided over the railing like one of the ghosts that was rumored to haunt the ship.

The dim light filtering through the open doorway cast an eerie glow in the dense fog and allowed Rylie to glimpse the man slipping through the opening. She managed to rush forward just in time to keep the door from completely closing by sticking her toe in the narrow opening.

Slowly, she inched the heavy door open a little wider, just enough to allow her to pass through. Keeping her foot wedged in the opening, she quickly scanned the interior. Rylie saw no one about but heard the squeal of another door opening, and a din of noise floated out. Rylie widened the gap enough to allow Colin to follow her in.

"Do you hear them?" Colin whispered.

"What was that?" Rylie asked.

"Barking, it's muffled, but it sounds like a bunch of different breeds. We need to check it out," Colin said urgently. The hair on the ruff of his neck and down his back was standing straight up. "Some of them sound very distressed."

"Okay, let's go," Rylie agreed.

The wisps of fog that slipped inside the ship swirled around them and were slow to fade away. Once Rylie's eyes adjusted to the dim light, it was easier for her to make out her surroundings.

"The man must have gone through that door over there," Rylie said, pointing to a door slightly hidden by a desk at the back corner of the room.

"I'm just going to crack it open a little and see what I can. You need to stay back in the shadows."

Realizing his cousin was planning to go in without him made Colin very uneasy. "You know, Ry, maybe we should go for help. This could get dangerous now."

Sounding braver than she really felt, Rylie said, "I'm only going to take a look. It's not like we really have anything to report anyhow. We need actually to see what's going on in there and then we'll get help. Okay?"

"Alright, just be careful and hurry," Colin cautioned. "And don't bump into anything."

Very slowly, Rylie eased open the door. She intended to crack it barely and only peer inside, but the heart-wrenching sound of the dogs barking and whimpering assaulted her. She was so stunned by the sight of so many dogs caged at the far side of the room that she didn't realize she had pushed her way through the door. The old hinges protested loudly and drew the attention of the two thugs.

One was the tall, thin smoker she nearly collided with earlier, and the other one looked very familiar to her in the dim light. His puffy face and mean, beady eyes searched the doorway for the intruder.

Frozen in place, it took Rylie a second to remember he couldn't see her and that he was searching for the culprit that opened the door. She recalled the tall guy mumbling about someone named Melvin, his partner in crime. That's who the other guy is, she thought, Melvin the dog catcher.

Carefully, Rylie stepped aside and released her hold on the door, letting it swing shut on its own. Then she edged further into the room, away from the doorway and out of the direct path of an enraged Melvin.

Melvin's normally flushed face was instantly leeched of color as he stared wide-eyed at the closing door. But fury overcame fear, and he stomped toward the door.

"Now look what you did, Darrell. You almost got me falling for all those stupid ghost stories you've been telling me. You're making me crazy," he railed.

The tall guy, Darrell, started laughing at Melvin's anger but his laughter died in his throat when Melvin yanked open the door and was staring face-to-face with the largest grey wolf he had ever seen.

Melvin was quick to react. He whipped out his loop, and before Colin could move Melvin had the loop securely tightened over his head and was dragging Colin toward a large steel cage.

Trying to keep his wits about him, Colin knew enough not to fight Melvin. Instead, he let loose a deep, rumbling growl and bared his teeth.

"I told you, you wild-eyed mutt, that I would get you. Now you'll see who's in charge," Melvin sneered, gleefully yanking harder on the noose.

"We'll see what the Doc thinks of you for one of his experiments." Melvin was so pleased with his catch that shrill giggles reverberated around the room.

Colin wasn't exactly sure where Rylie was at the moment, but he hoped she would stay cool and not reveal herself, at least not until he thought of a plan and a way to get them out of this mess.

"Whoa, man, where'd he come from? I heard a wolf outside when I was headed in, but I didn't see him. How'd he get in here anyway?" Darrell asked.

"And stop that giggling man, you're creeping me out." The little hairs on his arms were standing on end.

"How should I know how he got in here?" Melvin snapped as he slammed the cage door shut and twisted the latch. "Go look outside and see if that Donovan girl is out there. Last time I saw this mutt he looked a little different, but I'm sure he was running with her down at the beach."

Shaking his head, Darrell walked through the door, mumbling, "I am getting my cash, and I'm done with this business."

Rylie watched as Melvin dragged a chair over and set it a couple of feet in front of the cage. She saw him grasp one end of the wooden handle of his loop and drag it across the bars, taunting the beast.

"Well, two can play that game," Rylie thought. She searched the room, looking for something she could use. Don't think I'm going to find a sheet in here, she thought. Then, she noticed a coarse blue blanket crumpled in the corner of the room. That should do the trick.

Carefully, Rylie made her way over to the blanket dodging portable kennels of all shapes and sizes on her way. But what she didn't notice in the dim light until it was too late was the plastic watering can. She tripped over the long spout, spilling its contents over the floor. Water flowed everywhere.

"What the heck," Melvin shouted, "Who's in here." He jumped up from his chair, knocking it over backwards and searched the room.

He spotted the water flowing across the floor, but seeing no one in the dim light, he began to sweat. Then, out of the corner of his eye, he saw the blanket floating toward him. He screamed a high-pitched wail that had the dogs joining in frantically howling and barking. He flung his pudgy arms up in front of his face to ward off the evil spirit.

 At the same time, the outer door burst open. "What's all that screaming about?" Darrell shouted.

The blanket floating toward him caught him off guard for only a moment because he sure as heck didn't believe in ghosts. After all he was the one making all the ghost stories up that he'd been taunting Melvin with for the last few weeks.

He reached out and, grabbed a handful of the blanket and pulled. When he saw that, all he held was the rough blanket in his fist, and there was nothing solid standing in front of him, no human being playing at being a ghost. He gave a strangled cry, turned and bolted out of the door.

Melvin pulled a huge hunting knife from the sheath strapped to his right leg and waved it back and forth in front of him. "You, you brought this evil upon me," he shrieked at the wolf and headed menacingly toward the cage.

"Colin, change shape," Rylie shouted as she edged further away from Melvin and closer to the other dog cages. She watched in fascination as Colin changed before their eyes from the huge menacing wolf to a small brown mouse that easily scampered between the bars. The transformation was so fast it left a shimmering ripple in the air like heat rising off pavement. The distraction Colin created allowed her time to open cage doors, releasing every breed imaginable from their confinement.

Melvin stood frozen where he was, still brandishing the knife, his beady eyes looking like hard, black pebbles in his pale face, unable to comprehend the chaos erupting around him. His thick lips trembled, and his mind just couldn't accept what he had just seen: a huge wolf disappearing out of a locked cage to be replaced by a small brown mouse. Dogs barked and howled in a frenzy, the pounding of paws echoing like thunder against the concrete floor. Impossible. The place truly was haunted. His breath came in short, ragged gasps as the full weight of fear crept up his spine. The only other explanation possible was that he was going mad.

Rylie had just finished opening the last dog cage and was headed toward the cages that held a few cats when a door she hadn't noticed burst open, knocking her flat. In her dazed state, she was unable to maintain her invisibility.

Standing in the doorway was a tall man wearing a long, white lab coat spattered with blood, his sharp, penetrating eyes taking in the chaos around the room. He reached out and grabbed Rylie by the arm, jerking her up in front of him.

"What are you doing here?" he growled as he roughly shook Rylie's arm. "Did you come alone?"

The man stared past Rylie, his mouth gaping open in stunned disbelief. Standing just a few feet away was a fire-breathing dragon—real, massive, and magnificent. Even in the dim, flickering light, its turquoise and gold scales gleamed like molten jewels, casting glints of color onto the surrounding walls.

The dragon's eyes—piercing emeralds full of fury and ancient wisdom—locked onto the doctor. A guttural growl rumbled from deep within its chest before it reared back its head and let loose an earth-shaking roar. A stream of flame shot overhead, scorching the ceiling and singeing the stark white tips of the man's hair. The heat forced him back against the wall, trembling, his courage evaporating like steam.

Just then, the outer door burst open with a bang, and Aunt Molly rushed into the chaos, with Uncle Shawn only a step behind. The scene hit Uncle Shawn like a punch to the chest—he stumbled, eyes wide, frozen by the impossible sight before him.

But not Aunt Molly.

Without hesitation, she surged forward, cutting through the smoke and heat, her focus solely on Rylie. The presence of a dragon—however shocking—meant nothing compared to the well-being of her niece.

"Release my niece this instant," she demanded. The doctor struggled to drag his eyes away from the dragon to look at Aunt Molly.

"Now!" she growled, sounding as fierce as the dragon.

The doctor looked from Aunt Molly to the girl he had forgotten he was still holding and forced his hand open.

Rylie rushed to her aunt, and she wrapped her arms around her.

"It's okay now, Minx," Aunt Molly soothed, patting Rylie's back. She turned her head toward the dragon and said, "You can change back now, Colin. All is under control."

"Ah, Aunt Molly, I'm down here," Colin said, standing up on his little back legs and waving a tiny paw at his aunt.

"Oh my." Aunt Molly murmured. "Then who is this?"

"Please, let me introduce you to Draco."

"Glory," they all shouted at once.

Colin instantly shifted to his human form and smiled up at Glory as she hovered near Draco's head.

A visibly shaken Uncle Shawn managed to disarm and handcuff a stunned Melvin, who was too busy muttering to himself to offer any kind of resistance. "None of this is real," he kept repeating, over and over, as if clinging to that phrase could somehow undo what he'd witnessed.

Without a word, Uncle Shawn tightened the cuffs and turned his attention to the doctor, who had barely moved, his face pale and lips pressed in a thin, guilty line. He cuffed the man with practiced efficiency, then—almost with poetic justice—shoved both Melvin and the doctor into two of the largest cages they had once used to imprison others. They didn't protest. The clang of the cage doors echoed through the room like a gavel falling in a courtroom.

Uncle Shawn pulled out his radio and called for backup, his voice tight but steady. Once help was on the way, he cautiously made his way to the back room, unsure of what more he might find.

What greeted him stopped him cold. An operating table stood under a harsh fluorescent light, and on it—what remained of a small brown dog. The sight twisted something in his gut. Blood still pooled beneath the lifeless body, and scattered tools nearby hinted at the cruelty that had taken place.

His jaw clenched. With a heavy exhale, he stepped back and pulled the door shut, sealing the horror behind it. Whatever had happened here, it was over now. But he knew the memory wouldn't leave him anytime soon.

"Does someone want to tell me what the heck is going on here," Uncle Shawn shouted over the hubbub, a scowl on his face.

Once everyone quieted down and turned their attention to him, he grinned. "Am I really going to have the pleasure of meeting Glory?"

Glory floated over to Uncle Shawn and kissed him on the cheek. "You have an extraordinary family, Detective. And I can see that your niece and nephew are going to follow closely in your twin's footsteps, keeping things exciting for all of us."

"I can't believe Draco is here. He saved our lives," Colin said in awe.

"You and Draco have a very special connection, I believe." Glory said. "He sensed you were in danger and merely tried to rescue you."

"But how is that possible? He was just an ornament on Grandpa's old sea chest," Colin said.

"Actually, Draco comes from very old Fairy magic. He has been in my family farther back than anyone can remember. His resting place, until he is needed, is the old sea chest. But it grows late, and we need to take our leave. I believe your backup, Detective, will be arriving shortly," Glory laughed, "and with us gone, there will be less for you to try to explain."

With a smile and a twirl, she and Draco vanished into thin air, leaving the small group speechless.

Uncle Shawn looked around the room at the unsettling number of dogs. They had all quieted down, probably due to Draco's appearance, and were lying down huddled together around the room as if unsure what was going to happen next.

So much had happened so fast that Uncle Shawn was having trouble comprehending everything. "So, which of you plans to start explaining?" he asked, looking from one cousin to the other.

Rylie and Colin started talking simultaneously, tripping over each other in their haste to tell their story.

Uncle Shawn merely held up one hand, and Rylie stopped talking. She decided this was a good time to let Colin explain.

Colin told them how he had heard the dogs barking the other day while on patrol and how he and Rylie had decided to check it out at night when no one would be around, or so they thought.

"We intended to go for help once we found out for sure what was going on," Rylie interrupted. "But somehow, things got out of control before we were able to do that."

Uncle Shawn looked at Colin and grimaced. "I can't believe I am going to ask this. So, I take it your gift from Glory is the ability to Shapeshift?"

"Uh, yeah," Colin shrugged. "We didn't want to freak you out, so we kept that to ourselves."

"So, you were the one that received the gift. I always thought it would be Rylie, she's so fanciful and all.

"I guess I owe you an apology, Rylie. I sure didn't see this coming," he said, looking around the room.

"You were on top of this one right from the very beginning. I'm sorry. But my apology doesn't change the fact that I don't like the way you and Colin handled the situation, going out at night alone and putting yourselves in such a dangerous situation. If your aunt hadn't called me with one of her feelings, I don't know what would have happened."

Rylie walked over to her uncle and hugged him. "I am really sorry, Uncle Shawn. Next time, I promise we'll be more careful."

"Well, there better not be a next time, or you two will be off the squad. Got that?"

"Yes sir, Detective," Rylie and Colin solemnly answered.

"So, do you see the little poodle, Samson or Paul's boxer, Sarge?" Uncle Shawn asked.

Rylie giggled and looked around the room. "With everything happening so fast, I really didn't even think to look."

Colin spotted a bit of white fluff cuddled up next to a black Labrador and checked the dog tag. "Hey, Samson's right here, and I bet that is Sarge over in that corner," he said, pointing to a boxer with a white star on his forehead.

Aunt Molly smiled encouragingly at Rylie. "I'll help sort all this out in a few minutes, but first, wasn't there something else you want to share with your uncle?"

Rylie signed. "Yeah, I guess I better."

Seeing that the backup had arrived and was taking charge of the bad guys and trying to round up all the dogs, Rylie looked at her uncle. "Ummm, it's getting a little crowded in here. Maybe we should go in the back, so it's a little more private when I tell you. Okay?"

"Okay, but not in there," Uncle Shawn said, nodding toward the back room. "Let's try this door." He opened another door that led to a large room and motioned Rylie to enter. "Okay, Ry, let's have it."

"Well, Colin wasn't exactly the only one that Glory gave a gift to."

"Oh, no," he groaned, shaking his head. "What exactly was your gift?"

"Well, Uncle Shawn, I think I better just show you."

Poof, Rylie disappeared then in a flash, she was back.

"Heaven help us," Uncle Shawn mumbled. "You couldn't ask her for something like a new computer or some fancy jewelry?"

Then, pinching the bridge of his nose with his fingers, he shook his head again and asked, "Does anyone else know about your abilities?"

"Ah, well, just the two crooks in the other room and Grandpa. Grandpa didn't think anyone else should know right now."

"I guess we'll keep it our little secret then. As for those other guys, who's going to believe them?"

The entire town was buzzing with the shocking news of the dognapping escapade—and the even more surprising revelation that two members of the newly formed Junior Detective Squad had been the ones to stumble onto the crime scene. Whispers turned to chatter at every corner café, market stall, and front porch. Parents clutched their pets a little tighter, and children reenacted dramatic versions of the rescue with flashlights and stuffed animals.

Detective Donovan found himself juggling a full plate of statements, evidence logs, and a very nosy press. More challenging, however, was the delicate task of wrapping up the case without disclosing too many of the more *extraordinary* details—like the fact that a wolf had turned into a mouse and helped set dozens of dogs free.

He addressed the public with practiced calm, assuring the anxious townsfolk that their beloved fur babies would be reunited with them very soon. He left out the part where magic and mayhem had collided in a ghost ship.

The only silver lining in the whole bizarre ordeal was, ironically, a political one: the mayor now had the perfect reason to fire Melvin—his good-for-nothing nephew—without invoking the wrath of his wife. After all, Melvin had been caught red-handed in the middle of a criminal operation and now faced some serious jail time.

With the help from Glory and a little Fairy dust they were able to blur the memories of Doc and Melvin, so they had trouble recalling exactly what took place just prior to the police arriving. And with Rylie's description of Darrell, an officer found him at the local bus terminal. All in all, it was a good outcome to a horrible event.

Later that afternoon Rylie and Colin met at the treehouse to talk about what they planned to tell their friends. "We need to really think about this, Rylie. If we tell Stretch, J.D. and Sam the truth about our gifts, it could end in disaster."

"We could do a pact like we did with Grampa," Rylie said.

"And what if they can't handle it or just think we are crazy?" Colin asked.

"Well, it would make everything easier, Colin, and I trust them. Even Stretch." Rylie confided. "We could feel them out and see how they feel about magic and if they thought it could be real. See how they react."

"I don't know. We told our folks we would keep it to ourselves." Colin said.

"But didn't Molly say not to say anything unless we were sure about who we shared it with? I really trust our friends Colin."

"Let's just ask them, and maybe they will be cool with it. But we probably should make them swear to never talk about it to anyone. On their honor. I just must share it with Sam, and I know you want to tell Stretch and J.D.," Rylie said.

"Yeah, I do. I just hope we don't screw it up." Colin sighed and then said, "Okay, Rylie, let's call them and have them come over. I know they are dying to hear our side of everything that went down last night."

"You make your calls, and I will call Sam. I'm going to snag some cookies from the kitchen and will be right back."

It wasn't long before they heard their friends climbing the stairs. "It's show time," Rylie giggled.

After everyone found a place to sit and grabbed a cookie, Colin looked around the room.

"I know you guys want to know more about what went down last night, but there is something else we need to talk about first."

"Oh, come on, Colin, nothing else can be more exciting than what happened last night," Stretch said.

"You just might be wrong about that," Rylie smirked.

Not wanting to drag it out, Colin looked at each friend and said, "We want to ask you something. Do you think magic can be real? I mean like, really, real magic? Like Fairy magic?"

Stretch looked at J.D. and started to be snarky but saw the serious expressions on the cousins' faces. "Well, I don't know. It would be cool if it were."

"What about you guys?" Colin asked J.D. and Sam.

Sam just shrugged her shoulders and said, "I don't think it is." J.D. grinned and said, "Don't you wish it was, though?"

"Okay, the thing is," Colin began, "What we are going to share with you guys, you must swear you won't tell anyone. No one at all. Can you do that?"

"Sure," "Okay," "No Problem," the three spoke at once. Then Colin proceeded to share the Donovan family legacy. He watched as disbelief morphed into awe. "Do you think you can handle a demonstration of our gifts?" Colin asked.

"Oh yeah," Stretch said with a huge grin. J.D. and Sam, eyes wide, just nodded their agreement.

"But first, you guys must make a pact with us, like we did with our Grampa, that you won't tell anyone. Are you good with that?" Colin asked.

With all heads nodding affirmative, Colin put his hand out, and Rylie topped it with hers, then she looked expectantly at Stretch. Stretch placed his on top, followed by J.D. and lastly by Sam.

"We pledge to carry your secret to our graves," Stretch solemnly said, with J.D. and Sam adding their agreement.

Just as Colin said, "Okay, that seals it," gold and silver strands gently wrapped around the stack of hands, magically sealing the pact and quickly disappearing. Colin looked at Rylie and smirked, "I didn't see that coming." "Neither did I," she said, laughing, as she looked at the startled faces of their friends. "I guess Glory approves."

"Okay then, do you want to go first, Rylie, or should I?"

"You go ahead, Colin."

Colin took a breath to steady himself and promptly turned into a black cat, thinking it was the safest, non-threatening one to choose. The three friends were speechless for exactly five seconds, and then chaos erupted. "That is awesome," Stretch shouted, "Can you do other animals?"

"I can," Colin said and obliged by turning into his favorite, the wolf. Sam surprised everyone by readily accepting Colin's wolf. "Wolves are my all-time favorite animals," she admitted. J.D. was so overwhelmed that he just kept saying that's cool, over and over.

Once everyone had calmed down and Colin returned to himself, they all expectantly looked at Rylie.

"Well, I can't do any awesome animals, but I can disappear!" And in a flash, she was gone.

Once again, shouts of "awesome" and "wow" were heard. When Rylie reappeared, Sam laid her hand on her arm and said, "Thank you guys for sharing this with us. I know it had to be hard for you to take a chance on us."

"You are my best friend, I had to tell you," Rylie said as she hugged her.

So now that you guys know our Donovan clan secrets, I can explain exactly what happened last night. Once Colin finished the tale with Rylie filling in her part of the story, the first thing Stretch said was, "I can't believe you guys got to have all the fun. Draco must have been awesome."

Colin looked at the chest he was sitting in front of and let his fingers stroke Draco's wings. "He totally was amazing."

"Wasn't it scary before Draco showed up?" Sam asked. "I'm so glad you were okay and all of those poor dogs were rescued."

"So, you were completely right about there being a dognapping problem," J.D. said.

"Yeah, but Uncle Shawn was not at all happy that we checked it out on our own," Colin admitted.

"I might be part of the squad, but I would never have been brave enough to go down to the wharf at night in the fog," Sam admitted.

"That really was brave of you, Shorty. I'm impressed," Stretch said with a grin.

The friends talked about everything for a while, going over all the events again and again, and then headed home, leaving Colin and Rylie looking exhausted.

"I am so happy we told them, Colin." "Yeah, I am too. It will be more fun now with them knowing everything." Colin agreed.

About The Author:

Although Las Vegas has become my home, I actually grew up in a small town in Connecticut. My time is spent with my husband, Roy and with Moses, our sweet and very spoiled Boston terrier. Since I was a child, I've always been a daydreamer with my head in the clouds or in a book. I have a love of Fairies, fantasy, and mysteries with a dash of romance and magic. The things I am most passionate about, apart from my husband and my pup, are reading, writing and baking.

Karen Cotton